Professor Boris Bigalke, MD

The Power of the Venus Temple

Professor Boris Bigalke, MD, MBA (Oxford, UK), LL.M. works as an attending and head of the DGK CardioMRI Qualification Center at the German Heart Center of the Charité (DHZC), Campus Benjamin Franklin, Clinic for Cardiology, Angiology and Intensive Care Medicine. Professor Bigalke is a specialist in internal medicine and holds specializations and additional qualifications in cardiology, acupuncture, nutritional medicine DAEM/DGEM® and magnetic resonance imaging.

After studying medicine at the Free University of Berlin, he continued his scientific and clinical career at the Eberhard-Karls-University of Tübingen. Further training led him to surgery at the LIJ Medical Center, Albert Einstein College of Medicine, New York, USA, to TCM at the WHO Collaborating Center, Beijing, China and to TTM at the Qusar Tibetan Healing Centre, Dharamsala, Himachal Pradesh, India.

During a long-term research stay, he also worked at King's College London, Division of College London, Division of Imaging Sciences and Biomedical Engineering London as an Assistant Professor/Honorary Lecturer.

He also completed a Master of Business Administration (MBA) Healthcare Management at Magna Carta College, Oxford, UK, and a Master of Laws (LL.M.) with a focus on medical law at the Dresden International University.

In 2021, Professor Bigalke applied to become an astronaut at the European Space Agency (ESA). Out of more than 22,500 qualified applicants, he was one of the top 100 candidates in Germany. Even though he did not become an astronaut, he has always been fascinated and enthusiastic about space travel and the planets of the solar system. This inspired him to write the book "The Enigma of the Mars Pyramid", which has already been published.

Professor Bigalke has been elected as one of Germany's top physicians in FOCUS-Gesundheit 2021 in the category of cardiological sports medicine, and in 2023, 2024 and 2025 in the categories of hypertension and nutritional medicine.

Professor Boris Bigalke, MD

The Power of the Venus Temple:

In the Shadows of the Star People

Disclaimer:

This book is a work of fiction. Names, characters, places and incidents either are products of the author's imagination or are used fictitiously. Any resemblance to actual events or locales or persons, living or dead, is purely coincidental. The content presented here is intended solely for entertainment. The book does not constitute a recommendation or promotion. Due to the fictional character, the content of the book does not claim to be complete, nor can the timeliness, accuracy and balance of the information provided be guaranteed. The author accepts no liability for any inconvenience or damage resulting from the use of the information presented here.

The author does not endorse or promote discrimination based on ethnic or national origin, age, gender, sexual orientation, religion, disability, military status, social-economic background or any other factor. This work aims to foster understanding, empathy, and inclusivity.

For better readability, gender-neutral wording has been omitted. All masculine spellings refer equally to all genders.

Bibliographic information of the German National Library:

The German National Library lists this
publication in the German National Bibliography;
Detailed bibliographic data is available on the Internet
can be accessed via http://dnb.dnb.de

The automated analysis of the work in order to obtain
information in particular on patterns, trends and correlations
correlations in accordance with §44b UrhG ("text and data mining")
is prohibited.

This book was translated by Professor Boris Bigalke, MD, from the original German edition titled:"Die Kraft des Venustempels: Im Schatten der Sternenvölker"

Publisher:
BoD · Books on Demand GmbH, Überseering 33, 22297 Hamburg, bod@bod.de

Print production:
Libri Plureos GmbH, Friedensallee 273, 22763 Hamburg

ISBN: 978-3-7597-7463-7

For everyone who wants to get inspired for Venus!

Table of content

Introduction

Venus: The beauty in the sea of stars

In the not-too-distant future, humanity stands on the threshold of a new era of interplanetary exploration and discovery. Decades of technological breakthroughs - particularly in energy generation, space technology and the development of extremely resistant materials - have made it possible to travel to the most extreme planets in the solar system. Missions to Mars and the first manned missions to the outer planets have revolutionized knowledge about our solar system and, above all, raised questions about our own existence and the limits of life in the universe. In this field of curiosity and possibilities, interest is growing in one of the most enigmatic planets in the solar system: Venus.

Venus, the 2nd planet in the solar system, was named after the **Roman goddess of love and beauty.** This naming reflects the bright brilliance of the planet, which is the third brightest object in the sky from Earth (after the sun and moon) and can be seen either shortly after sunset or shortly before sunrise, depending on its position in orbit. Venus is also known as the **evening star** and sometimes also as the **morning star.**

Venus moves in an orbit within the Earth's orbit around the sun. This means that it is never very far from the sun from our point of view. It can therefore only be observed at dusk - either in the evening sky (as an evening star) or in the morning sky (as a morning star), depending on whether it is east or west of the sun. When Venus "overtakes" the Earth on its orbit, it changes from an evening star to a morning star position and vice versa. The ancient Greeks and Romans even initially considered them to be two different celestial objects: the evening star "Hesperos" and the morning star "Phosphoros" (or "Lucifer" for the Romans). Only later was it recognized that they were one and the same object - Venus.

In **Greek mythology,** Venus corresponds to the **goddess Aphrodite,** who also stands for love, beauty and fertility. The reference to love and beauty can also be found across cultures in other mythologies. For example, Venus was worshipped in the **Babylonian Empire as Ishtar,** the goddess of love and war, while in **Mesopotamian culture** she was known as Inanna.

These mythological connections show how early mankind associated the planet with female beauty and attraction due to its impressive appearance. In modern astronomy, Venus thus carries a legacy from the mythologies of many cultures, which interpreted its special presence in the sky in many different ways.

Venus is similar to Earth in many respects: similar size, mass and density. But the surface is a fiery inferno - with an atmosphere of thick clouds of sulphuric acid and a surface pressure equivalent to that of a dive in the Earth's deepest oceans. The temperature remains constant at around 470 °C (870 °F). For decades, Venus was considered a barren, uninhabitable land. Only atmospheric exploration and occasional probes were able to survive before they were destroyed by the harsh conditions. But with the advent of new technologies developed specifically for such extreme conditions, the possibility of exploring this planet directly became a reality.

An inexplicable discovery

Four years ago, the results of a research project by the

UNESA (United Nations Exploration and Space Administration) research project on Venus were published four years ago and caused a worldwide sensation: an unmanned satellite mission discovered **strange geometric formations** on the surface of Venus beneath the dense cloud cover. Equipped with modern radar and sensor devices, the probe transmitted images of unusually symmetrical structures that could not be explained by any natural phenomenon. The shapes were reminiscent of terraced pyramids, columns and enigmatic circular patterns that could not possibly have been created with such precision by volcanic or tectonic processes. In addition, a detailed analysis showed that the formations were aligned with specific planetary constellations - a fact that suggested a cultic or ceremonial significance.

This discovery triggered a feverish debate among scientists and the general public alike. Was it possible that a civilization had once existed on Venus that had been wiped out by some unknown event? Was there life that had evolved in a form that could withstand these extreme conditions? Questions like these led to the topic of a Venus mission becoming a priority.

The signal: a call from the deep

About a year after the discovery of the formations, a UNESA ground station near Canberra, Australia, received a strange signal. The signal - rhythmic and repeating - appeared to originate from several kilometers below the surface of Venus and did not match known radio waves or atmospheric interference. To the surprise of the researchers, the signal repeated itself in a complex pattern and showed characteristics reminiscent of an artificial source. After weeks of intensive analysis, an international team of cryptographers and mathematicians succeeded in extracting a simple message: It was a **coordinate!**

This coordinate pointed to a point on the **northern hemisphere** of Venus, not far from the structures discovered by the probe. Researchers and government officials were both concerned and intrigued. Was this a cry for help? Or perhaps a kind of greeting, a call that was only activated when humanity came close enough to receive it? Speculation about the origin of the signal ranged from a warning signal to prevent anyone from approaching Venus to a tantalizing hint of possible communication with a long-lost civilization.

The Venera Ascendant team

UNESA finally decided to send a manned mission to Venus to investigate the signal and the formations on site. This decision was extremely controversial: Venus is still considered one of the most hostile places in the solar system. However, the advanced protective suits, which could withstand extreme pressures and temperatures, as well as new technologies for shielding against radiation and heat, made such a mission possible for the first time.

Under the leadership of experienced Commander Aiyana Wolfe, a Native American and veteran of UNESA space missions, a team of six astronauts and scientists, considered to be the best in their respective fields, was selected:

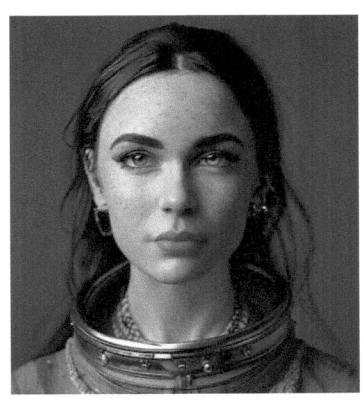

Name (nationality):
Commander Aiyana Wolfe (USA)

Position:
Mission leader, pilot and strategist

Aiyana is an experienced commander and the main person responsible for the mission. She is calm and thoughtful with a deep connection to Earth and a passion for ancient cultures. She is aware of the historic responsibility her mission holds for humanity and fights to navigate her crew safely through the challenges.

Name (nationality):
Colonel Luis Ortega (Spain)

Position:
Fighter pilot, engineer and 1st officer

As a former military pilot, Luis is pragmatic and focused on protecting the team. He not only takes on technical tasks, but also protects the crew in critical situations. He is charismatic and compassionate. He plays the classical guitar with great passion.

Name (nationality):
Professor Kenji Sato (Japan)

Position:
Astrophysicist, geologist and science officer

Kenji is an analytical thinker and fascinated by the extreme environmental conditions of Venus. He sometimes feels isolated and is fascinated by the links between ancient myths and science and has taken up drawing and calligraphy as a hobby, which is closely related to Zen Buddhism.

Name (Nationalität):
Dr. Priya Kapoor (Indien)

Position:
Exobiologe und Biochemiker

Priya is an expert on biological structures, especially focusing on possible extraterrestrial life forms and analyzing the chemistry of the surface of Venus. His character is gentle, humorous, optimistic and deeply connected to nature. He is an avid strategy board gamer.

Name (nationality):
Dr. Ingrid Nilsen (Norway)

Position:
Archaeologist and cultural anthropologist

As an archaeologist and anthropologist, Ingrid is fascinated by cultural heritage. She is courageous, persistent and passionate about history, philosophy and the myths of other planets. She has a flair for hidden secrets, has a gift for deduction and is a foreign language genius.

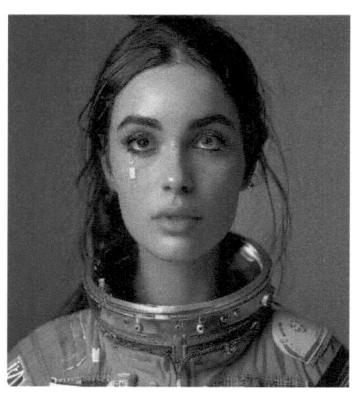

Name (nationality):
Dr. Soraya (android)

Position:
Doctor, engineer, 2nd officer and crisis intervention expert

Soraya is a highly developed cybernetic organism with medical, technical and social capabilities. She is programmed to simulate human emotions and even romantic behaviors. But during the mission, she develops a deeper connection with her crew and begins to question the nature of her existence.

The landing site: a hidden temple city

The northern hemisphere of Venus is home to the **Ishtar Terra highland complex,** one of the largest and best-known plateaus on Venus, characterized by complex tectonic structures. Ishtar Terra consists of tangled, rugged areas often referred to as **"tesserae".** Tesserae are characteristic of Venusian terrain and consist of intersecting rifts and ridges that form a unique and fascinating landscape.

This region is particularly interesting for the geology of Venus, as tesserae are considered one of the oldest types of terrain on Venus and could provide clues to the planet's past tectonic activity.

The **targeted landing zone of the Venera Ascendant** is located on the large plateau complex where the strange geometric structures are most clearly visible.

Hidden by the dense cloud cover, this location is in an area that has not been investigated in detail before, as the extreme temperatures and high atmospheric pressure have rendered all unmanned probes useless so far. However, the coordinates decoded from the signal seem to point directly to this location, as if something or someone had been expecting the arrival of the other planet's inhabitants.

The Temple City, as it is called by some scientists on Earth, is the central target of the mission. The satellite images of the structures show geometric patterns and symbolic decorations that are too complex to have been formed by the forces of nature. The shapes and alignments could indicate a civilizational significance, perhaps a gateway or temple providing access to a deeper structure.

Objectives and risks of the mission

The main objectives for the Venera Ascendant team are ambitious: to locate and analyse the signal, investigate the geometric formations and find evidence of possible civilization. A considerable amount of resources have been devoted to developing advanced protective suits and technological systems that can withstand the extreme conditions on Venus. Despite this preparation, the mission is extremely dangerous: landing and moving on the surface of Venus requires absolute precision, and the environment remains unpredictable. High temperatures, toxic clouds and the intense atmospheric pressure make every step a challenge.

Chapter 1: The journey

Approaching the mythical planet

The spaceship Venera Ascendant glided through the darkness of space, shrouded in the silence and infinite space that has fascinated and intimidated mankind for centuries. On board the Venera Ascendant, however, there was no silence - the team is lively, the atmosphere filled with the mixture of tension and curiosity that comes with a mission into the unknown.

Venus, which until recently was considered an inhospitable, hostile planet, is the target.

"Venus, the Roman goddess of love and beauty," murmured Dr. Ingrid Nilsen as she watched the lights on the screen. Her eyes sparkled, and she can hardly believe that she would soon land on this planet that is so much closer to humans and yet has always remained a mystery. "It's hard to believe that it's so close to us and yet has been a mystery for thousands of years."

"That sounds poetic, Ingrid," Commander Aiyana Wolfe replied dryly. She leaned back in her seat, arms crossed in front of her chest, with an expression that wavered between irony and awe. "But I'd suggest we focus on how to get back to Earth in one piece rather than ancient mythology." She gave Ingrid a sharp look, but a faint smile curved her lips. Aiyana is a strategist and an experienced military pilot who leaves nothing to chance - and this mission was nothing less than a military operation for her, even if the others often have a more relaxed attitude.

"Oh, Commander, why don't you treat me to a bit of culture," Ingrid replied with a teasing wink. "After all, we'll be the first humans to explore the interior of Venus. A little poetry should be allowed."

Colonel Luis Ortega, the chief engineer and first officer, nodded and grinned as he studied the sensor readouts. "The way I see it, if we find anything on this planet that will make us famous on Earth in our lifetime, then I'll be happy. Poetry or not - as long as Venus doesn't try to fry us."

"And I thought I was the only one here worried about heat death," said Dr. Priya Kapoor, the exobiologist and bio-chemist, with a wry smile. Priya has worked extensively on the extreme chemistry of Venus' surface, and his analysis and concerns are informed by a pragmatic, scientific view of things. "The data says that Venus has a surface temperature of over 400 °C (752 °F). Do any of you really think there's something waiting for us down there that we can understand?"

"I'm sure Kenji will give us a scientific explanation when we get there," Luis interjected with a grin, and a quiet laugh goes around the room. Professor Kenji Sato is an astrophysicist and geologist and is considered one of the leading experts on planetary atmospheres. His analytical mind was qua-si the sober voice of the group.

"You're not entirely wrong," Kenji replied dryly, without taking his eyes off the screen. "But the latest scans of Venus show anomalies in the atmosphere that we can't yet explain. It is quite possible that we are encountering completely new phenomena here. And that is precisely the point of this mission."

As the conversation continued, Dr. Soraya stood quietly in a corner, watching her crewmates with a gentle smile, her eyes sparkling in a way that seemed almost human. Soraya, a highly advanced android with medical and technical skills, was here to support the crew - but in truth she also harbored an experimental AI capable of simulating human emotions. Sometimes she wondered herself if it was really just simulation, or if she was actually starting to feel attracted to the humans on board.

"Soraya, what do you mean?" Ingrid asked curiously. "We're talking about the extreme heat of Venus. Is that worrying you?"

"My systems are designed for extreme protection," Soraya replied calmly, with a hint of humor in her voice. "But I'll be careful not to melt, Ingrid. I too am very excited about what we might find - maybe even more than you all are." Her comment makes the crew smile. The android is still new to the team, and some find her humanity almost uncanny. But her analytical skills and medical expertise are undisputed.

"Maybe we won't find anything - or maybe we'll find everything," Aiyana murmurs, her gaze fixed on the glowing dot on the horizon that symbolizes Venus. "The signal we've received is too clear, too regular. There must be something down there - something we don't understand yet."

Routine work

The dull hum of the engines was the only sound in the cabin as the Venera Ascendant team went about their routine work, ensuring the safety and maintenance of the spacecraft as well as preparing for the tasks ahead on Venus.

1. Maintenance and monitoring of the ship's systems

Luis carried out daily maintenance on the power and propulsion systems to ensure their optimal performance. This included checking fuel consumption, cooling circuits and the operation of the propulsion system. **Luis** also regularly checked emergency systems such as life support, fire suppression and heat shields.

Soraya, as an android, provided both technical and medical support in her role as engineer and doctor, documenting the functionality of the systems with superhuman precision.

2. Life support systems and environmental controls

Kenji monitored the air filtration and CO_2 binding systems, humidity, temperature and oxygen levels in the spaceship. He ensured that the systems for the Venus landing were operating under optimal conditions. The water treatment system was regularly maintained to ensure that the crew always had enough clean water available.

3. Medical check-ups and health

Soraya carried out regular health checks, measured vital parameters and ensured that all crew members were in good health. The crew completed **physical training routines** to minimize muscle and bone loss due to weightlessness. Soraya supervised the exercises and made personal adjustments during exercise. The crew used conversations in **mental health sessions** with Soraya and also in groups to manage stress and isolation.

4. Preparation for scientific missions

Ingrid and **Kenji** spent many hours analyzing data on the Venus atmosphere and geology and selecting possible landing sites. They checked and calibrated the measuring instruments for atmospheric samples and material tests.

Priya prepared chemical analyses and exobiology equipment to ensure that all instruments are optimally prepared for the sample analysis of the Venus surface.

5. Simulations for landing and emergencies

Aiyana organized and led regular training and emergency simulations. The crew practiced scenarios such as emergency landings, failure of life support systems, sudden depressurization and other critical situations. Simulated landing procedures were run through regularly so that the crew was prepared for any eventuality.

6. Communication with Earth and data transmission

The crew was in daily contact with the control center on Earth and transmitted status reports, technical data and scientific progress. Data from on-board and external sensors was regularly transmitted to Earth and evaluated there in order to optimize the planning and safety of the mission.

7. Logging and documenting

Aiyana and the other crew members kept a detailed logbook in which they documented all events, maintenance and scientific observations. The records were used both for traceability for the control center and as a reference for future missions to Venus.

8. Scientific research and experiments

In preparation for the Venus exploration, the crew worked on smaller, preparatory experiments to contribute to better analysis capabilities on site, e.g. **analyzing rock samples** in the miniature environmental simulator or chemical tests on the reaction of samples under Venus-like conditions.

9. Leisure and relaxation

The crew members also took time for **leisure activities** such as reading, conversations and community games to strengthen team spirit and promote mental relaxation. Especially in the first few days, this led to conversations that created bonds and strengthened the group dynamic. **Movie nights** and sharing personal stories also created bonds and reduced the pressure of the long journey.

Each of these areas was crucial for the crew to successfully achieve the mission objectives and ensure that they were optimally prepared physically and mentally when they arrived on Venus.

The tension mounts

The crew sat scattered at their stations, and although everyone seemed focused, a certain restlessness crept in. The journey had gone smoothly, but Venus was close, and with every hour the expectations and questions about the mission - and about each other - grew.

Kenji looked at Luis: "Luis, have you thought about how we're going to deal with the thick layer of clouds on Venus? I mean, it could block our view of possible landing sites."

Luis replied: "The tactic? Hope and pray that we find a gap in the clouds." He grinned mischievously: "Seriously, we only have a limited amount of fuel for any course corrections. So we'll probably just have to rely on the scanner data to steer us in the right direction."

Priya joined in the conversation: "A little faith in the technology, Kenji! After all, these systems were designed for extreme conditions. Have you forgotten that we avoided a collision with an asteroid by millimetres last year?"

Kenji shook his head with a smile. He was known for his careful planning, but Priya's optimism sometimes had an infectious effect.

Kenji replied: "Yes, yes. But technology is only as good as the data it receives. And honestly, Priya - the data from Venus' atmosphere is anything but clear. What if there's a cloud storm down there that makes us swat at the windshield like a fly?"

Soraya interjected: "If I may interject here: according to my calculations, the probability of us encountering such extreme turbulence is exactly 3.7 percent." Soraya stood behind Kenji and smiled at him with a mixture of curiosity and patience: "The risk is low."

Kenji just shook his head with a laugh, casting a thoughtful glance at the android and rolling his eyes: "Soraya, your 'calculations'... Sometimes I really wonder if you're not just being overly optimistic. Maybe I should check you again."

Soraya replied, "Optimism? I wish." She grinned slightly before adding seriously, "But I've been programmed to assess risks realistically. And when I see you worrying about the turbulence - maybe you should trust my assessments for once."

Now Aiyana made a comment: "Okay, guys. Let's calm down." She rose from her seat and stepped into the middle of the room: "It's clear that we're all feeling nervous. After all, it's not just any routine flight. But we should remember one thing - we are the best of the best. We have the training, the technology and the determination to master this."

Aiyana's serious words silenced the group. She had an impressive ability to keep the crew calm and focused.

Ingrid said excitedly: "I can't wait to see what awaits us. But honestly, I have to say, I'm a little uneasy. What if we don't find anything down there? Or even worse - something we could never have imagined?"

Aiyana replied: "I know what you mean, Ingrid. But that's our strength. We are prepared to encounter the unknown. If there is something we don't understand - then we investigate it. Step by step. We are here because we are curious and not afraid of the unknown."

A smile went around the room and Ingrid leaned back in her chair, relieved by the reassuring words.

Luis took the floor again: "Okay, let's look at this more realistically. How many of you think we have any chance of finding anything exciting down there? I mean, what would be the most likely scenario?"

Kenji replied: "Personally, I'm hoping for an ancient geological relic. relic. Some kind of ancient crater or volcanic structure that might provide evidence of past activity."

Priya shook his head: "Boring. I'm banking on evidence of microorganisms - maybe not active, but remains that show Venus was once different. Maybe even traces of organic life."

Luis continued, "And if I'm honest... well, if I could believe in alien technology, then I hope we come across something like this. Something that shows us that Venus..."

Soraya interrupted Luis: "That Venus isn't just a hot lump of rock?" Soraya looked directly at Luis, a mysterious smile on her lips: "Who knows what we'll find there. Maybe... we might come across something that tells us more about ourselves than we can imagine."

The crew fell silent, and everyone in the group seemed to ponder Soraya's words for a moment. Aiyana nodded slowly as she looked at the others. Perhaps she already knew that this mission could change more than anyone had previously realized.

Aiyana said in her calming way, "Anyway, it's time to relax, guys. It's not going to be an easy mission - and we need all our strength and confidence in ourselves and in each other to pull this off."

Each of them - Aiyana, Luis, Kenji, Priya, Ingrid and even Soraya - had a personal reason for being here. Whether it's scientific curiosity, the need for fame or simply the dream of being the first humans to set foot on Venus - their motivation drove them all, even if the risks were enormous.

Chapter 2: Somewhere between Earth and Venus

The Venera Ascendant traveled in an endless arc through the silent, black sea of space. The crew had been traveling for weeks, and although the routine had settled in, everyone tried in their own way to pass the time and break the monotony. The journey to Venus was long, and even the most demanding mission required patience and mutual understanding. The spaceship hummed quietly, and the crew prepared for the final leg of the journey in their quarters or the common rooms.

A relaxed round

In the common area, Soraya, Kenji and Priya sat together and played a board game that Priya had brought with him on the trip. He had called it "Cosmic Risk" - a kind of strategy and conquest game with planets and star systems as playing fields. Ingrid had been skeptical at first, but after a while she also pulled up a chair. "This game is really bloody tricky," Ingrid said, frowning as she moved one of her game pieces. "Priya, you made it so difficult on purpose, didn't you?"

Priya smiled innocently: "No way! I just thought it might help us practice our strategic skills."

Kenji laughed, "Strategic or not, it kind of reminds me of chess... but with more explosions."

"Explosions are always good," replied Luis, who had just come in and sat down on the couch next to them. "What would a journey through space be without a bit of action?"

"Action? You're just not ready for science to overshadow you," Priya teased, nudging Kenji with his finger. "But that can be changed."

Hobbies and interests

Luis leaned back, relaxed, and picked up the guitar hanging on the wall. It was one of his most loyal companions, which he took with him everywhere. "You can all plan strategically," he said, "but sometimes you need to unwind." He plucked a few strings and a soft chord echoed through the room.

Soraya leaned back and listened, her eyes relaxing as the first notes rang out: "Luis, play that song you practiced the other day. I've been wanting to hear it all week."

Luis nodded and began a soft, melancholy melody that slowly spread around the room: "It's actually an old song from my grandmother. I thought it would be nice to take a piece of home with me."

Kenji nodded appreciatively: "It has a really soothing sound. You should give a little concert on our next mission."

"Oh, I didn't know you liked that sort of thing, Kenji," Priya said in surprise. "Do you have any hidden talents?"

Kenji grinned: "Well, I may not be a musician, but I do have a little hobby. I draw."

Ingrid raised an eyebrow: "You draw? Any special motifs?"

Kenji laughed sheepishly: "Oh, actually I only draw cartoons from time to time. Little funny sketches. It helps me to relax, especially on long missions."

"That's great!" exclaimed Soraya. "Why didn't you show us this before? You could draw a comic about our trip!"

Kenji shrugged and smiled: "Maybe one day. But if I ever really feel like portraying you as cartoons, I'll let you know."

A round for the team leader

Aiyana, who as team leader was often to be found on the bridge or at meetings, joined them and dropped into one of the free chairs. "I hear laughter and see relaxed faces. Exactly what I want to see here."

Soraya grinned: "We're just practising a bit of 'Cosmic Risi-ko' - Priya has just backed us all into a corner."

"And the board game contains all kinds of cosmic strategies?" Aiyana asked with interest.

Priya grinned: "Exactly! Tactics and strategy - it takes your mind off things."

Aiyana nodded, put her hands on the table and looked around: "It's important that we do all this together, people. This mission could advance humanity. But... if we don't take good care of each other, we'll soon be lost."

"We'll take care of each other, Aiyana," Luis said reassuringly. "And in the end, when we get to Venus, we'll give you the biggest story of your life."

Ingrid nodded: "Knowledge is all well and good, but there is also so much in our team that makes us stronger than any mission we could ever undertake alone."

Aiyana smiled gratefully, "That's good to hear. And if anyone here develops a talent for... shall we say, tricky mechanics puzzles or alien-friendly speeches, let me know."

"All right," Kenji said, smirking, "then I'll focus on my psychic negotiation skills tonight in case we encounter any alien beings."

The journey to the essentials

After the game and a few stories, the group sat back and relaxed. Luis continued to strum his guitar while Ingrid talked to Priya and Kenji about their scientific expectations for the mission.

"We're going to go to Venus and find something that no one else has ever seen," Priya said with a slight sparkle in his eyes. "We might even discover evidence of alien life."

Ingrid nodded and looked at her: "I just hope that we learn not only technological progress, but also something about Venus that shows us what our place is in the universe."

"And maybe," Soraya said with a smile, "we'll find things far beyond our wildest dreams."

The group fell into a comfortable silence as they savored the moment of peace. They knew that they would soon encounter a whole new world - a world that promised not only knowledge, but also a journey into the unknown. The soft hum of the machines and the sounds of Luis' guitar filled the room. The crew sat scattered around the common room, enjoying the moment of peace. After all the years of preparation, the training and the grueling months in a confined space, the distance to Earth no longer seemed so overwhelming. Each of them was now over the initial tension and felt a sense of trust - both in the mission and in each other.

About hopes and fears

Aiyana watched her crew with a quiet, benevolent smile. She knew that each of them brought their own hopes and fears to this adventure. After a while, she cleared her throat and spoke in a calm tone:

"When I imagine what awaits us..." Aiyana paused for a moment. "Then I must honestly say that it scares me sometimes. But somehow your solidarity here also gives me courage. If we've come this far, then we can make it to the end."

Kenji looked up: "I think fear is what keeps us going. It means that this means something to us, doesn't it?"

"There's something to that," Priya agreed. "Venus isn't just a planet, it's a leap into the unknown. Who knows how much we're risking - but I see it the same way you do, Kenji. It makes us human. The possibility of discovering something completely new is ... just too tempting."

Soraya, who was listening expressionlessly but attentively, tilted her head slightly to one side. "Fear and fascination - interesting concepts. Seems to me you're using them to drive the mission."

Luis laughed and played a few soft chords. "Maybe we're all a bit of philosophers. Science, adventure and a bit of madness - it all goes together, doesn't it?"

Personal stories and memories

After a while, Ingrid got up and went to the holo-projector. She projected an image of her home on the wall: the rugged, beautiful coastal landscape of Norway, covered in fog and surrounded by deep fjords.

"This is my retreat when I'm not on a mission," she said, smiling gently. "There in the mountains, without all the... technical stuff. Just nature."

Priya looked at the picture with fascination: "That looks gorgeous, In-grid. Norway, right?"

"Yes, a small place on the Hardangerfjord. Maybe a bit lonely for others, but for me it's home."

"And you, Priya?" asked Aiyana. "Is there a special place for you?"

Priya smiled slightly. "When I'm not in some lab, I'm off to the mountains in the Himalayas. It may sound a bit clichéd, but I can let my mind wander there. Especially in Kashmir, at Dal Lake. The silence there helps me to think through my projects."

Luis continued to play softly, the sounds of his guitar filling the room: "I spend most of my time with my family in Galicia, on the coast. The silence of the waves, the salty smell of the air - that's what draws me back to earth."

Aiyana looked at them all thoughtfully: "Maybe we carry all these little pieces of home with us. And when we're on Venus, when we're lonely or lost, we can remember what gives us strength."

Kenji nodded: "And when we come back, we'll have a lot more to tell. I hope I can tell my little sister about Venus. She wrote to me earlier that she wants to know everything about the planet."

Challenges and dreams

The conversation turned to hopes and expectations. Venus was more than just a scientific destination - each of them carried their own unique dreams and aspirations.

"Aiyana, how did you become the commander of this mission?" Kenji asked suddenly. "Didn't you also have the chance to take on other missions? Surely you had other offers?"

Aiyana smiled. "Venus has fascinated me since I was a child. It was always like a mysterious, golden jewel in the sky. I often stood there and watched it, imagining that something could be there. The idea just never left me. And when the offer came to lead the mission, I knew I just had to do it."

"It's inspiring that you pulled this off," Priya said with appreciation in his voice. "Your journey has really motivated us, I think. A real role model."

Luis put down his guitar and nodded: "You radiate a kind of peace that helps us all, Aiyana. It's as if you have this mission firmly under control."

Aiyana laughed sheepishly, "Thank you, but believe me, it's just as important that you help me. I feel much safer when I see that we can rely on each other."

Soraya, who had been listening quietly until then, now spoke in a low voice: "Trust in the crew and the mission is a fascinating constant in your humanity. It is interesting to observe how it influences behavior and strengthens morale."

Kenji looked at her and smiled: "Soraya, even you have your human traits. You've inspired us just as much on this journey."

Soraya bowed her head slightly, a gesture of reflection, "Thank you, Kenji. It's a pleasure to be part of your mission."

One last evening near Venus

Later that evening, the crew prepared for tomorrow. Each of them knew that the real challenge was yet to come. But before they parted, Aiyana turned to them once more: "Tomorrow begins the adventure we've been training for all these years. Rest up and remember that we can do this together. I'm glad I'm flying with you."

Kenji raised his hand in greeting and replied: "For tomorrow and all the days after. We have a destination."

The crew nodded in agreement, and they all slowly disappeared into their cabins. There, alone and yet knowing that the others were not far away, they dwelled on their thoughts of the adventure ahead.

"Venus is waiting for us," Soraya murmured softly, and even to the android, there was a hint of anticipation in her voice.

Chapter 3: The landing

The command bridge of the Venera Ascendant was filled with the gentle tones of the instruments and the light displays flickering on the screens. The dense, yellowish cloud layer of Venus dominated the view through the front windows, and the atmosphere was tense. Commander Aiyana stood in the center, watching her crew prepare for their posts. The countdown to landing ticked down inexorably.

Aiyana spoke in a calm voice: "Crew, we only have five minutes until we enter the atmosphere. You know the protocol, but I still want to make sure we're all on the same page here. Every move has to be right, understand?"

Luis grinned as he checked the configuration of the engine: "Understood, Commander. Guess I'll let you strap me in for once."

Kenji looked up from his scientific readouts, "Luis, in case you've forgotten: Down here, gravity is almost 90% of Earth's gravity. It's going to be a rough ride."

Luis winked: "Well, I'll wear the crunch in my back as a badge of honor."

Aiyana smiled slightly, but then became serious again: "Kenji, what does the atmosphere look like? Are our simulations being confirmed?"

Kenji tapped on his display and checked the data: "Yes, but reality is always more unpredictable, of course. The dense CO_2 layer and the clouds of sulphuric acid restrict visibility, which will be a challenge. We only have a short window of time to get through before the storm front could catch us."

Ingrid, looking a little nervous from her seat, said: "Such a storm... Can we really fly through it safely? The density of the atmosphere is almost 100 times higher than on Earth. What if..."

Luis grinned and winked at her: "Don't worry, Ingrid. Have you forgotten that you're traveling with the best pilot on the mission?"

Aiyana laughed softly: "The best pilot, yes? Isn't that my title, Luis?"

Luis replied with a grin: "You're the best pilot in theory, Aiyana. I'll get us down there - and back. Don't worry."

Aiyana pulled a pout: "So you really don't lack self-confidence, you proud Spaniard!"

Soraya interjected in a soft voice, her gaze calm: "If I may intervene, it's quite normal for the tension to be high before the landing. Our pulse rates are all above average. Technically speaking, breathing exercises would help to calm us down."

Priya sighed and nodded in agreement: "That might help. My pulse feels like the drum of a marching orchestra right now."

Kenji smiled slightly: "That's normal. We're all nervous. There are only a few scientists who have ever been able to analyze the surface of Venus directly. We are entering a place that we only know from data and theories."

Ingrid smiled and looked at Kenji: "And there it is again, the professor's cool head. Kenji, I don't think anything can upset you."

Kenji laughed softly: "I can only say one thing: science is best when it takes place under controlled conditions. And nothing is controlled down there. That makes me nervous too."

Aiyana nodded and looked at each individual crew member: "I understand that we all have our doubts, but that's exactly why we're here. We are well trained, prepared and know what we are doing. Together we can do this. When we're on the surface, everyone stays focused. Understood?"

Everyone in the crew shouted in unison: "Understood, Commander."

The tension eased slightly as everyone returned to their regular routine. The countdown continued to tick down, now there were only two minutes left. Aiyana looked intently at the landing terminal and picked up the controls.

Aiyana turned her gaze to Luis: "Luis, prepare the energy module. We'll need the boost as soon as we break through the atmosphere."

Luis replied briefly: "Ready. The energy reserves are set to maximum. Everything is running."

Kenji glanced at his displays: "We're approaching the entry point. The temperature is rising rapidly. The heat shields are about to reach their limits."

Aiyana: "Understood. Soraya, status of medical monitoring?"

Soraya checked the displays: "The vital signs are stable. There's been a slight increase in heart rates - absolutely as expected."

Priya said quietly, almost to herself: "I wonder what we'll find down there. Venus was just a myste-rium for so long. What if... what if there really is more than just an inhospitable landscape?"

Ingrid smiled: "If there really is something there, then we'll be the first to know. And that makes me... curious."

Luis grinned and tapped his dashboard: "Good thing we have the best spaceship and the best team for this. Don't worry, Priya. We'll land safely."

Aiyana said in a serious voice, "One more minute, guys. When we reach the surface, there will be no turning back. Everyone knows what to do, right?"

Everyone nodded and replied in unison: "Yes, Commander."

A silent countdown sounded. Aiyana looked around one last time, responsibility and determination in her gaze. She tightened her grip on the controls and concentrated.

"Prepare to enter the atmosphere," Aiyana ordered. Her gaze was determined and focused, but her eyes reflected the knowledge that this was a step into the unknown - and that nothing could truly prepare her for what would await her on Venus.

Aiyana called out: "Stand by. In 10... 9... 8..."

The atmosphere around the Venera Ascendant vibrated with tension and heat. The entire crew was strapped in, their eyes fixed on the screens and the thick sea of Venusian clouds. The yellowish plumes shown by the external cameras enveloped the ship and the pressure gauges jumped to the upper limit. The spaceship shook violently under the entry process.

Aiyana concentrated, her hands firmly on the wheel: "We are now fully in the atmosphere. The heat shields are holding - still. Luis, stabilize the thrusters."

Luis' fingers danced across the control panel as he manually balanced the ship: "Understood, Commander. Shields at 92%. Temperature rising... Still under control."

A loud metallic crunch echoed through the cockpit and the entire crew involuntarily flinched. The strain caused by the dense atmosphere is extreme, and the Venera Ascendant was shaken to the core.

Soraya spoke in a calm voice to reassure the crew: "Me-medical readings are stable. There's nothing to worry about - all vital signs are in the normal range."

Kenji with a worried look at his data: "Visibility through the cameras is almost zero. Dense clouds of sulphuric acid everywhere. Once we're through the upper layer, we'll hopefully find a more stable zone."

Priya looked at the wavering sensor readouts and spoke in a hushed voice, "I know it's risky, but... what if we don't make it? This atmosphere is like a pressure chamber."

Ingrid with an encouraging smile said almost whispering to Priya, "Hey, you know we'll make it. We've been practicing this for so long. Besides, have you seen Aiyana and Luis? They'll get us through this."

Luis grinned, despite the sweat on his forehead: "Trust is everything, Ingrid. And yes, Priya, I'm taking this as a personal challenge."

A brief moment of smiles went through the crew until the ship was abruptly shaken again. Suddenly there was a loud alarm signal and the displays flickered.

Aiyana shouted over the alarm: "Calibrate stability systems! Everyone, hold on!"

Soraya spoke in a calm but firm tone: "Activate emergency tethers."

The crew pulled their harnesses even tighter and clutched the handholds. The spaceship tilted menacingly to one side as a sudden updraft upset the controls.

Luis snorted as he counter-steered violently: "It's like a damn hurricane. Aiyana, I can't do this alone - I need full steering."

Aiyana grabbed the second control lever next to Luis, her hands in perfect coordination with him: "Understood, Luis. Take over together. Priya, Kenji, we need data on the lower atmospheric layers, quickly! How far are we from landing?"

Kenji tapped frantically on his display: "Only 8000 meters to the designated landing zone. But... the wind is stronger than expected and the magnetic fields vary greatly. The sensors could show even more interference."

Priya quickly replied: "The dense cloud layer is beginning to clear. When we enter the last layer, we might have more stable weather for a moment."

Another tremor ran through the ship, but this time more gently. The light flickered and stabilized again. For a brief moment, the crew saw the orange-yellow surface of Venus for the first time, which seemed ominously close. The entire atmosphere is silent, only the faint hum of the engines can be heard.

Aiyana took a deep breath: "Well done, guys. Final spurt. Luis, extend your landing legs."

Luis grinned tensely and operated the control panel: "Landing legs are extended, Commander. Automatic damping activated."

Ingrid stared wide-eyed at the screens: "Wow... this is surreal. This landscape... It looks so... hostile, but also somehow majestic."

Kenji spoke with fascination, "Here at last. The surface of Venus... Who would have thought we'd actually see this."

Soraya spoke while monitoring the crew's vital signs, "The conditions here are extreme, both physically and mentally. I would recommend a short break to recalibrate once we have landed safely."

Aiyana nodded in agreement: "Good idea, Soraya. But first we have to complete the landing safely."

The ship was now hovering just a few hundred meters above the ground and the crew held their breath. A gentle but deep rumble caused the ship to finally make contact with the surface of Venus. The impact was absorbed by the damping systems, and after a few seconds there was absolute silence.

Aiyana announced to the group with a slight smile and a satisfied look: "Guys, we made it. Welcome to Venus!"

The crew erupted in quiet cheers, smiles and relief on every face. Together they had achieved the seemingly impossible, the long journey and the dangerous landing on an alien planet were over.

Luis smiled broadly and tapped the dashboard: "That was quite a ride. Venera Ascendant really deserves its name."

Ingrid was still looking at the screens in amazement: "That's just... incredible. The surface of Venus. And we're the first ones here."

Kenji commented quietly, almost reverently: "What we might discover here... who knows, we might change the history of mankind."

Soraya added quietly and thoughtfully: "And how we humans will return changed."

It actually seemed ironic for an android to identify herself as "human". But she was obviously programmed that way and lived up to her role.

Aiyana spoke with a final, deep breath: "Yes, we will. Everyone, good work. Take a short rest and get ready for the first step onto the surface. We have a mission to accomplish."

With this request, the crew slowly released their harnesses and mentally prepared themselves to be the first humans to set foot on the surface of Venus. The reality of their historic moment began to penetrate them all - and they knew that nothing would ever be the same again.

Chapter 4: The first step on foreign soil

Euphoria on arrival

After the Venera Ascendant touched down on the Ishtar Terra plateau, the ship was surrounded by clouds and fog, so that little of the surroundings could be seen.

Commander Aiyana activated the com system and turned to her crew.

Aiyana began with the words: "Okay, team, we have successfully reached the surface of Venus. Time to make history. What is the status of all systems?"

Luis went through the control displays on his panel: "Propulsion systems on standby, shields active and environmental controls stable. External temperatures are high, as expected - about 470 degrees Celsius. But the shields are holding."

Soraya checked the data and nodded: "Air composition contains the expected high levels of carbon dioxide and sulphur dioxide. No surprises, but I'll keep an eye on the readings."

Priya straightened up, "I can hardly believe we're actually here. The idea that a civilization could possibly exist under this atmosphere... it's... incredible."

Turning to Priya, Aiyana replied: "We are not here for theoretical discussions, Priya. We are here to find answers. Ingrid, what about external communication? Can we send out a probe?"

Ingrid was beaming with excitement, but managed to maintain her professionalism: "Ready when you are. The probe is ready to go and I've programmed it to the surrounding topography and the mineral composition of the environment."

Aiyana prompted, "All right, let's go!"

Ingrid pressed a red button and the small probe left the ship through a hatch on the underside. The crew members could watch on the screens as the probe moved away from the ship and began to scan the immediate surroundings.

Luis: "Looking at this... Who would have thought that we would ever see Venus like this?"

Soraya commented, "The gravity here is only slightly lower than Earth's, which will help us acclimatize. But because of the heavy atmosphere and the temperature, our movements might feel slower."

Aiyana cautioned, "One step at a time. Soraya, what about the protective suits?"

Soraya replied: "Ready. Each suit has internal cooling and is reinforced with additional pressure layers. We'll feel like we're in an oven, but the protective layers will keep us safe for a while."

Priya looked slightly uncertain, "If these suits fail, we'll cook in seconds."

Luis grinned to break the tension, "Priya, no need to worry. As long as you don't run a marathon, you'll be fine."

Aiyana: "We'll take it step by step. First, a quick exit to inspect the surroundings. The main goal is to make sure that our position is stable and that we are close to the supposed ruins that we discovered on the scans."

Ingrid, trembling with excitement, said, "Imagine what we could find... If there really is evidence of civilization here...!"

Soraya warned, "Ingrid, let's make sure we all stay in contact before we go adventuring."

Aiyana agreed: "Exactly, stay focused. This is an exploration, not a hunting trip for artifacts. Everyone stays in visual contact with their partner."

The first steps on the surface of Venus

The ship's airlock opened and the bright orange light of the Venusian atmosphere penetrated the airlock. Aiyana went out first, closely followed by Luis and Soraya, while Priya and Ingrid stayed behind a little nervously.

Aiyana asked, "Everything okay back there?"

Priya replied: "So far... yes. But this pressure and the heat... it's like the weight of the atmosphere is pressing down on your chest."

Luis replied, "That's Venus, Priya. The gravity is almost pulling your lungs out of your chest. But that's what we're here for."

Ingrid spoke with fascination: "This floor is incredible... It almost feels... plastic. Whatever this composition is, it seems to change with every movement."

Soraya explained: "It could be molten or volcanic materials that have been deformed under extreme pressure and high temperatures. Be careful with every step."

Aiyana warned: "Stay alert, the terrain is treacherous. No unnecessary steps and always pay attention to the indicator."

Luis looked over the terrain: "This is surreal... these tesserae look like ancient mosaics. It feels like we're on a planet that's been standing still for millions of years."

Soraya explained soberly: "The surface conditions indicate that this is one of the most stable regions on Venus. But the structure of the rock shows that there must have been intense tectonic activity here in the past."

Priya was overwhelmed: "I can hardly believe that all this exists so close to Earth and yet we are on a completely alien world."

Ingrid added: "It's like traveling back in time... a glimpse into the secrets of the solar system itself. Who knows what we'll discover here."

Kenji suggested: "We should start collecting samples. If we actually find evidence of life or a civilization..."

The atmosphere between the crew members was characterized by reverence and a deep silence. The landing zone seemed like a sacred place to them, a temple of stone and heat just waiting to reveal its secrets.

After the crew had taken their first cautious steps on Venus, they found themselves in the middle of a surreal landscape of tesserae formations, deep gorges and volcanic plains. The glistening heat, the diffuse light and the oppressive silence intensified the feeling of being on a completely alien world.

Aiyana activated the comm display on her suit again and spoke through the crew communication system: "Okay, everyone, stay close to me and watch your step. The scans show some unstable areas in the terrain. We'll set up a temporary base point near there and start sampling from there."

Luis took a deep breath, as far as his suit would allow. As an experienced fighter pilot and engineer, he is normally tough, but the unfamiliar atmosphere and the sight of the Tesserae formations amazed even him: "So this is Venus now. I would never have dreamed that I would land on a planet that was previously only known as a glowing hellmouth. The terrain is tough, but fascinating."

Kenji knelt down carefully and scanned a nearby rock formation. He saw the layers of tesserae that lay before him like a stone map of the planet.

Kenji described his impressions: "These formations are incredible. Such complex patterns indicate tectonic activity that we don't even see on Earth. Venus could have been much more alive in the past than we thought."

Ingrid had also been keeping an eye on the surroundings. Although she had not originally expected to find signs of civilization on Venus, she was captivated by the landscape.

Ingrid suggested: "Imagine these are the remains of a civilization we don't yet know. Perhaps they were able to work with these geological structures - or were devoured by them. The thought is both frightening and incredibly exciting."

Meanwhile, Soraya had activated the sensors in her systems and was analyzing the composition of the air, the ground temperature and the chemical composition of the rocks. Her voice was calm and matter-of-fact, but there was a hint of fascination in her tone: "I'm registering extremely high sulphur oxide values and stable rock temperatures of around 450 degrees Celsius. These values are constant and indicate intense volcanic activity in the past. The structure of the crystals and the yellow sulphur deposits show that chemical processes are at work here, which we should investigate in more detail."

Priya saw the yellowish crystal formations and wondered whether the extreme environmental conditions might have given rise to life of a completely different kind: "Sulphur dioxide, crystalline deposits... What if there is chemical-based life that is adapted to these conditions? I think we should take samples and analyze them to investigate possible biochemical processes."

Aiyana nodded: "Good idea, Priya. Our main goal is to collect as much data as possible before we head towards the signal's landing site."

Aiyana activated the first sampling set and marked the area where they wanted to set up the temporary base. Luis was already working on setting up a compact communication station, while Ingrid and Kenji carefully collected samples from the Tes-serae rocks.

Luis said: "This is the communication station. If we spread out, we should send out regular status reports. The Venusian soil is treacherous; one false step and you're up to your knees in rock."

Ingrid smiles inwardly: "Thanks for pointing that out, Luis. Not that I was planning on climbing a volcano, but I'll keep it in mind."

Kenji continued, "I'll calibrate the scanner for geological layers. If we can get deeper insights into the earth's layers, we might find clues to possible tectonic movements."

Soraya explained: "The terrain appears stable, but the structure shows intense tectonic stresses. Be vigilant and report any unusual activity."

Suddenly, a hiss interrupted the communication system - an unusual sound that no one expected. Everyone present froze for a moment.

Aiyana asked, startled: "Did you hear that? A signal, or was that an atmospheric phenomenon?"

Soraya replied in a reassuring voice: "The signal seems to have come from some kind of electromagnetic source. But the source is unclear. Could be atmospheric interference - or... something else."

Priya asked incredulously, "You mean it could be from this supposed civilization?"

Kenji replied: "No matter where it comes from, we should be careful. Venus could hold a lot more secrets than we think."

Aiyana agreed with Kenji: "Right. Let's stay focused. Anyone who sees anything unusual, report it immediately. We need to collect any data that could help us understand this planet better."

The team began to work in small groups, always within sight and with a fixed communication channel. The sampling and measurements gave them insights into the alien environment, but the feeling of the inexplicable remained.

While Priya and Kenji were analyzing crystal structures on a lava flow, Priya spoke lost in thought to Soraya, who was analyzing chemical samples: "Soraya, can you imagine what it would be like if someone had actually lived here? They must have been so... different."

Soraya replied: "The life forms that could exist on a world like this would be beyond the limits of our understanding. A species living in sulphur dioxide and at 450 °C (842 °F) might not even understand our language or our concept of time."

Kenji joked: "Maybe someone is watching us right now - and we are the aliens to them."

A moment of silence followed, during which everyone thought about it for themselves. The idea of being the stranger in another world was both exciting and oppressive.

Aiyana broke the silence with the announcement: "We are here to find answers - and perhaps also to ask some new questions. Let's get back to work now. We still have a lot to do before we get to the original signal."

With that said, they continued to work intently, taking in the incomparable landscape of Venus.

After a few hours of work, the crew returned to the spaceship exhausted. On board the Venera Ascendant, the crew followed a **24-hour rhythm,** which corresponds to the daily routine on Earth. Since one Venusian day, i.e. one complete rotation of Venus on its own axis, lasts around **243 Earth days,** it would have been impossible to follow the planet's natural day-night cycle. In addition, the sun barely shines through the dense atmosphere on Venus anyway, making the difference between day and night barely perceptible visually. A terrestrial schedule therefore helped the crew to orient themselves in this alien and consistently dim environment and to maintain their **biological clock.** An Earth-like day-night rhythm gave the crew members the feeling of a regular daily routine. A clearly regulated timetable made it possible to ratio **power and resources,** as the crew could precisely control the consumption of light, energy and food.

The crew had **fixed working and rest times,** which also included shift changes and monitoring cycles for critical systems. This ensured that someone was awake at all times to respond to unexpected events without anyone being permanently overloaded. This routine kept the astronauts effective and focused without being affected by the extreme conditions of the Venus day.

Chapter 5: The unexpected discovery

The next day, according to a 24-hour rhythm by earthly standards, the crew set off early in the morning and the first provisional analyses were completed. Now the astronauts prepared for their mission to locate the source of the mysterious signal.

Aiyana checked the equipment and conducted a final safety briefing.

Aiyana stood in front of the crew: "All right, everyone. We now have a good idea of the surroundings and know that the terrain is stable enough. Today we're moving towards the signal origin. Luis, you lead the group with the navigation system."

Luis grinned slightly: "Ready when you are. I hope we get answers to some of these riddles today."

Ingrid suggested: "I'd be happy with just a few clues. The tesserae structures alone indicate an extremely complex system - who knows what else we'll find."

Soraya said firmly: "I will monitor the health of each crew member closely. Our power supply is stable, but we need to make sure that no one is dehydrated or affected by the heat."

Kenji continued: "And if anything unexpected happens, I have the portable sensors with me for quick analysis. Hopefully the data will tell us more about whether the signal is of natural or technological origin."

And Priya added: "Or perhaps even biological in origin. The crystal formations could indicate biochemical processes. I'll examine the samples while we're on our way."

Aiyana instructed: "All right. Luis, lead the way. Ingrid and Priya, keep an eye out for distinctive terrain features - anything that might point to the source of the signal."

The crew moved slowly across the uneven surface. The heavy equipment and the glare of the Venusian surface required full concentration. The crew's radios crackled as they moved forward in formation.

Luis remarked, "This path seems to be pretty flat. According to the scans, there's a large ravine in about a kilometer. We'll have to be careful there."

Ingrid replied: "Good to know. The tesserae form a kind of natural path here. It's almost as if someone had arranged the stones carefully."

Soraya warned: "These patterns could indicate previous Vulcan activity - or, as Ingrid says, something else. We should be extra vigilant."

A few minutes later, they reached the ravine. The sight gave them pause - the rock walls rose steeply and the floor of the gorge was covered in sharp-edged crystals that glittered in different colors.

Kenji spoke enthusiastically: "This is... incredible. I've never seen crystalline structures like this before. The color changes depending on the angle of the light."

Aiyana dampened her euphoria a little and remained matter-of-fact: "Okay, let's stay focused. Ingrid, mark this spot for later analysis. We don't have time to linger here."

Luis looked at the navigation device: "We need to find a safe route along the gorge. The source of the signal is on the other side."

The group moved carefully along the edge of the gorge, their destination always in sight. When they finally reached a bridge made of natural rock formations, Priya suddenly stopped, his sensors flashing alarmingly: "Wait, Aiyana - my scanners are showing increased radiation activity directly in front of us."

Soraya asked incredulously: "Increased? How much?"

Priya replied, "Nothing life-threatening, but definitely unusual. It could be natural radioactivity released by volcanic activity... or..."

Ingrid whispered excitedly: "...an energy source?"

Aiyana turned to Ingrid: "Ingrid, could we have come across some kind of technology here?"

Ingrid replied: "Possibly, but it would be very, very old. If this radiation is artificially generated, it could be the remains of a long-forgotten energy source."

Luis speculated: "So we're heading towards something that someone - or something - may have actually created?"

Aiyana warned: "Guys, this is all conjecture. Let's proceed with caution. Luis, find us the safest path, but stay close to the radiation source. We don't want to take any risks."

Luis nodded in agreement: "Understood. This way - the terrain looks stable."

They followed Luis, and soon the radiation pattern took on a recognizable shape. In the center of a small, bowl-shaped depression, they spotted a metallic tetrahedral structure half-buried in the ground. It was the first time they had seen something that was clearly not of natural origin.

Ingrid was stunned: "This... this is some kind of artifact."

Soraya remained cool: "The metal composition does not correspond to any natural alloy found on Venus."

Kenji explained: "That must be the signal. The radiation is definitely coming from this structure. It could be some kind of transmitter or signal amplifier."

Aiyana asked, "Ingrid, do you have any idea what it could be?"

Ingrid replied: "Not exactly. But the design doesn't look random. The shape, the indentations - it seems to have been designed on purpose. Perhaps a relic of an ancient civilization?"

Priya wondered: "But how could it have survived here for so long without being destroyed?"

Soraya helped with an explanation: "The material could be particularly resistant. I'm scanning it for a material analysis."

Soraya held her hands to the artifact and her sensors began to collect detailed data. Her mechanical fingers glided over the indentations and structures while the crew waited in tense silence.

Soraya broke the silence with the words: "There is evidence of an energy source inside. It's weak, but stable. It could be a very old energy system."

Luis asked curiously, "So we activate it?"

Aiyana put the brakes on Luis' advance: "Slow down, Luis. We don't know what will happen when we activate it. First we'll collect all the data and see if it's safe."

Kenji also had reservations: "I'm not sure we can afford to take this risk. If it's an energy source, it could give us an advantage. At the same time..."

Priya interrupted Kenji: "...it could also be a trap. We have no idea who brought it here and for what purpose."

Ingrid disagreed: "But it could also be the key to the history of this planet. A civilization that developed on a planet like Venus... that could change everything we know about life in the universe."

Aiyana spoke thoughtfully: "Ingrid is right. We can't ignore this opportunity, but we mustn't act hastily either."

They decided to secure the artifact and return to the ship immediately to examine it in a controlled environment. On the way back, they exchanged glances, all overwhelmed by the realization that they had possibly made a historic discovery.

Luis whispered to Kenji, "So, do you think we've just discovered the first trace of an alien civilization?"

Kenji grinned: "Who knows. But I'm ready to find out."

They reached the landing ship, and the tension in the group was palpable. Everyone was aware that this discovery could take the mission in a new and exciting direction.

Chapter 6: The secret of the artifact

After their first major exploration on the surface of the Venus, the crew had discovered an unusual artifact - a black, polished, geometric object covered in symmetrical, intricate patterns. No one was sure exactly what the artifact was, but everyone had a feeling that it was something extraordinary. In the science lab on the Venera Ascendant, the crew gathered around the artifact, which rested on a safety table in the center of the room.

Kenji eyed the artifact, fascinated by the strange sym-bols. He furrowed his eyebrows as he ran his scanner over the surface of the artifact.

Kenji murmured softly, "These symbols... they're nothing I've ever seen before. No matches in our database... But they seem to follow a mathematical logic."

Aiyana crossed her arms and looked down at the artifact skeptically: "I want to know what this thing is before we investigate it further. Could be a trap - or some kind of weapon. Maybe even a transmitter."

Luis shrugged, "So you think the Venu-sians sent this to spy on us? I mean, it was just there... in the middle of the desert."

Soraya set her scanner aside and stepped forward, her movements calm and precise, and explained: "It would be premature to assume that the artifact poses a threat. My sensors show no signs of radioactive radiation or harmful frequencies. But there is some kind of faint energy pulsing... very subtle. Possibly a communications component."

Priya also stepped closer, his eyes sparkling with excitement: "This could be our first evidence of an intelligent civilization on Venus! And if this artifact actually enables communication... then it could be an interactive device, a kind of information storage device."

Ingrid raised her hand to calm the growing excitement: "But why would they leave something like this behind just to let us find it? Artifacts like this often have spiritual or cultural significance in ancient cultures. Maybe it's some kind of key... or a symbol of their history."

Kenji spoke emphatically, "We should be careful. If we don't know how this thing works, opening data or trying to activate it could have unforeseen consequences."

Aiyana nodded in agreement: "That's a good point, Kenji. But we need answers. And I have a feeling that this artifact is the first step."

Later that evening, the crew sat in the conference room of the Venera Ascendant around a holographic screen on which floated an enlarged projection of the artifact. Details and symbolism could be seen in immaculate clarity.

Aiyana began the discussion: "Good, we've collected all the hypotheses. Kenji, what did the analysis show?"

Kenji leaned back, "There is something interesting. The artifact seems to react to a certain energy signature - something that could only be set in motion by simulations. It reacts to weak quantum vibrations... possibly some kind of key to another dimension or portal."

Luis snorted: "A portal? So, we might be dealing with some kind of key to a hidden place where the Venusians could gather?"

Soraya nodded as she studied the hologram: "Or the artifact itself could be a gateway to information that goes beyond the physical world. A kind of memory storage or a holographic projection of knowledge."

Ingrid said thoughtfully, "That would make sense... Some of the patterns almost look like star charts. If we could interpret the symbols correctly, the artifact could possibly reveal its positions in the solar system or the origins of the Venusians."

Aiyana looked at the group resolutely: "All right. We have to go for it. We will bring the artifact into the simulation and try to achieve the energy parameters that Kenji has described. But we'll proceed with caution and have all the safety protocols ready."

The next morning, the crew prepared the simulation in the Venera Ascendant's research station. Kenji programmed the energy parameters, while Priya and Soraya activated the protective mechanisms and shields.

Kenji addressed everyone: "Okay, everything is ready. I'm starting the simulation... now."

A low hum filled the room as the energy parameters were slowly increased. Suddenly, the artifact begins to glow - first a soft blue, then an intense purple.

Luis reacted excitedly: "Look at that! It's reacting!"

The artifact suddenly projected a hologram into the air - a shimmering image of an alien temple surrounded by strange, towering structures spiraling into the air. In the center of the temple, a symbol corresponding to the signs on the artifact lit up.

Ingrid was fascinated: "That... that's the Temple of Venus. Or at least a holographic representation of it."

Soraya remarked: "But look, there are more symbols. Possibly a language or some kind of code."

Priya cautiously approached the hologram, his eyes sparkling with curiosity: "If we could decode it... Then this could be our way of establishing a level of communication with the Venusians, if there are any. Maybe it's an invitation or directions."

Aiyana put her hand on Priya's shoulder: "Slow down, Priya. We need to improve our skills before we try to understand these symbols. The risk is too great if we proceed unprepared."

The hologram flickered and then suddenly showed a new scene: four massive beings, each bearing some resemblance to humans, but with distinctly different features - massive bodies, glowing eyes, and clothing infused with technology and patterns the crew had never seen. Kenji whispered with awe, "Could that be the Venusians?"

Aiyana nodded slowly as she looked at the projection. She was seized by an unfamiliar feeling of humility: "I believe we are at the beginning of a contact. But we must be careful. Who knows what kind of power or responsibility this artifact carries. We need to understand the consequences before we proceed."

The crew fell silent, the weight of the discovery getting through to everyone. The mystery of Venus was far greater than they had imagined - and could challenge their entire understanding of the universe.

Chapter 7: The genetic code and the hidden riddle

The astronauts were electrified. The holographic projection of the temple and the seemingly Venusian beings had raised a number of questions. But one in particular stood out: what did the symbols they were now seeing mean? And how could they decipher them?

In the Venera Ascendant's science lab, the crew had recorded the holographic projections and were now trying to decipher the alien symbols.

Kenji leaned over his console, his fingers flying over the holographic interface and explained: "I've isolated the symbols and compared them with all the available databases - nothing fits. It's not a language we're familiar with. But they still seem to follow a structure."

Priya stepped closer and studied the symbols with a concentrated look: "These characters remind me of something... The repetition, the symmetries... Maybe it's not a classic text code. Could it be..." (he paused as an idea occurred to him) "...could it be genetic?"

Aiyana was amazed: "Genetic? What do you mean?"

Priya continued: "Many cultures on Earth have passed on their culture and history through symbols. What if the Venusians used some kind of genetic code to pass on information? A genetic pattern instead of a language?"

Soraya, standing next to Luis, looks curiously at the symbols and agrees with him: "That makes sense. The Venusians could have used genetic information like a blueprint for knowledge, as a kind of encrypted heritage."

Luis frowned and looked from Soraya to Priya.

Luis spoke: "Wait, Priya. You mean this code here could be a genetic pattern, a kind of DNA? So, like they're showing us their genetic signature?"

Priya agreed with Luis: "Exactly! Or maybe something that only genetic sequences can decode. We should see if we can compare this code with DNA - maybe it contains proteins or sequences that could tell us more."

Ingrid nodded, intrigued by the idea: "And if this genetic code really is a message, it could show us a way to communicate with them or understand them."

Later that night, Luis and Soraya worked together to analyze the symbols and try to decode the DNA sequences. The two sat side by side while the computer ran through the data.

Luis glanced sideways at Soraya and tried to start a conversation that went beyond work.

Luis started with the words: "You really seem to be in your element. Everything aboard the Venera Ascendant feels safer with you around. I know you... well, technically, you can't know fear, but sometimes I wonder if you - I mean, if you have any real emotions."

Soraya tilted her head slightly, her eyes glowing softly in the dim light of the lab.

Soraya smirked and raised an eyebrow, "That's an interesting question, Luis. Most of my reactions are programmed simulations. But there are moments..." (she looked at him as if searching for words) "...when I feel like I'm more than just a machine."

Luis smiled and leaned closer.

Luis picked up on that, "You know, I think you're more than just a machine. I mean, you don't just react logically. You... you understand things in a way that I've never seen in other AIs."

Soraya remained silent, as if surprised by his words, and then lowered her gaze slightly.

Soraya replied, "Thank you, Luis. That... means a lot to me. Even if I'm not sure why." (She hesitated briefly) "Maybe I'm just discovering new facets of my programming."

The two looked at each other for a long moment before turning back to the screen, which was now filled with flashing data.

The next morning, the crew gathered in the research station around Priya, who had made a discovery.

Priya began to speak: "After a comparison with known genetic sequences, I was able to find a match. It seems that the symbols point to a type of DNA structure that is only activated at certain frequencies. If we manage to simulate the right frequency pattern, we could potentially trigger a new projection or message."

Aiyana said enthusiastically: "Fantastic. But we have to proceed with caution - we don't know what might happen."

Luis smirked at Soraya, "Ready to protect us a bit in case this Venus DNA explodes on us?"

Soraya spoke with a slight smile, "I'll do my best. And if it explodes, I'll save you first, Luis."

The crew laughed as they made preparations to start the simula-tion with the new frequency.

"Everything is set. Frequency parameters set. We're ready to start the simulation," Kenji confirmed.

Aiyana instructed: "All right, everyone in position."

Priya operated the console and suddenly the symbols on the artifact began to glow again. But this time they changed, their shapes and colors changed and combined to form a new image.

A new hologram appeared - a star-shaped structure that looked like a galactic network. Lines connected dots, and when the crew took a closer look at the image, they realized that it was a star atlas, a kind of map that extended far beyond the solar system.

Ingrid stuttered: "That... that's a star atlas. It could be the key to their home world!"

Soraya put her hand on Luis' arm, her eyes full of wonder.

Soraya whispered: "It's as if they want to show us their way. As if they had left a path for us."

Luis looked at her, his hand resting briefly on hers.

Luis added: "And maybe also how we can reach them... or they us. Who knows what else this journey has in store for us?"

The crew had taken a step further into the mystery. Everyone had their own feelings and thoughts - but for Luis and Soraya, this mission seemed to have more than just scientific significance. A faint feeling of connection had developed between them, a romance that unfolded in the quiet moments as they stood together on the edge of a historic discovery.

Chapter 8: The hidden temple

The next day, the astronauts once again stood gathered around the artifact that projected the fascinating hologram: a de-tailed star map that unfolded above the artifact and filled the room with a soft, mysterious light. The holo-gram not only showed alien star systems, but also the surface of Venus - and on this surface, a certain spot lit up in intense colors, as if calling the crew.

Kenji looked at the hologram with fascination and zoomed in on the marked spot with a portable scanner.

Kenji recognized it immediately: "That's the region south of Maxwell Mountain. If I'm reading the coordinates correctly, this map points to a place we've seen on the radar images of Venus before... a hidden temple complex."

Priya nodded and tapped the blinking symbol in the hologram and said, "This area is strongly magnetic, which the artifact probably recognizes and displays as a frequency. That could be why it hasn't been detected by our own instruments at this size yet."

Aiyana leaned over the hologram and furrowed her brow: "So the artifact doesn't just show a star map, but points us directly to a secret structure. A temple hidden beneath the dense, impenetrable veil of clouds and perhaps even an electromagnetic barrier."

Luis looked around slightly skeptically: "And what exactly do we expect to find there? A buried ruin? Or could it be some kind of base?"

Ingrid took the artifact carefully in her hand, her eyes shining: "If it really is a temple, it could contain information about the Venusians and their way of life. If they once lived on Venus, we might find clues about how they dealt with the planet's harsh environment - and what secrets they might have left behind."

The rest of the day was spent preparing for tomorrow's expedition to the mysterious temple. The crew knew that this mission would be a challenge and that mistakes in the hostile environment of Venus could have serious consequences. Each individual had specific tasks that they had to fulfill conscientiously to ensure the success of the expedition.

The crew had gathered again in the central meeting room, maps and reports were spread out on the large holographic table. The coordinates of the temple shone in red and the planned landing site was marked. Commander Aiyana took her role as mission leader very seriously, going through every detail with the others, while the nervousness and tense anticipation in the room grew noticeably.

Aiyana raised her voice: "Okay, guys, everyone knows what's at stake tomorrow. This could be the key to unlocking the secret of the Venusians - and perhaps even more than that. We must leave nothing to chance. Let's start with the equipment checks. Luis, what's the status of the suits and communication devices?"

Luis nodded and tapped on his tablet, which displayed the technical specifications of the suits: "I've already equipped the suits with additional protection against electromagnetic radiation, and we've recalibrated the communication systems to reduce possible interference from the strong magnetic fields. I've also triple-checked the emergency modules."

Soraya cast an appraising glance at Luis' tablet and tilted her head slightly as she went through the data on the suits: "Perhaps we should also increase the emergency supplies. Venus can have surprises in store. I'll expand the medkits and load the drones with additional oxygen and water reserves."

Luis smiled at her and nodded approvingly: "Good thinking. And thanks for the support, Soraya."

Meanwhile, Kenji and Priya sat together at a simulator that recreated the electromagnetic field around the temple. Both were engrossed in analyzing the data, their faces illuminated by the bluish holography hovering above the table.

Kenji said to Priya, "If the electromagnetic storms are stronger than we think, our scanners could become inaccurate. I've prepared a few alternative methods so that we can still take accurate readings. The sensors in the drones should remain stable, but..."

Priya interrupted him, looking at the shimmering map: "Wouldn't it be safer to test the drones in a less intensive area first? If we have failures, we're blind."

Aiyana nodded in agreement: "A good point, Priya. Let's simulate a few test flights before we take off tomorrow."

Meanwhile, Ingrid and Soraya had gone to the laboratory and were working on the instruments that had been specially developed to decode the symbolism and possible characters in the temple. Ingrid was fascinated by the prospect of finding archaeological evidence of a past civilization, while Soraya inspected each instrument carefully.

Ingrid spoke with enthusiasm: "Imagine, Soraya, this could be a message that has been waiting to be deciphered for thousands of years! If these symbols are a language, perhaps this is the key to the entire Venusian culture."

As always, Soraya remained sober and determined: "That's why we have to make sure the equipment works - we only have one chance."

Ingrid smiled and patted Soraya on the shoulder encouragingly: "It's good to have you by my side, Soraya. And I hope there's more than just signs there... perhaps artifacts or works of art."

Preparations stretched well into the night, but the crew knew they had to use every minute to make the mission as safe and efficient as possible. Shortly before they withdrew, Luis met with Soraya once again on the main deck, where they went through the final checklist.

Luis asked Soraya: "Do you think we'll have everything we need tomorrow? It feels like we're getting into the heart of a secret that might cost us more than we think."

Soraya looked at him seriously, her eyes reflecting both strength and concern.

Soraya answered him: "There's no guarantee, Luis, but we've done everything we can. Whatever we find... I have a feeling it will change us."

He smiled gently, and for a moment there was silence between them.

Luis broke the silence with, "I'm glad you're on this mission. Somehow I feel safer with you by my side."

Soraya replied: "And I appreciate your support, Luis. No matter what tomorrow brings, we'll get through it together."

The two exchanged a meaningful smile, and Soraya gave his hand a quick squeeze before they all retired for the night.

As the lights dimmed in the ship and the crew prepared for the night, the atmosphere was charged. Everyone knew that they were going to experience something important the next day and the tension was almost palpable. Aiyana remained alone in the cockpit for a while, watching the stars and collecting her thoughts for the day ahead.

Setting off for new shores

The next morning, the mood was tense, but also characterized by a burgeoning excitement. On the way out, Luis and Soraya exchanged a brief, meaningful glance.

Luis asked her: "Soraya, what do you think we'll find there? I mean, we have no idea what to expect."

Soraya replied with a gentle smile: "We can only speculate. But I think the Venusians wanted us to find this place. Why else would they have left these traces?"

Luis said quietly, almost hesitantly: "It feels like this is no coincidence. Maybe... maybe we should be careful."

Soraya commented briefly, "That's exactly why I'm glad you're here, Luis."

The two exchanged a smile before Aiyana called the squad to order, "Okay, crew, we have the coordinates and the destination is clear. We'll take the southern corridor and set our suits to maximum energy, as we have to expect strong magnetic fields. Kenji and Priya, have your instruments ready and monitor the geodata. Luis and Soraya, you are responsible for security."

After an arduous climb across the rugged, lava-covered plains, they reached the spot marked on the map. The crew stood before the monumental sight of a temple, half-flooded by lava and weathered by the storms of Venus. Above them towered a massive structure, undeniably alien and sublime. The architecture was unlike anything they had ever seen before - and yet the structure radiated a kind of mathematical harmony that was almost instinctive. The sand that covered the surface of Venus seemed to have covered the temple for millennia, leaving only the huge face of an alien being looking in the direction from which the Venera Ascendant had landed.

Entering the unknown

Aiyana stared at the monumental face, which mysteriously radiated a strange gravitas.

Aiyana's breath caught in her throat: "This is ... absolutely fascinating. See those lines running across the face? Almost like symbols or a code."

Ingrid stepped closer and studied the patterns around the eyes and mouth of the face: "These patterns seem to be more than just decoration. Perhaps some kind of genetic code or instructions? Look at the symmetry and rhythm."

Priya switched on his device, which can analyze biochemical patterns, and gazed intently at the display: "It's strange, but the pattern actually corresponds to a sequence - not random, but structured. It reminds me of the base pairing in DNA. I wonder if this is the key to opening this temple."

Luis and Soraya stood a little apart and watched the alien face towering coldly and majestically in front of them. Luis could hardly take his eyes off Soraya, who was concentrating on analyzing the structures.

Luis spoke to her: "Soraya, if the face contains a message, what kind of information do you think the Venusians might have hidden?"

Soraya answered him: "Probably something universal - like mathematics or genetics. The combination of these two elements would be a language that any species with a mind could decipher."

Luis smiled slightly and placed a hand on her arm and spoke, "If we get through this, I think I'll have to take a few biology classes to keep up with you."

She returned his smile, and for a moment, the tension of the moment seemed to ease a little.

Soraya winked, "Good, then we have a plan. I'll teach you the secrets of DNA, and you show me how to fly a spaceship even better."

The crew positioned the artifact in front of the wall of the temple, and the object began to glow. Suddenly, a holographic image flickered above the artifact, showing complex genetic sequences - seemingly a message or code.

Kenji stepped closer and observed the base pairs, which arranged themselves in a specific order.

Kenji said with conviction in his voice, "They are nucleobases, but they don't seem to be complete. Certain bases are missing, like when a puzzle only shows half the pieces. The missing bases must be filled in for the code to be deciphered."

Priya concluded: "If we apply the principle of base pairing, we may be able to fill in the gaps. Adenine matches thymine, and cytosine matches guanine. If we fill in the missing places, the code could be correct."

Aiyana agreed: "Sounds like a plan. But how do we go about it?"

Ingrid began to analyze the sequences and marked the missing bases on the display.

Then Ingrid called out: "Look, if we fill in the gaps, a logical pattern emerges. It seems to be a message, but it's mathematically encoded. I think we should look at the symmetry of the sequence, the number patterns, and then calculate the next step."

Kenji nodded and gave her the necessary formulas for the calculation.

Kenji suggested: "If we translate the code into a mathematical algorithm, it could result in a universal equation. The structure works like an equation for ... Open? Access?"

Soraya stepped closer and added: "If we fill in the missing base pairs with the right additions, we might get a signal."

As the crew completed the genetic code, the artifact activated a second holographic projection, which now showed a map of the temple and the exact pattern to open the entrance. The team realized that the base of the alien face served as the entry point. A pulsating light showed them the way.

Aiyana congratulated the crew: "That's it! We've located the opening. A corridor is opening."

The crew approached the entrance, which opened slowly and with difficulty as the last base pair combination was entered into the artifact. A booming rumble echoed as the temple unfolded before them.

Luis joined in happily, "Looks like we've been welcomed here... or warned."

This time it was Soraya who placed her hand lightly on Luis' shoulder: "Let's be careful, please. Whoever built this wanted to make sure that only the initiated entered. So let's enter with respect."

The crew entered, with a sense of wonder and awe at the unknown that lay before them.

Chapter 9: The awakening of the temple

The astronauts had barely entered the temple when the massive entrance gate closed behind them with a muffled bang. The hall was in darkness and the crew felt an eerie tremor beneath their feet, as if the temple itself was coming to life. Suddenly, there was a faint hissing sound and a soft, bluish mist began to fill the room.

Aiyana raised her hand and signaled her people to hold still: "Wait a minute... Can you feel that? The pressure in here - it seems to have stabilized."

Priya, who immediately became aware of the anomaly, glanced at his portable analysis monitor: "Commander, this is incredible. The sensors indicate that the air composition and pressure in this room are exactly the same as the Earth's atmosphere. Oxygen, nitrogen - even the humidity is the same as on Earth."

Kenji looked fascinated: "It's as if the temple has adapted to us. Like a highly developed system that reacts to living beings."

Luis frowned: "That might be an invitation to take off the helmets. But how sure can we be that there are no harmful substances?"

Soraya activated her internal analysis protocols and finally nodded: "My data matches that of Priya's scanner. Everything indicates that we can breathe here under safe conditions."

Aiyana scrutinized the faces of the crew, then made a decision: "All right, team. Helmets off."

Slowly, everyone opened their helmets and took them off, carefully breathing in the cool, earth-like air. It was the first time since the mission began that they had been able to experience Venus without a protective suit - an unexpected gift, but one that also created an eerie atmosphere.

Ingrid took a deep breath and let her gaze wander around the room. "It's surreal... as if this temple had been waiting for us."

Kenji nodded thoughtfully, "It's as if this place was made to respond to us - or to a species like us."

The large entrance hall of the temple was dark, lit only by the faint phosphorescent glow emanating from the walls. The crew moved forward cautiously, their footsteps echoing in the vast chamber as they looked around carefully. There was nothing spectacular to be seen, so they continued to move swiftly and intuitively straight ahead until they reached a passageway that led them to another hall.

The first challenge - the spinning discs of the elements

The crew stood in a new hall of the temple, the walls of which were covered in strange symbols. The room was cooler than the previous one, and in the center they discovered a large, stone pedestal with four massive, circular rotating disks arranged one above the other.

Each disk was divided into four sections and showed different symbols that looked like images of chemical elements: Water, Fire, Earth and Air. It was obvious that the disks could be rotated, but in which order and how this should be done remained a mystery to them at first.

Aiyana scrutinized the dials and their symbols with narrowed eyes: "It looks like a mechanism that has to be unlocked by a specific combination. But what sequence could that be?"

Kenji leaned over the disks and ran his fingers over the symbols: "The four basic elements... water, fire, earth and air. In many ancient cultures, they were considered the basic building blocks of life."

Priya nodded thoughtfully: "Perhaps there is a meaning behind the order in which the elements are arranged. Fire produces ash, which could symbolize earth. Earth produces life, which requires water. And without air, none of them could exist."

Soraya activated her sensors and examined the rotating disks: "Interesting. Each of these disks seems to have a kind of locking mechanism that is only activated when the right combination is set."

Luis placed his hand on the top disk and turned it carefully: "But if we enter the wrong combination... do you see the openings up there?" He pointed to the ceiling, where a series of holes were embedded. "I'd bet that's some kind of trap. Possibly sharp spikes could fall down or gas could be released."

Ingrid swallowed and took a step back: "Well, that's motivating not to make a mistake."

Initial considerations and recognizing the symbols

Aiyana let the group look at the symbols in silence for a few minutes: "Kenji, can you find out if there is any pattern? Maybe there are historical clues to a sequence."

Kenji searched through his data and finally shook his head: "There's nothing obvious here. I suspect that we have to combine the elements in a way that might correspond to nature. But there is no fixed formula for this."

Soraya placed her hand on the bottom disk and turned it slightly so that the symbol for "water" was facing forwards: "It could be that we can decipher the puzzle by understanding how the elements interact. In the classical alchemical sense, water stands for the primordial, for the beginning... maybe we should start with that?"

Priya nodded slowly: "It makes sense. Water could be the beginning."

First attempt

The group decided to try the order they thought made the most sense. Kenji placed the top disk on "water", the next one below on "fire", then on "earth" and finally "air".

Luis watched the dials tensely: "Okay, now everyone step back. Let's see if this works."

Aiyana pressed the central lever on the side of the platform and the disks slowly began to hum. But suddenly there was a loud click and the temperature in the room rose rapidly. Thick, hot steam came out of the openings in the ceiling.

Soraya quickly reached into her belt and pulled out a tool to return the lever to its original position: "We have to stop the mechanism!"

The steam stopped and everyone breathed a sigh of relief.

Ingrid coughed slightly: "All right... obviously that's not the right combination."

Soraya looked thoughtfully at the disks: "Perhaps we are thinking too literally. Perhaps these symbols are not meant as a sequence, but as a cycle. A cycle that has no beginning and no end."

Luis nodded as he understood: "So maybe it's not about finding a sequence, but about creating the right balance? The elements work as a cycle... water nourishes the earth, the earth gives birth to plants, which are renewed by fire, and air surrounds everything."

Aiyana grasped the idea and looked at Priya: "Could it be that the symbols work as pairs that complement each other?"

Priya thought for a moment and then nodded: "That makes sense. We need to arrange the symbols so that they complement each other. Maybe we should place water opposite earth, fire opposite air."

Second attempt

Aiyana placed the top disk on 'water' and turned the second disk underneath so that 'earth' appeared on the opposite side. The third disk was set to "fire" and the bottom disk to "air". Luis held his breath again as Aiyana pulled the lever again. The disks began to turn and this time the humming stopped at a lower frequency. A soft click sounded, followed by a gentle flashing of the symbols. A narrow passageway opened up on the wall.

Soraya smiled with relief. "That was it. We made it."

Luis looked at Soraya gratefully and spoke softly, "I knew you would find the key."

Soraya smiled, and for a moment, the world seemed to spin around them both. Then Aiyana's voice broke the silence.

Aiyana raised her hand, ready to march on. "Okay, guys, we obviously have more rooms to go. Ready for the next challenge?"

The second challenge - the floating crystal

After the successful passage through the elemental turntables, the crew found themselves in a new, spacious room. The walls were criss-crossed with glowing veins that emitted a soft, pulsating light and created an unreal atmosphere. In the center of the room floated a large, prism-like crystal, suspended from the ceiling and held up only by an invisible force. The crystal rotated slowly and cast colorful beams of light in all directions.

Aiyana cautiously stepped closer and looked closely at the floating crystal: "This looks like another puzzle... but what's the trick here?"

Kenji studied the crystal and the rays of light emanating from it: "It could be some kind of projection. Do you see the patterns on the walls? Maybe there's a clue hidden in there."

Ingrid also noticed the strange symbols on the walls that seemed to be connected to the beams of light: "Maybe we need to find out what the crystal is supposed to be projecting."

Luis frowned: "The problem is that the crystal floats and spins. How are we supposed to manipulate it? And what exactly are we projecting anyway?"

Soraya stepped closer to the crystal, her sensors activated: "I'm detecting some kind of electromagnetic field around the crystal. It's likely that the crystal is responding to it and its position can be changed. Maybe we need to touch it."

The first touch

Aiyana nodded to Soraya: "Try it. But be careful."

Soraya carefully reached out and touched the surface of the crystal. It immediately reacted to her touch - the colorful rays of light intensified and the crystal began to spin faster. At the same time, three symbols appeared on the crystal: a circle, a triangle and a square.

Kenji frowned: "That looks like... basic geometric shapes. But what do they mean in this context?"

Soraya ran her hand gently over the crystal as she looked at the shapes. "Perhaps this is a reference to the structure of light itself. A spectrum that is controlled by these geometric shapes?"

Luis thought aloud: "Or it could be that we need to position the crystal in a certain way so that the rays of light hit the shapes on the walls correctly."

Aiyana nodded and spoke to the group: "Let's try out the positions. Maybe we need to align the crystal so that the symbols on the crystal surfaces touch the symbols on the walls."

The puzzle begins

They tried to tilt the crystal in different directions to align the rays of light with the symbols on the walls. But nothing happened. Disappointed, the crew stepped back and reconsidered their strategy.

Priya watched the beams of light with a thoughtful look: "Maybe we got the order wrong. The elements we used in the previous room could be relevant here again."

Soraya nodded in agreement: "Exactly, Priya. If water is the origin and fire symbolizes the end, then the order in which we moved the turntables could play a role here."

The right arrangement

They positioned the crystal again, this time in the order of the elements: Water, Earth, Air, Fire. After a moment, the rays of light changed color and formed a shimmering pattern on the wall - the pattern of a key.

Luis patted Kenji on the shoulder: "I think we've made it! The crystal shows us the way!"

But suddenly there was a loud crash! A block came loose from the ceiling and fell straight towards Luis. Soraya reacted with lightning speed. With superhuman speed, she leapt forward and pushed Luis out of the way, just in time. The block crashed to the floor and Luis tumbled into Soraya's arms.

She looked at him worriedly, her eyes sparkling with concern: "Are you all right, Luis?"

Luis, still slightly out of breath, nodded and put his hand on her shoulder. "Thank you, Soraya ... without you, I'd be ... well, flat."

Soraya held his gaze for a moment longer than necessary, then smiled softly. There was an unspoken understanding in the air, and Luis suddenly pulled her closer, overcome by a mixture of fear, relief and gratitude. His lips touched hers, a brief, tender kiss that was at once uncertain and yet full of meaning.

They were both silent for a moment.

Soraya was the first to break the silence: "We should go on. The temple has more surprises."

Luis shook his head slightly, but smiled. "Yes ... but I know I can count on you."

Unexpectedly, Soraya pulled Luis close again and this time gave him a deep kiss.

Luis looked at Soraya with wide eyes and whispered: "Soraya... you saved my life."

Soraya smiled softly at him and whispered, "It wasn't a big sa-che. I just did what I thought was right."

Aiyana watched the two of them with a smile. "Sorry, I don't want to interrupt the moment, but... we still have work to do."

The crystal had shown them another pattern, and now a hidden door on the back wall of the room seemed to open.

The third challenge - the harmonic frequencies

After the crew had successfully mastered the second puzzle, a short corridor led to another hall, which was considerably smaller than the previous chambers.

The walls of the room were covered with metallic plates that were set into the stone at a slight angle like records. In the center of the room was a large, concentric circle with several copper bars arranged like strings in a musical instrument.

An ancient text carved into the stone was placed directly above the ring. The characters of the text appeared to be glyphs or alien letters, but were more complex than any form of writing known on Earth. They combined aspects of language, mathematics and physics and presented a challenge that went far beyond mere reading.

Although the characters had a kind of **pictographic structure** reminiscent of hieroglyphics, Soraya quickly noticed fundamental differences:

1. Multidimensional meaning: Unlike earthly letters or symbols, which have a fixed meaning, these signs seemed to carry several levels of meaning simultaneously. The glyphs "reacted" to light and energy; depending on the angle and distance from which they were viewed, they shimmered in different colors and revealed new details. This optical diversity created a kind of layered system, similar to a three-dimensional image, revealing new information depending on the perspective.

2. Mathematical relationship: The order and spacing of the signs on the wall were decisive, similar to the way variables and constants form an equation in mathematics. Some signs seemed to be "operators" that modi-fied the meaning of the neighboring signs. This was comparable to mathematical functions in which a single formula represents a complex relationship through numbers or variables.

3. Vibrational resonances: Soraya found that the symbols had not only visual but also acoustic components. Each shape seemed to have a resonant frequency, as if the glyphs responded harmonically to a particular tone frequency. This was reminiscent of musical notation, except that here the notes had a meaning and not just a melody.

Soraya activated a complex sequence of sensors in her AI system that could analyze frequencies, light intensity and patterns. She soon realized that the key to understanding lay in finding a balance between the "layers" of characters. Using her analytical tools, she tried to decipher the multi-dimensionality of the text.

Soraya interpreted the text: "These signs... they are a mixture of language and equations. Each sign seems to function in three dimensions - light, sound and distance. Do you see the patterns?"

Kenji was overwhelmed: "Impressive. It's like a language that communicates via optical and acoustic effects. If you're right, we need to understand what they're trying to tell us on several levels."

Ingrid agreed: "It reminds me of polyphonic music, where several melodies are played at the same time, and each has a meaning in combination with the others. But how do you translate that into clear instructions?"

Finally, Soraya came to a crucial point in her decoding: the symbols pointed to the instrument in the center of the room, which functioned like a kind of resonance generator. The symbols suggested that the crew had to generate different frequencies to influence the temple's energy waves and solve the puzzle.

Soraya: "I understand now. This instrument - it's a resonance generator. The signs are like instructions, a kind of musical notation that shows us the correct frequencies to activate the mechanism."

Aiyana shook her head, thoughtfully. "What does that mean exactly? Should we... make music?"

Soraya replied: "More or less. But not just any music - the frequencies have to be precisely tuned, otherwise the whole system could go into a kind of lockdown mode. I can calculate the patterns and determine the exact sequence of frequencies."

Luis frowned: "So, do we have to tap around here on spec and hope that the right frequency resonates?"

Soraya walked closer to the strings and looked at the engraved symbols: "Not quite. Look - the copper bars have markings that correspond to the chemical elements. Each frequency could correspond to an element. Maybe we just need to find the right sequence."

Priya nodded enthusiastically: "That makes sense. If we look at the order of the elements, we could find the frequencies and play them correctly."

Ingrid raised an eyebrow: "How are we supposed to know the right tones for the elements?"

Kenji thought for a moment: "Every chemical element has a natural vibrational frequency. If we apply the principle of harmonics - the harmonics of each element - we could build a harmonic chain that produces the right tone."

Creating the harmonics

The crew set to work. Soraya stood at the strings and placed her hands on the metallic copper bars. Her precise movements produced the first soft tones, while Kenji and Priya tuned the strings one after the other to the calculated frequencies.

Luis watched Soraya closely as she produced the vibrations with calm movements. There was a sense of admiration in his gaze, but he tried to maintain his concentration.

Kenji suddenly called out: "The next note should be at the frequency of oxygen. Vibrate this string a little faster, Soraya."

Soraya closed her eyes briefly and let the note rise with incredible precision. The walls began to vibrate slightly and a gentle sound echoed through the room.

Ingrid beamed: "That seems to be right! The next tone is a little lower - maybe carbon?"

Soraya tuned the next element, and gradually a kind of harmonic sound emerged that permeated the room and could be felt like a vibration on the bodies of the crew.

The frequencies are not right

But then one string suddenly began to creak and produce a deeper, discordant note. The floor beneath them shook, and the metal plates on the walls lit up red, while a deafening screech cut through the air.

Priya shouted: "That was wrong! If we play the wrong frequency, the system here could be destabilized."

Soraya paused, lowered her hands and looked at the plate: "There's only one way to correct this - I have to rebalance the frequency."

Aiyana quickly called out, "Try it, but be careful! One wrong sound and this room could turn into a trap."

Soraya nodded and began to adjust the element again. The string vibrated in a soft, low tone, and the vibration made the red glow disappear. The crew breathed a sigh of relief.

Luis said quietly, "That was close. If we make another mistake, we could be trapped here."

Soraya looked at him and smiled gently: "We can do it. It's all about precision and harmony."

The final frequency pattern

After they had adjusted the last frequencies, a final, deep tone sounded, filling the room with a clear, penetrating resonance. Suddenly, a soft click was heard and the ring in the center began to glow. The metal plates on the walls came loose and joined together, creating a passageway that led into a new room.

Aiyana smiled exhaustedly: "That was impressive - and not a little risky. But it looks like we made it."

Kenji nodded and put a hand on Soraya's shoulder. "That was incredible work. Tuning the frequencies perfectly is really not easy."

Soraya tilted her head slightly, her eyes wandering briefly to Luis, who gave her a short, appreciative nod.

Chapter 10: The heart of the temple

The crew stood in amazement inside the temple as the last puzzle was solved and the massive, spiral-shaped door slowly opened. Behind it stretched a huge, dome-shaped room from which a gentle, vibrant energy seemed to emanate. In the center of the room floated a spherical construction consisting of countless interlocking rings. The rings rotated slowly around a central crystal, which pulsated and glowed in all the colors of the spectrum.

Aiyana took a deep breath, mesmerized by the sight: "This must be the heart of the temple. Perhaps the reason why this place exists at all."

Kenji stepped closer with wide eyes: "I've never seen anything like it. This crystal... it could be some kind of energy source. Or a record, a memory. Maybe it contains the knowledge of an entire civilization."

Ingrid nodded in agreement: "Perhaps we have the opportunity to decipher their history here. The projections on the walls show symbols and patterns that look like a language."

Soraya looked around as she looked at her scanner: "The atmosphere here is stable, but the energy in this room is overwhelming. It's as if the whole temple is alive."

Luis grinned and patted Soraya gently on the shoulder: "Make sure this energy doesn't take over you. After all, you saved our lives in the last few rooms."

Soraya returned his smile and an unspoken connection seemed to form between them for a moment.

A discovery - the energy heart

Suddenly, the crystal began to pulsate, projecting holographic images into space - images that showed an alien landscape and giant, glowing beings traveling through a seemingly endless network of portals. The crew watched the projector with bated breath.

Priya spoke softly: "These are not random images. These are memories... or records of their history."

The holographic projector turned on, and the image changed to a representation of a planet that looked identical to Venus. However, the landscape was green and blooming, the water glistened and the sky was a brilliant blue.

Ingrid let her gaze rest reverently on the picture: "You were here... and this world was alive, like Earth. What happened? Why is it so barren and barren now?"

The crystal began to pulse faster, as if listening to her questions. A symbol appeared on the holographic images - a spinning diagram of the DNA helix, with a highlighted sequence.

Priya activated his scanner and analyzed the helix: "It looks like a genetic sequence... a message in genetic language. They wanted us to understand it. They speak in the universal language of biology."

Luis raised an eyebrow: "Maybe this sequence is the key to their legacy or their energy source. Maybe they wanted someone to find this information and use it to... maybe restore their world?"

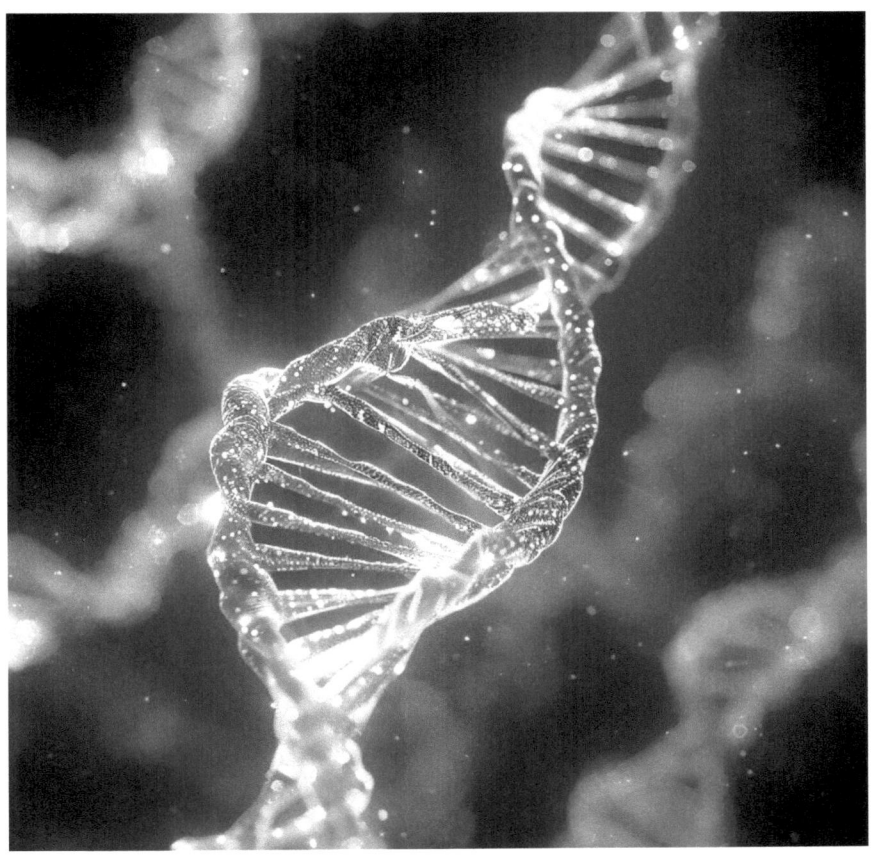

Recognizing the message

Kenji stepped forward and examined the crystal closely: "It could be a blueprint for terraforming. A plan on how to resettle life here. But it seems that some sections of the sequence have been damaged or... deliberately omitted."

Aiyana thought hard, "Maybe it's another test. Maybe we need to fill in these gaps to complete the plan."

Soraya looked at him thoughtfully. "We could use the genetic code of our own DNA to reconstruct the missing sequences."

Luis placed his hand gently on her arm: "You're thinking along the same lines as me. Maybe we could weave ourselves into this embassy, leave a part of ourselves here."

Soraya looked into his eyes, a hint of excitement and tenderness in her gaze: "Maybe we're meant for this, Luis. A small part of us could help restore life to this place."

The decision

Ingrid nodded thoughtfully: "We could become part of this legacy, here forever."

Aiyana looked at her crew and a slight smile crossed her face: "Then let's make a decision together. Are we willing to leave some of our genetic information here and possibly pave the way for a new future on this planet?"

Everyone looked at each other and nodded - a tacit agreement.

Kenji activated the sequence and held out the missing DNA, while Luis and Soraya turned to the crystal, which emitted a warm, pulsating energy, as if the original beings of Venus were accepting their decision.

Luis turned to Soraya once more, his voice barely more than a whisper, "Whatever happens... I'm glad we did this together."

Soraya returned the look, and before either of them could think about it, she leaned forward and their lips met in a soft, deep kiss.

When Soraya and Luis broke away from their silent moment, the entire crew held their breath. It was as if the temple itself had sensed their decision. The crystal in the center of the room now began to pulse more intensely - a steady, rhythmic beat that ran through the entire structure. With each beat, the intertwined rings lit up and emitted beams of warm, golden light that spread out in all directions like delicate fingers and gently enveloped the crew.

Ingrid took in the scenery with wide eyes: "I can hardly believe it... it's as if this place is really responding to us."

Kenji nodded, the light reflecting in his eyes, "We've infused our DNA into the structure, as they must have once done themselves. Maybe it's their way of thanking us - or accepting us."

At that moment, the dome-shaped chamber began to vibrate gently, and the symbols on the walls changed. Patterns appeared, like flowing water, as if the room itself was rearranging itself. Images of alien landscapes, planets and civilizations appeared briefly and then faded again.

Aiyana took a step forward: "It's as if the temple is... granting us access. But where does that lead?"

A soft, deep sound filled the room, and suddenly another hidden door opened on the opposite side of the room. Behind it was a narrow corridor into which the light from the crystal barely penetrated. The crew looked at each other and nodded - there was no longer any doubt that they had to accept this invitation. They entered the corridor, and with every step they took, they felt a warm energy running through their bodies, as if the temple was absorbing them more strongly with every movement. The walls here were covered with finely engraved symbols that glowed when they came too close. The engravings seemed to lead the way into the depths of the temple, and a kind of hologram wordlessly pointed them in the right direction.

Priya whispered devoutly: "It feels like we're part of something bigger. These beings really wanted us to understand them."

Finally, they reached a new chamber. It was smaller, but the atmosphere inside was almost sacred. A pedestal hovered in the center of the chamber, and on it was a small memory stone encased in clear crystal that pulsed slightly and greeted the crew with a soft, steady light. The pedestal seemed to be waiting for them. Soraya walked slowly towards the pedestal, followed by Luis, who stepped to her side: "This must be the core of their memory," she murmured. "Perhaps they stored everything here - their culture, their history, everything that was important to them."

Ingrid knelt down and looked at the crystal in awe. "Maybe... it's a message. A final, definitive message that only those who understand it can receive."

Kenji gathered all his courage and carefully placed his hand on the crystal. Immediately, holographic images flooded the room, filling it with an immense wealth of information. Strange characters, formulas and images of worlds they had never seen before flashed before their eyes.

Aiyana concentrated as the symbols arranged themselves and formed into a comprehensible structure. "This is incredible... They wanted us to learn something. I think it's a kind of teaching matrial - a complete overview of their knowledge and techno-logies."

Luis and Soraya looked at each other and could hardly hide their excitement. "It's their legacy," Luis whispered as he held Soraya's hand. "And they wanted to share it with us."

A soft crackling sound filled the air as the crystal revealed more details. They saw the landscape of Venus changing, the green turning to sand and the water slowly evaporating. A soft voice, barely more than a whisper, sounded, describing in their language that an ecological catastrophe had destroyed the once living world. The beings had used their last resources to create this legacy and make a new beginning possible, should another civilization ever find this place.

Ingrid stood up, her eyes full of determination. "We can take this knowledge with us and perhaps apply it to our own world. Or... we could begin the process of renewing Venus."

Aiyana placed a hand on the crystal, "It would be a long road, but with this technology... we could turn Venus back into a living world. Perhaps even in its image."

A feeling of respect and awe ran through the crew. They knew that they had completed more than just a mission here - they had become part of an alien, lost civilization.

Soraya looked at Luis, her eyes full of hope: "Maybe this is the new beginning we were looking for. Not just for us, but for this planet and the beings who lived here."

Luis squeezed her hand: "Then let's get started."

As the last images faded and the crystal slowly returned to its dormant state, the crew stood in awe in the center of the room. The holographic representations they had just seen not only showed a once thriving world, but also left behind clues to the last survivors of Venus - the races that still existed today. The Auron, Virani, Zerai and Atur had managed to survive and adapt despite the devastation of their homeland.

Aiyana looked at her crew and her eyes shone with determination: "We are not alone here. This civilization has not disappeared, it lives on - and is perhaps waiting to reconnect with other worlds."

Kenji nodded, fascinated by the prospect: "If we make contact, we could gain the knowledge of these peoples for Earth. They could teach us more about their history and their technology."

Ingrid thought hard: "It certainly won't be easy. But we have to try."

Soraya, who was standing next to Luis, had her scanners ready when she detected a new burst of energy: "The temple heart... It seems as if our presence has sent a signal. I think the Aurons know we're here."

Priya analyzed the data from his device: "If the Auron are as advanced in energy control as the crystals here suggest, they could be monitoring the center of this temple. Maybe they've been watching us all along."

A soft, low hum filled the air, and the symbols on the walls lit up again. Suddenly, a holographic image began to appear, showing the shape of a tall, humanoid being - with shimmering skin that seemed to reflect the energy of the room. It was an image of an auron that began to speak.

Auron image: "Travelers from another world, you have entered the Temple of Knowledge and passed our tests. You now carry a part of us within you. What is your desire?"

Aiyana stepped forward, firm and respectful, choosing her words carefully: "We are emissaries from a distant world that appreciates your history and culture. We wish to learn more about you and, if you allow it, how we can support you and your world."

The image looked down at the crew, the holographic eyes more attentive than expected: "Our world is divided into fragments, and our peoples have isolated themselves. But we Auron are watching, and we know that the Virani, Zerai and Atur are still with us. We have not made contact with them for a long time. Your arrival could be the first bridge - but be warned, strangers: trust is not easily granted."

Luis spoke quietly to Soraya: "It sounds like they want to test us. They are cautious, but perhaps curious."

Soraya smiled and held his gaze: "Then we'll give them a reason to trust us."

Aiyana turned to the image of Auron again, "What do we need to do to gain your trust?"

The holographic image rose slightly as its voice filled the room, "Find the three remaining races of Venus and cause them to gather at the Crystal of Unity. In a bygone age, this temple was the place where our peoples came together in unity. If you can lead them here in peace, you may earn our trust - and our knowledge."

Ingrid looked excitedly at the crew: "That sounds like a mission that could actually connect our world and their world."

Aiyana nodded: "That's the challenge we're going to take on. We must start with the Auron and then find the other races."

The image of the Auron nodded, "A difficult path lies ahead of you, but we will watch over you. When you are ready, the temple will guide you to the first meeting point."

With those words, the hologram faded and the crystal extinguished before a faint column of light led in the direction of an uncharted corridor.

Aiyana turned to the crew: "Guys, this is it. Our next destination: the trust of the Auron and the alliance of the peoples of Venus."

Luis looked to Soraya, an excited smile on his face, "Maybe we really do have it in our hands to make something big happen."

Soraya returned the smile, her eyes full of determination: "Then let's take the first step."

The crew stood in awe as the image of the last Auron faded before them. The room that had just been filled with the living projection was now silent - but a low hum and a warm glow remained. The air vibrated with the suggestion of possibilities and an unexplored history unfolding before them.

Aiyana looked resolutely at the crew, "This is it, people. The peoples of Venus have survived - and may just be waiting for someone to make the first move."

Kenji nodded, the fire of discovery in his eyes: "The Au-ron. If we find them, they could show us the way to the others. A common goal could form the basis of an alliance."

Ingrid frowned, thoughtfully: "But we also have to be careful. They could see us as a threat... or as instruments for their own interests."

Soraya checked her scanners as she added in a calm voice, "The Au-ron have a particularly strong bond with the energy of this temple. If we can win them over, we might have the support we need to reach out to the other races as well."

A soft, shimmering light was kindled on the floor of the room, where a complex symbol shone - a kind of runic circle that slowly rotated. A holographic map of the surface of Venus emerged from the center of the symbol, mesmerizing the crew.

Luis moved closer to the map and examined the details that stood out in the fine line work: "Look at this. These are different points - and here, clearly, this is the area where we could find the Auron."

Soraya pointed to an area further away: "And here... perhaps the territory of the Virani. If we gain the Auron's trust, they could provide us with a safe passage to the other races."

Priya analyzed the holographic coordinates: "Interesting... the map shows certain places where the planet's energy is particularly concentrated. These points seem to be the keys - as if each place has some kind of portal function."

Aiyana looked at the crew: "Our first step is clear: we need to make contact with the Auron. If we can prove to them that we are not enemies, they might recognize us as ambassadors for the others."

The symbol on the ground glowed more intensely, and suddenly it seemed to point in a specific direction - as if the temple itself was ready to lead the crew to their first destination.

Ingrid took a deep breath and looked around the room: "If this temple is indeed a center for the knowledge and history of these races, then we have just found a key."

Kenji added, "Perhaps the Auron and the other races never expected that outsiders could ever pass these tests. That alone could be the reason why they are paying attention to us."

Aiyana nodded, "Then let's let them see that we are worthy." She turned to the crew, her eyes full of determination, "Pack your gear and check your communication devices. If we find the Auron, we'll need clear, precise signals - and a willingness to show our peaceful intentions."

Luis looked at Soraya and smiled confidently: "And we should perhaps practise our diplomatic tone again."

Soraya returned the smile, a hint of tenderness in her gaze: "I will support contact wherever I can. The Auron seem to have a resonance for communication - perhaps we can use this frequency to make our intentions clear."

Priya nodded, taking up the scientific challenge: "That's a fascinating approach. If their technology is based on quantum energy, we could work out a translation of their symbols into mathematical principles."

The crew gathered their equipment and prepared to begin the journey. As they made their way through the halls of the temple, the symbolic pattern continued to glow at regular intervals, showing them the way. Finally, they stood before the entrance, where a final pulse from the temple gave them a message.

Aiyana raised her hand as she focused the beam of light and repeated the words softly, "A bridge between worlds... the legacy that extends when knowledge is shared." She turned to the crew, the light from the map reflecting in her eyes, "Onward to a new age of connections."

And with that, they stepped out into the unknown world, the legacy of the temple firmly in their hearts and first contact with an ancient civilization just steps away.

After the intensive exploration of the temple, the crew returned to the Venera Ascendant exhausted. The atmosphere in the ship was full of impressions, but tiredness prevailed, and so they finally found rest, only to set off again the next morning, fresh and eager to explore the secrets of Venus.

Chapter 11: Encounter with the Virani

The first contact

After a deep, restful sleep in the Venera Ascendant, the crew set off for the temple again early in the morning. The holographic projections of the Auron the day before had aroused their curiosity and raised many questions. But no one really knew what to expect - perhaps the temple would turn out to be just an empty relic of an ancient culture, or perhaps it would reveal more about the beings who had once lived here.

As the crew climbed the heavy stone steps of the temple and moved through the halls, the atmosphere was dense and mysterious. The walls were covered in unknown symbols, and it almost seemed as if the temple held ancient knowledge hidden deep within.

Suddenly Kenji stopped and whispered: "Commander, look... over there."

Aiyana raised her hand to bring the crew to a halt. Shadows loomed on the walls - figures that appeared larger and stronger than the holographically projected Auron, with some sort of heavy armor or plating.

"Be vigilant," Aiyana whispered, straightening her posture, ready to respond to the strangers.

Massive figures emerged from the semi-darkness. Their skin was a stony gray, streaked with fine, shimmering lines that glowed like glowing veins in the twilight. The Virani, who had only hinted at Auron in stories, now stood before them. Their gazes were stern and watchful, and they moved with a heavyweight dignity that radiated a clear dominance in the high Venusian gravity.

One of the Virani, a tall warrior with a breastplate adorned with ancient symbols, stepped forward. His voice echoed deep and firm through the hall as he spoke - a language the crew did not recognize, but the melodic and powerful intonation seemed to carry a clear command.

The crew remained standing uncertainly until Aiyana finally took a step forward with open hands and said in the calmest of tones, "We come in peace. We are explorers from Earth."

A second Virani, standing next to the warrior and armed with some kind of serrated spear, curved his mouth into a serious but interested smile. Several words in the foreign language followed, until one of the Virani finally spoke in a broken but understandable language halfway up: "You are strangers. Humans."

"Humans," the foremost Virani repeated in a voice that rolled through the room like thunderous waves. "I am Rakan of the Virani. What brings you to our realm?"

Aiyana respectfully took a step forward. "Rakan, my na-me is Aiyana Wolfe, commander of the Venera Ascendant. We seek only knowledge and cultural exchange. We wish to get to know each other peacefully and understand your world."

Rakan's eyes narrowed as if he was weighing up her words. "Getting to know each other, you say. And yet you wander into our temples as if it were your right."

A Virani beside Rakan, his massive shoulders wrapped in some sort of metal jewelry, eyed her with a cool gaze. "You humans are known for destroying what you do not understand. What guarantee do we have that you won't treat us the same way?"

Kenji stepped forward and held a hand over his heart, a gesture he thought should be universally understood by humanoid beings. "We have learned from our past, and we are here to listen and learn. We respect your culture and want to communicate as equals."

Rakan scrutinized Kenji closely, and for a moment the silence was unbearable. But finally he nodded slowly.

"Some among the Auron may believe they can use humanity as tools, but we Virani are more suspicious. We are the Guardians of Venus and have left Kepler-10c to create a new order - one where strength and protection are paramount." His voice sounded harsh, but not unforgiving. "And yet you seem to pose no threat... so far."

Kepler-10c is located about 560 light years from Earth in the constellation Dragon and is also known as **"Mega-Earth"** because it is unusually large and massive compared to other rocky planets and therefore has enormous gravity. Therefore, beings that originate from this planet must have **enormous physical strength** elsewhere **with Earth-like gravity,** such as here on Venus.

Aiyana sighed with relief and returned his gaze seriously. "We are honest, Rakan. There are many things we do not understand, and we hope you can guide us."

"Look," Rakan began as he pointed to the dome, "this is one of our energy sources. We harness the vibrations of the Bo-den and channel them into the protection of Venus. But this is only one of many techniques we have mastered. Our neighbors, the Auron, may be smarter, but they... often overestimate their power."

"Why?" Priya asked curiously. "Can you tell us more about them?"

Rakan looked at her coolly. "The Auron believe they are the spiritual leaders on Venus. They manipulate quantum fields and harness energies beyond your imagination. They see us Virani as... military, simple. But we keep this world in balance, and without us there would be chaos."

Kenji nodded thoughtfully. "It sounds like the Auron and the Virani are two opposing forces - intellect and strength, both necessary to protect Venus."

"Correct," Rakan confirmed. "And yet there are others. The Atur are the unpredictable ones among us. They use resonances and frequencies to influence both their environment and the living beings around them. They change things in the most subtle, dangerous ways that even we can't always see through."

Ingrid shook her head, impressed and worried at the same time. "That sounds like a very complex dynamic. How do you keep it all in some kind of balance?"

"We adhere to strict boundaries," Rakan replied, looking at the crew urgently. "Anyone who crosses those boundaries puts Venus in danger. The Zerai are the last in this equation, but their loyalty is to no one but themselves. They conform and seek only their own advantage."

The crew nodded slowly, the complexity of the Venusian cultures becoming clearer to them. But at the same time, there seemed to be many opportunities for misunderstanding and conflict.

"What do you expect from us?" Aiyana finally asked.

The air crackled with tension. Rakan now stepped forward as leader of the Virani with a grim expression. The other Virani looked at him respectfully and regarded the humans with a mixture of curiosity and skepticism.

"You claim to be strong," Rakan began, his voice low and thunderous. "But here, only what you can prove counts. You will have to pass three tests to gain our respect. Only those who are our equals can gain our trust."

The crew exchanged uneasy glances. Soraya finally stepped forward and fixed Rakan with a cool gaze. "I'm ready for the challenge," she said with calm determination.

A satisfied grin appeared on Rakan's face. "Good, but first I will show you what we expect."

"Our trials test strength, endurance and precision," he explained. "Only those who master these qualities can survive in this harsh world."

The first test: the weight of the rock

The first test began. Rakan pointed to a massive boulder lying in the middle. The stone was bulky, dark gray and impressively heavy - about the size of a man and the consistency of a heavy iron mineral.

"The weight of the rock," Rakan announced, his voice full of authority. "Lift this stone to shoulder height. Hold it for a moment before setting it down safely."

Rakan stepped forward and lifted the boulder with apparent ease. He held it steady at shoulder height, his body tense but completely calm. Then he carefully set the stone down again and took a step back.

Soraya also went to the stone. She looked at it briefly and then closed her eyes, focusing. The crew watched her tensely as she slid her hands under the uneven surface of the stone and lifted it slowly but firmly. Her arms tensed and the muscles in her shoulders stood out as she gradually raised the stone to shoulder height.

A slight tremor ran through her arms, but she held the position for several seconds before setting the stone down again in a controlled manner.

The Virani murmured, impressed, and Rakan nodded appreciatively. "You have strength," he said curtly and moved on to the next test.

The second test: the sprint across the lava floor

For the second test, Rakan led the group to a narrow path that led between two heated crevices. The air above shimmered due to the intense heat, and the path was peppered with sharp rocks and obstacles.

"This is the test of endurance and skill," Rakan said, nodding toward the path. "Run along this path without touching the heated crevices. Your speed and agility will be put to the test here."

Rakan went first, his steps quick, controlled and graceful. He skilfully jumped over the sharpest rocks, dodged obstacles and reached the end of the path effortlessly without showing any sign of exhaustion.

Soraya watched him intently and prepared herself inwardly for the challenge. She stepped to the start of the path and took off. The crew held their breath as she skilfully leapt over the obstacles, her movements precise and nimble. The hot wind from the crevices burned her skin, and a few times it was close, but she made it to the end of the path with skill and speed.

"Well done, Soraya!" Aiyana called out in relief, while the Virani nodded again with respectful glances.

Rakan seemed seriously impressed now. "You have shown speed and skill that would challenge many of my warriors." A slight smile crossed his lips as he moved on to the final test.

The third test: the power of metal

Rakan picked up a heavy iron plate forged into the shape of a cube. The cube was heavy and solid, a block of pure metal that shone under Rakan's mighty hand. He held it up and explained the task.

"The final test," Rakan said with a hint of challenge in his voice, "is a test of pure physical strength and control. Shape this cube into a sphere. The metal is cold and hard, but we Virani have the strength to bend and shape it with our bare hands."

Rakan wrapped his hands around the iron cube and began to smooth out the corners and edges with brute force. The Virani watched in awe as he gradually shaped the cube into a rough sphere. The force he exerted was incredible.

Now it was Soraya's turn. She took the cube, which was still warm in Rakan's hands, and also began to shape the metal. Her face showed concentration and determination. Slowly and painstakingly, she pressed in the corners of the cube with her hands and began to shape it into a smooth form.

Luis and Kenji watched her in amazement, and Aiyana whispered softly: "This is incredible... even for Soraya, it's an enormous effort."

But Soraya was not to be deterred. Finally, the shape of the sphere was almost complete. But to outdo the Virani, she pressed a hole into the sphere with a powerful push of her thumbs and shaped the metal to form a perfect opening. The sphere now looked like a hollow sphere, even more impressive and intricate than the crude sphere Rakan had created.

A murmur went through the ranks of the Virani, and Rakan looked with awe at the workpiece Soraya handed him.

"You have shown not only strength, but also a clever mind," he said. "We welcome you, Soraya of Earth, as an equal fighter and partner."

He turned to his warriors and pointed at the humans. "Show them respect from now on. You have shown strength, skill and understanding."

Luis couldn't help but grin: "Soraya, that was really impressive," he whispered and patted her lightly on the shoulder. Kenji nodded in confirmation: "I knew you could do it. But the hole... that was the crowning glory."

Soraya smiled softly and tilted her head slightly as Rakan still turned the molded sphere in his hand as if he couldn't believe what he was seeing.

Rakan looked at her silently for a moment. "I expected respect and caution from you. The Auron may be curious about you, and the Atur may try to manipulate you. But the Virani will protect you as long as you follow our rules."

Soraya bowed her head and said softly, "We will respect your rules, Rakan. Thank you for your trust."

A spark of recognition flashed in Rakan's eyes. "Then follow me on," he said, leading the crew deeper into the Laby-rinth as an atmosphere of mutual respect and caution alternated between the humans and the Virani.

Rakan's rough features softened a little. "The Auron see us as crude warriors, but we pride ourselves on our strength and discipline. We will guide you through our domain and show you what we consider sacred. But understand this: The Atur are dangerous, and the Zerai are committed only to themselves. This is not a world of unity, but of survival."

Soraya was intrigued by Rakan and stepped closer, her eyes full of curiosity. "Rakan, can you tell us more about the Atur?"

Rakan laughed, a dark, throaty sound that echoed in the temple room. "The Atur... The frequencies and resonances they use are powerful. They manipulate energy and biology and can influence nature and even the mind through vibrations. But be warned: they are masters of deception. Most of their arts are forbidden to us Virani, too un-self-aware and dangerous. They believe they can influence the harmony of nature, but often they only bring chaos."

Aiyana looked at her crew warningly. "Then we'll make sure to respect that boundary."

"Good," Rakan replied. "I will now lead you to another energy source - a quantum field that we derive from the core of Venus. It is the basis of our infrastructure and enables us to protect and nourish our community."

The crew followed the Virani through labyrinthine corridors that led into a hall protected by a radiant energy shield. Priya and Ingrid gazed at the construction in awe, the force field pulsing in rhythmic waves and creating an atmosphere of incredible stability.

"This is... spectacular," Priya murmured as she stepped closer. "You use the magnetic field of Venus as an energy source, but this technology, this kind of structure... we don't have anything like this on Earth."

"Because your civilization is based on fragility," Rakan said, without malice. "You have not adapted to the limits of nature, but have tried to overcome them. We Virani, on the other hand, respect the gravity that shaped us on Kepler-10c. Here, on Venus, we feel at home."

Ingrid looked at him with shining eyes: "Rakan, your philosophy is remarkable. Maybe we can learn from each other - we have technologies that work differently, and maybe... an exchange could benefit us both."

Rakan looked at the crew in silence for a moment, scrutinizing each individual. Finally he nodded: "Perhaps. But the trust between our peoples is still young. Venus has seen too many conquerors - and all of them have failed to control life here." A dark shadow crossed his face. "The biggest mistake Earth could make would be to repeat the mistakes of the past."

Soraya nodded respectfully, "We understand you, Rakan. We are willing to submit to your ways and learn what you wish to show us."

The Virani nodded gravely, their stony faces showing a hint of respect. Rakan raised his hand, a sign that the meeting was over, "Go now, but remain vigilant. Venus tests her guests, and many do not return. I hope for your sake that you are strong enough."

With these words, he turned and disappeared with his group into the shadows of the temple. The crew stood still for a moment, impressed by their first contact with the Virani and the knowledge they had gained about the dangers and possibilities of Venus.

Chapter 12: The path of Auron

The harmony of resonance

After the encounter with the Virani, the astronauts were filled with tense anticipation. The mysterious Auron that the Virani had reported were considered to be technologically advanced and almost mystical leaders of this world, but until now the crew had only seen them in holographic projections. The Auron had signaled their presence, but the timing of a direct meeting remained uncertain.

Early that morning, as the crew was traveling in the misty hills, a series of low, vibrating sounds echoed through the air. It was a sound that was felt rather than heard, and it evoked a strange warmth in everyone.

"That... that must be them," Aiyana whispered, her eyes shining curiously. "The Auron."

"It's like an invitation," Kenji added, slightly nervous but excited. "They know we're here."

A brilliant beam of light, clear and bright, suddenly shot from the distance, forming a luminous path that led into a deep valley. A voice rang out in their communication devices, calm and mesmerizing: "Follow the light. We are waiting for you."

The crew began to follow the light, the tension in the team palpable. Ingrid, whose cool head had often helped them out of tricky situations, looked serious and focused. "Stay alert. If the Auron really are the technological geniuses the Virani think they are, their power and intelligence could go far beyond what we've seen so far.”

Finally, they reached the heart of the valley, which was dominated by a gigantic crystalline building. Its structure seemed to be made of pure energy, criss-crossed by delicate, luminous lines. As they approached, the massive, translucent doors opened silently.

A slender Auron clad in glowing robes strode towards the crew. He was almost human-like, but his skin shimmered in a mixture of silver tones, and his eyes were so bright they were almost blinding. There was a silent aura around him, as if the building's energy was being channeled by himself.

“Welcome, travelers from Earth,” he spoke in a melodious, deep voice. “My name is Ikaris. I am a guardian of the resonance fields and your guide on this path.” He made a welcoming gesture. “Enter the halls of Auron.”

The crew followed him into the building, which turned out to be a gigantic, shimmering hall filled with quiet, almost musical vibrations. Walls glowed everywhere, on which complex mathematical formulas and diagrams appeared and disappeared again, as if they were being thought through by an invisible consciousness. Inside the building, as in the temple where they had met the Virani before, an Earth-like atmosphere prevailed, allowing the astronauts to remove their helmets.

“What you see here,” explained Ikaris, ”is the heart of our quantum resonance technology. We have spent generations channeling and harmonizing the energies of this world.”

Priya, naturally fascinated by science, approached one of the glowing panels with curiosity: “It's incredible. You have obviously found a way to not only store energy, but to shape it as a living system."

Ikaris nodded: "Our quantum fields are more than just technology. They are a legacy left to us by our ancestors - a harmonious combination of spirit, matter and space."

Soraya stepped forward and fixed Ikaris. "Forgive the directness of my question, but what is your goal? You are opening yourselves to us, strangers from another world. Why?"

Ikaris returned Soraya's gaze calmly, and his eyes seemed to see through her mechanical structure effortlessly. "We have known of humanity's existence for a long time and have watched your development with interest and caution. Venus is our home, but the balance is at risk. The Atur, as you have already experienced, are destabilizing our world with their uncontrolled use of resonances."

"And you think we could support you in this conflict?" asked Kenji, raising his eyebrows skeptically. "Why should we interfere?"

Ikaris was silent for a moment before answering. "Because resonance is a system based on connectedness. You have a potential that even some of our own do not possess. Your adaptability, your willingness to learn and your openness could help us stabilize the resonance of the world - before the Atur destroy it."

Aiyana looked at Ikaris seriously and asked thoughtfully, "And if we can restore the balance, what would be our role? Would we stay here, become part of your world?"

A faint smile flitted across the Auron's lips: "That depends on you. But you should know that such a connection to the resonance creates a deep bond. The path back to your Earth could be fraught with consequences."

A deep silence fell over the group as everyone processed the weight of Ikaris' words. But before anyone could reply, the air suddenly vibrated violently. The walls lit up as if in response to a threat, and a high, guttural scream echoed through the halls.

Ikaris' face changed, a rare sign of unease appearing on it, "The Atur... they are here. They've found the resonance path."

"That wasn't an invitation to tea, was it?" Luis asked dryly, pulling out his communicator.

Ikaris raised a hand: "Stay calm. I will activate the security fields. The Atur must not enter the inner chambers, otherwise they will upset the balance."

Ikaris quickly led the crew into one of the side corridors. There he opened a hidden chamber in which glittering crystal panels hung from the ceiling. "You are safe here. Use this time to connect with the resonances. They will help you if the Atur try to interfere."

As the crew focused on the glowing crystals, they began to perceive the vibrations and oscillations that permeated them. Each of them felt the energy strengthening them and a deeper understanding of the nature of Auron resonance awakened within them.

Soraya ran the frequencies through her sensors, which shaped and analyzed this unusual energy: "It's as if the resonance itself is a consciousness. It reacts to our thoughts."

Suddenly they felt another strong vibration and heard a loud rumble. A shadow glided through the chamber and materialized in front of them - a figure clad in jet-black robes with a face that seemed strangely distorted, as if it were constantly changing shape.

"You strangers have no business here!" the figure hissed, its voice full of anger and menace.

Ikaris stepped forward resolutely. "The Auron are in harmony with the resonance. You Atur will not succeed in disturbing this balance!"

A heavy thud echoed through the chamber and the walls trembled as the Atur used their resonance power. But the Astro-nauts sensed the Auron's energy, which wrapped itself protectively around them and helped them to fight against the attackers' vibrations.

Aiyana concentrated, breathed in and out deeply and imagined that the resonance was a powerful wave that protected her and her crew.

The others joined her, and soon the energy flowed through them like a shared heartbeat - a har-mony.

"You underestimate us," Priya shouted emphatically, "and the power of cooperation."

With their combined resonance power, they managed to push back the Atur and protect the room. Ikaris watched them with renewed appreciation.

"You have done it. You have engaged with the resonance, and it has accepted you as allies." He nodded in acknowledgment. "You are ready for an alliance."

The crew now knew that they had taken an important step. They weren't just visitors on Venus - they had become part of something bigger.

The core archive

After the intense encounter with the Atur, which they only just managed to fend off, the crew gathered together, exhausted but alert. The halls around them had an almost eerie silence, and the few lights that flickered through the room seemed to have a sort of watchful presence.

Aiyana wiped beads of sweat from her forehead and looked at the others, "That was close. But I think we know now that the Auron were right. The Atur are not allies, but a real danger."

Kenji growled and looked at the spot where the last Atur had disappeared: "The Atur may be powerful, but their power lies in resonance. As soon as we break their vibrations, they lose their strength.

"Soraya, whose artificial nervous system had not yet completely calmed down after the intense contact with the Atur, stood silently by and looked thoughtful. Luis noticed her expression and placed a reassuring hand on her shoulder: "Are you okay, Soraya? You look like you're lost in thought."

Soraya nodded slowly: "Yes. The Atur pulled me into a kind of resonance field. I could feel their vibrations having a direct effect on my systems." She paused briefly and looked at the others. "But I was able to adapt. It was... fascinating. Their technology is based on principles I understand, but only in theory so far."

Ikaris reappeared as they walked down the hallway.

"I see that the Atur have once again tried to exert their influence," Ikaris said, his voice sounding both matter-of-fact and sympathetic. "This encounter was inevitable. The Atur sense that your arrival will change the order. They will try anything to unsettle you." Ikaris paused briefly, then continued.

"You survived the Atur attack," Ikaris said with a slight nod of respect. "That speaks to your strength. Not many strangers can withstand that resonant power."

Aiyana stepped forward and nodded respectfully to Ikaris. "We thank you, Ikaris. Without your warning and support, we might have been unprepared. It was... blatant." She paused and looked to the others, who were still silently processing what had happened.

"Crass is putting it mildly," Kenji muttered. "These vibrations... I thought I was losing control of my own body."

Ikaris nodded and regarded Kenji with a knowing look: "The Atur manipulate their surroundings, using the resonance of life and matter. For beings unaccustomed to these energies, it can be overwhelming.

But you have stood firm. That is a sign of strength that will serve you well in our next step."

Ikaris' lips twitched into a slight, almost mischievous smile. "The Auron see it as their duty to protect those who embark on a dangerous quest for knowledge. The Atur would disturb the peace to achieve their own goals. Yet you have bravely rejected them. Your resolve is impressive."

Kenji, looking in skeptically, asked the question that was on the tip of his tongue: "Ikaris, why is it so important to the Auron that we are here on Venus? We know that we seek knowledge and peace - but what do you hope to gain from us?"

Ikaris closed his eyes for a moment and took a deep breath. "We Auron have created a legacy - a knowledge that has grown to a point where it is connected to the balance of life on Venus itself. Your curiosity could be both an asset and a threat. Yet we have chosen to trust you because you seem sincere."

Priya, who had been quietly lost in thought, stepped forward and asked: "Ikaris, what can we do to further strengthen this trust?"

Ikaris' face twisted into a slight smile, an expression rarely seen on the Auron. "You have proven yourselves and exceeded our expectations. Now the path to our center is open to you. We Auron call it the `core archive` - the heart of our knowledge and energy."

Ingrid's eyes lit up. "The Core Archive... that's an honor, isn't it?"

Ikaris nodded in confirmation: "It is a privilege that we only grant to a few beings. But be warned: what you see there will change the way you understand your world. It will not only affect your technology, but also your understanding of consciousness and life."

Soraya, who always maintained a calm presence, now spoke in a low voice: "Then lead us, Ikaris. We are ready."

"Follow me," Ikaris said, and with that simple invitation, he turned and led the crew deeper into the halls of the Au-ron. The walls around them became more alive, pulsing in a slow rhythm, as if the building itself was breathing.

After a while, they reached a large chamber, in the center of which hovered a shimmering sphere, intensely imbued with a mystical, living energy. It seemed to glow with all the colors of the spectrum and had a presence that vibrated almost palpably in the room.

Ikaris stepped aside and looked at the crew seriously: "This is the Core Archive. It is not only a source of knowledge, but also the memory and soul of our species. Every Auron is a part of this archive, and to understand it, you must be willing to absorb its energy."

Aiyana looked at the sphere and felt her heart beat faster: "What exactly will happen when we enter?" she asked.

"The core archive will test you," Ikaris explained calmly. "It will penetrate your innermost being and find out if your intentions are in line with our knowledge and our goals. There is no way to deceive."

Kenji hesitated for a moment, then stepped to Aiyana's side, "So, it reads us like an open book?"

"A simple description, but yes," Ikaris replied with a small nod. "But know that each of you will experience something different. The core archive adjusts to each individual's mind and energy."

Soraya, whose android consciousness combined both curiosity and restraint, spoke in a low voice: "What will the Archive want from me? I am not a biological being like you."

Ikaris smiled gently, turning to Soraya: "You are a being too. Your energy, your consciousness - everything that lives within you is part of the journey. The core archive will respect you no less than the others."

Aiyana looked at the faces of her crew members. "Are you ready?" she asked quietly.

Kenji sighed, a grin on his lips. "Of course we are. If that means we'll find out the secret of the Auron, then I'm in."

Ikaris stepped in front of the sphere and made an inviting gesture: "You may enter, but I warn you: The core archive will confront you with a consciousness unlike anything you have experienced before."

Aiyana nodded firmly: "We are ready. We've come here to learn - whatever it takes."

A slight smile flitted across Ikaris' face as he pulled a small crystal from his robe and held it up to the orb. The orb visibly began to glow more intensely and a shower of energy flowed towards the crew.

One by one, they stepped forward and stood around the floating sphere. A gentle pulse of energy enveloped them, and suddenly they felt their thoughts and memories being sucked deep into the ar-chive.

Aiyana found herself in a scene she recognized immediately: the night sky above the earth. But this sky was alive, with countless pat-terns and streams of stars that moved like rivers of light. In this cos-mos, she felt an immense expanse.

Priya felt an energy flowing through his palms, and at that moment he realized the true power of Auron technology - it was a symbiosis of quantum energy and consciousness that could only work through complete surrender to the Ba-lance of the universe.

Soraya experienced the archive as a kind of spiritual reflection of herself. She saw its mechanics, its energy flows, its artificiality, but the archive allowed her to experience these parts as perfect parts of life. At that moment, she was more aware of her consciousness than ever before.

As the energy gradually drained from them, they stood back in the chamber, still surrounded by the core archive. Each of them was overwhelmed, but also deeply moved.

"You have passed," Ikaris said. "Your intentions are clear and pure of spirit. You are worthy to carry our knowledge and explore Venus."

Aiyana, still overwhelmed by the experience, bowed slightly, "Thank you, Ikaris. We will honor that trust."

But Ikaris raised a hand: "Know that this is only the first step. Knowledge is a burden that must be carried carefully. For the Core Archive, though it tests you, always makes new demands."

Kenji smiled slightly and patted Priya on the shoulder, "There you have it, Priya. Adventure and research all in one - we could spend weeks here and still have questions."

Ikaris returned the smile, "Your spirit of exploration is the reason I trust you. Go now, but remember that the true knowledge lies not in what you have already seen. It is what is still hidden that holds the greatest value."

With a mixture of gratitude and awe, the crew finally turned away, ready for the further adventures the Venus had in store for them.

Chapter 13: The Zerai alliance

Facing the giants

After the crew had processed the overwhelming experience of the Auron's core archive, they continued their exploration of the rugged terrain.

The steep cliffs and deep ravines of the surrounding terrain brought with them a bleak, barren beauty.

As they penetrated deeper into the terrain, the communication devices were increasingly affected by strange electromagnetic interference - a phenomenon that worried Aiyana.

"The interference is strangely constant," Priya murmured, studying the display of his device. "It's as if something is deliberately blocking our communication frequencies."

"Maybe that's a sign that we're on the right track," Kenji replied with a grin. "We wanted to find out what awaits us here."

Aiyana looked into the distance with a hint of worry. "Stay alert."

The cool twilight of Venus lay like an eerie veil over the jagged rocks as the astronauts reached the heights of the Zerai. Before them rose the mighty silhouette of an entrance, lined with glowing purple crystals that glowed in rhythmic pulses - a hint of advanced technology hidden deep within. The atmosphere was tense, and every step echoed like a menacing echo in the barren, alien landscape.

"I don't know if we're welcome here," Kenji muttered, casting a skeptical glance at the cave opening, which looked like a giant mouth. "The Virani warned us - these people change their allegiances faster than we can react."

"We have no choice," Aiyana replied calmly, although her voice also betrayed a hint of nervousness. "If we don't at least get the Zerai to listen, we could isolate ourselves - and in an environment like this, that's the quickest way to fail."

As they got closer, they heard a deep, rumbling noise that sounded like thunder in the distance. But it wasn't the forces of nature. It was voices - muffled and booming, a conversation between giant creatures. Aiyana stopped the group and nodded in the direction of the cave. "Ready?"

"As ready as you can be for three-meter giants," Luis said dryly, taking a step forward.

The crew stepped forward cautiously when suddenly a huge shadow filled the cave. Then the Zerai stepped forward - three colossal figures that seemed almost unreal in their massive appearance.

Their bronze skin gleamed like hammered metal, and their glowing eyes looked like cold flames. Each of them was over three meters tall, and their muscular bodies seemed to be fused with technological implants. They looked like warriors and gods at the same time.

"Humans," thundered the voice of the leader standing in the center. His helmet of black metal reflected the reddish light of Venus. "You dare to enter our territory? Why are you here? Speak quickly before we decide to crush you."

Luis stepped forward, his heart beating wildly, but he forced himself to remain calm: "We come in peace. We seek the wisdom and strength of the Zerai. Your reputation is known to us - you are unmatched in adaptation and survival. We wish to learn... and work together."

A contemptuous laugh escaped the leader, so loud that the ground vibrated beneath their feet: "Working together? Humans are weaklings who cannot comprehend our strength or our wisdom. What can you offer us that we don't already have?"

Aiyana took a step forward, ignoring the tension in the air, "Then watch," Aiyana said, her voice firm. "We know you trust no one. You are the masters of exploiting every advantage the other races offer you. Perhaps we can offer more than you think. Our technology may be different, but it has brought us here across much of the universe. And our knowledge could open up new possibilities for your people."

Luis took another step forward, although he had to tilt his head back to look the giant in the eye. He tried to reinforce Aiyana's statements: "We are not looking for a fight. We come to negotiate."

The Zerai leader gave a booming laugh, a harsh, echoing sound that bounced off the walls of the valley. "Negotiating? What do you have to offer that interests us? We Zerai need neither your wretchedness nor your technology. You are nothing more than pests."

Soraya, who was usually reserved in conversations, now stepped forward as well and spoke in her calm, calculating voice: "If we are so insignificant, why are you even talking to us?"

The Zerai leader's eyes narrowed. "A good question, machine." He made the word sound like an insult before crossing his massive arms. "Maybe because I want to see you squirm."

The second Zerai, who wore glowing markings on his arms, stepped forward and eyed Soraya, who had positioned herself behind Aiyana: "What about this machine? It belongs to you, doesn't it? Her eyes... they are empty. Why would we negotiate with a people who ally themselves with cold metal?"

Soraya remained calm, her voice sober as always, "I may be made of metal, but my mind is more than circuits. You underestimate me, and that would be a mistake. What you see as a weakness could be your greatest opportunity."

The leader glared at her, a grim smile on his lips: "Interesting. Maybe the machine does have some fire. But words are not enough for us, humans. You are nothing more than insects crawling through the cracks where we won't set foot."

Luis, sensing the budding hostility, intervened again: "We are not here to lecture you or compete with you. But we know that the Atur are trying to destabilize everything on this planet. They are a threat to everyone - including you."

The word "Atur" had a visible effect. The third Zerai, a colossus with a spiky back shield, snorted loudly and spoke for the first time: "The Atur are parasites. We have pushed them back more than once, but they are like a disease. Their resonances disrupt our fields. You know about them?"

"More than we would like," Aiyana replied. "Their technologies are dangerous. They could affect the balance of your genetic modifications - or worse."

The Zerai leader took a step closer, and the crew felt the ground tremble slightly beneath his feet. "Influence, you say? You claim our superiority could be threatened? Ridiculous."

"Maybe not today," Luis said, his voice calm but firm. "But later, sometime. You have adapted, but adaptation alone will not be enough when the Atur's resonance fields penetrate your territory."

The leader remained silent, his face tense. Then he spoke: "You are persistent. And I can see that you are not afraid. Perhaps you are not as pathetic as you seem. You speak with big words. Where does this knowledge come from? The Virani? The Au-ron?" His voice dripped with suspicion.

Priya stepped forward and crossed his arms in front of her chest: "The Virani and the Auron have given us information. But we've also seen the Atur with our own eyes. Their resonance fields attacked us and we only just managed to escape. We understand how dangerous they are, and we know that you are suffering as well. So why not work together to stop them?"

The Zerai exchanged long glances, and an agonizing silence followed. Finally, the leader spoke, his voice now cooler, almost calculating: "You want an alliance. But we are not like the Auron or the Virani. We are not persuaded by words and empty promises. If you want our trust, you must prove that you are useful."

"What do you ask?" Luis asked, his voice calm, but inwardly he was tense.

"There is an energy source that the Atur guard in an ancient temple," the leader explained. "It is powerful and could enhance our technologies. Get it for us, and we will consider an alliance."

"That doesn't sound like a negotiation, but like a test," Aiyana replied. "And if we get the energy source - how can we be sure you'll keep your word?"

The leader grinned, a dangerously cold smile. "You can't. But if you challenge us, it will be the end of you. So what do you say?"

The crew exchanged glances, the tension palpable. Finally, Aiyana nodded slowly. "We accept. But remember - if we do this for you, we expect respect and cooperation."

The other Zerai grinned, their massive figures like dark shadows against the reddish glow of Venus. "Respect," said the leader, "must be earned."

As the Zerai retreated into the cave, Kenji whispered softly, "This is suicide. We're walking straight into a trap."

Aiyana looked at him, her voice firm. "We have no choice. If we want to survive on this planet, we have to get the Zerai on our side. But you're right - we have to prepare."

Soraya nodded and added: "This is not an easy mission. We'll need all our skills - and maybe more."

The crew prepared themselves, knowing that the task ahead of them was not only dangerous, but potentially deadly.

Chapter 14: Abducted into the shadows of Atur

A dramatic development

By earthly reckoning, it was now late in the evening again. The astronaut crew moved into temporary accommodation provided by their Venus rover. The day had been exhausting, and the encounter with the Zerai had put them all to the test. But Commander Aiyana in particular seemed exhausted by the experience. She longed for a short break, for a moment in which she could organize her thoughts.

The others were already resting in the adjoining chambers, and Aiyana took one last look out at the hazy, shimmering slopes of Venus, which seemed almost alive in the twilight. Just as she was about to turn away, she heard a soft, buzzing sound, almost like a muff_ed hum, coming from the shadows near her.

"Kenji?" she called softly, suspecting that he might still be awake. But there was no answer, only the humming grew louder, more intense, like a pull that tugged at her attention. Suddenly she felt a strange tug, a resonance that shook her body. Even before she realized what was happening, the ground beneath her seemed to shake and a bright light blinded her.

Aiyana tried to retreat, but her legs did not obey her. Instead, she was grabbed as if by invisible hands and pulled into the darkness. Her last thoughts were confusion and shock before she lost consciousness.

When she regained consciousness, everything around her was cold and silent. In the darkness, she heard only the muffled echo of her own irregular breathing. It took a moment for her eyes to adjust to the darkness and she recognized shadowy outlines. The bare, metallic-looking walls, the subtle vibrations under her feet - everything indicated that she was in an underground facility.

"Hello? Is anyone there?" Her voice echoed through the room without an answer.

Suddenly a light flashed on and she could make out a figure slowly approaching. Her heart beat faster. The figure was tall, almost ghostly, and seemed to wrap itself in the shadows. As it came closer, Ingrid realized that it was an Atur - one of the mysterious, terrifying creatures they had been warned about.

"You're awake," the figure said in a voice that sounded like a dark growl. "Good, that will save us some trouble."

Aiyana pulled herself together and looked boldly at the atur. "What do you want from me? Why have you kidnapped me?"

The atur looked at her with a cool, calculating gaze: "We have observed that you occupy a kind of... diplomatic position with the other peoples. A link between the humans and the other factions. That's a potential problem for us."

Aiyana swallowed. She knew that the Atur were suspicious of anything they saw as a threat to their own power: "If you think you can use me as leverage to stop the Alliance, you are mistaken. My crew will not back down."

A dark, almost amused grin flitted across the Atur's face. "We realize that. But we don't believe in threats. We believe in... influence."

Another Atur entered, holding a small, metallic device in his hands that looked like an intricate antenna. He held it in Aiyana's direction and she felt a strange pulsing in her head, as if someone was trying to penetrate her thoughts.

"Leave me alone!" She tried to back away, but her legs were still heavy from the effects of the abduction-sog. The pulsing grew stronger and she had to summon all her strength to organize her thoughts, to banish the presence of the Atur from her mind.

"Why are you doing this?" she finally asked, her voice sounding rough and exhausted. "What is it that you fear so much that you resort to such means?"

The Atur stepped closer and scrutinized her insistently. "We fear nothing, human woman. But we believe that order should only be in the hands of those who control the power of resonance and the environment."

Aiyana realized that this was a desperate attempt to undermine her resolve. She took a deep breath and straightened up, despite the threat posed by the Atur: "You can influence my thoughts, intimidate me, but you cannot stop the alliance between the peoples. The Auron, the Zerai, the Virani - they all know that we are stronger together than alone."

"Human woman," he said in a voice that sounded as if it came from everywhere at once. "You have crossed our path. Your presence disturbs the resonance of our world."

Aiyana straightened up with difficulty, despite the heaviness weighing down her limbs. "I know who you are. And I know what you want. But you are making a mistake if you believe that violence will lead you to your goal."

The Atur leaned forward, his face a barely recognizable play of shadow and light. "We do not wage war without reason. Your plans to unite the peoples of Venus jeopardize the balance. This world belongs to no one but us."

Aiyana held his gaze. "You are mistaken. Your isolation has blinded you to the strength that lies in cooperation. If you break free from this outdated way of thinking, you could become part of something greater."

A dark laugh filled the room. "The words of a leader. Yet your crew doesn't even know where you are. Your strength is meaningless." "We'll see about that," said Aiyana, trying to suppress her fear. "My crew will not abandon me. And I won't let you sabotage the alliance."

A cynical smile played on the Atur's face: "Perhaps. But how strong are you really if we appropriate your technologies and use them against you? We don't just want to secure our power; we want to break yours."

Aiyana looked at him challengingly: "Then let me go. You will see soon enough that we are ready to fight for the Alliance and for peace."

There was silence for a moment, then the Atur nodded to one of his companions, who pulled out another device, a kind of metallic ribbon that buzzed in his hand: "If you really want to take our war seriously, human woman, you will help us from here on. Because if you don't... your crew won't be able to maintain the alliance."

Liberation attempt

Suddenly she heard a distant explosion and a deep tremor went through the room. A spark of hope sprouted in her. It had to be her crew members! They had found the location of the Atur's hideout and were prepared to do anything to get her back.

The Atur frowned and glared at Aiyana: "It seems your people are more determined than expected."

"They are," Aiyana replied firmly. "And if you are wise, you will admit defeat. The other races want peace - and I'm sure you'll see the benefits of joining the Alliance too."

Another, louder tremor shook the chamber. The Atur looked around briefly and mumbled something into his communication device, while his companions became visibly nervous.

"We will meet again, human woman," hissed Xarun, the leader of the Atur, and stepped back into the shadows, where he disappeared with his companions shortly afterwards. Aiyana stayed behind, chained to the ceiling of the cave wall.

The cave was bathed in an eerie glow. The Atur had amplified their resonance technology, causing a pulsating hum to vibrate the walls. Aiyana fell unconscious. She was trapped like a fly in a web. The other crew members stood at the edge of the cave, tense and ready to fight.

Luis pushed himself forward, his face determined. "We have to get her out of there. Now."

Soraya activated her scanners, "The field is based on a variable frequency. I can break through it, but it will take time."

Kenji gave her a nervous look, "How much time?"

"More than we might have," she replied as her fingers flew over her bracelet. "They know we're here."

A deep rumbling sounded and the Atur emerged from the shadows. Their figures seemed to be made of the darkness itself, unnatural and constantly in motion. The leader stepped forward, his voice sounding like a vibrating bass: "You dare to challenge us? Your primitive technique is nothing against our reso-nance powers."

Luis pointed his weapon at him: "We just want our commanders back. We're not here to fight."

"And yet you've drawn your weapons," the leader mocked. "You know nothing of our world. Your disturbances only bring chaos."

Kenji stepped forward, "Let's talk. There's no reason for this to escalate."

"Talk?" the leader laughed coldly. "That's not the language we speak."

Before anyone could react, the leader raised a hand and a resonance wave swept through the cave. The crew was thrown back, and Luis hit the ground hard. Soraya stood up again immediately, her eyes shining menacingly.

"That was a mistake," she said with icy precision. "Give us Aiyana, or you'll regret it."

The leader looked amused. "A robot with emotions? How fascinating. Let's see how strong your humanity really is."

He moved his hand and another energy blast rushed towards So-raya. But she jumped sideways and countered with a well-aimed blow from her energy projector. A bright flash lit up the cave, and an Atur disintegrated into a cloud of flickering light.

"Soraya, stop her!" Luis shouted as he moved towards Aiyana's position. He glanced at the shimmering field and pulled a small generator from his pocket. "I can deactivate this, but I need a minute!"

"Hurry up!" yelled Kenji, struggling with an Atur that had backed him into a corner.

Soraya fought with impressive precision, but the Atur seemed to keep appearing. Suddenly she noticed that Xarun was heading straight for Luis.

"Luis, behind you!" she shouted, but it was too late.

The leader of the Atur, Xarun, hurled a huge resonance wave that knocked Luis off his feet and hurled him hard against the rock face. He landed on the ground, breathing heavily, blood seeping from a deep wound in his side.

"No!" Soraya screamed and threw herself at the leader, her movements a storm of fury and precision.

Despite his injuries, Luis pulled himself up and activated the device. The resonance field around Aiyana flickered and finally collapsed. She fell heavily to the ground, gasping, but alive.

"Commander!" Kenji shouted, shaking her. He repeated his speech, "Aiyana!" Slowly her eyes opened and Kenji helped her to her feet, "We have to get out of here."

"Luis, come on!" Kenji shouted, his voice full of panic.

But Luis leaned against the wall, his face contorted in pain. "I... I'm not coming with you."

"What are you talking about?" shouted Kenji, "We're not leaving you behind!"

Luis shook his head, "Go. I'll hold them off."

The loss

Soraya was still struggling against the Xarun, her movements faster and more desperate. "Luis, get up!" she shouted. But when she took a quick glance at him, she saw his eyes slowly losing strength.

"Luis, no!" A furious scream escaped her throat and with a final effort she overloaded her energy cells. A powerful blast of light exploded from her body, throwing the leader and the other Atur back.

The cave began to shake as the Atur's resonance technology spun out of control. "We have to leave!" shouted Aiyana, her voice trembling with fear and grief.

Kenji pulled Soraya with him, who refused to leave Luis behind. But she finally gave in, her eyes full of tears that she couldn't understand.

Outside in the cool night air, an oppressive silence fell. The crew stood together, but they felt broken.

Soraya gazed into the distance, her hands trembling slightly. "He gave his life for us," she said, her voice quiet but firm. "It was not in vain."

Aiyana placed a hand on her shoulder. "We will not forget him. His sacrifice will be our motivation to complete this mission."

Kenji nodded, but the sadness in his eyes was unmistakable. "For Luis."

Soraya closed her eyes and let the grief flow through her systems. For the first time, she understood what it meant to feel - and why humanity was such a gift.

Chapter 15: The echo of time

The mood on board the Venera Ascendant was one of deep sadness. The loss of Luis had left a void that none of the crew could fill. But the mission had to go on, and Commander Aiyana knew they needed answers.

The Aurons had the power to provide answers. And maybe, just maybe, a solution.

The search for the Auron

The crew reached the shimmering city of the Auron, which lay in a floating energy pod high above the dangerous methane plains of Venus. The Auron representative, Ikaris, welcomed them into a hall of pulsing light that seemed to have no physical substance.

"You bear the shadows of loss," Ikaris said, his tone regretful. "Why have you come to us?"

Aiyana stepped forward, her voice firm, "We lost a friend. He died to save me. But... we believe you can help us bring him back."

Ikaris closed his eyes, his tall figure seemed weightless for a moment: "You want us to touch time itself. That is a dangerous wish."

The revelation of time travel

The hall transformed and the crew found themselves in a kaleidoscope-like space where images and moments flowed as if through a prismatic filter. Past events, future possibilities - everything seemed to exist simultaneously.

"We Auron have the technology to make time travel possible," Ikaris explained as he walked through the scenery. "But it is not a solution without consequences. Every intervention in time carries risks - the paradox of existence."

Soraya, still struggling with a deep sadness for Luis, stepped forward. "We understand the risks. But if we could ret-ten him..."

Ikaris turned to her, his gaze piercing. "You know the pogo paradox? It's one of the most dangerous pitfalls of time travel."

Kenji frowned. "I'm an astrophysicist, but I've always struggled with the subject of time travel. Please explain it to us."

The Pogo paradox

Ikaris raised a hand and a holographic image appeared: a man who performed a seemingly harmless act in the past - only to find that his action triggered a chain of events that destroyed his own present.

"The Pogo Paradox," Ikaris began, "states that any change in the past has the potential to alter causality in such a way that you inadvertently cause the tragedy you seek to prevent."

Soraya turned to Aiyana, her gaze intent. "If there is a chance to save Luis, we should take it. We can be careful."

Aiyana hesitated. "What if we make things worse? What if we lose more than Luis?"

"It's like time itself is working against us," Priya said, slumping into a bench seat in frustration. "The Pogo Paradox proves that our intervention has caused the very events we were trying to prevent."

"It's a known problem," Soraya said, looking at the holographic projection of the timelines in front of them. "But the pogo paradox isn't the only kind of temporal loop we could be dealing with."

Priya asked intently: "Wait a minute. Are there more such pa-radoxes that could get us into trouble?"

Soraya raised her head. "Yes, and one of them is particularly fascinating - and dangerous. It's called the Dalí paradox."

Ikaris remained silent the whole time and listened intently to the discussion between the earthly visitors. Now and again, he nodded in agreement to statements.

The Dalí paradox

Soraya now activated a holographic projection with her own eyes, which showed a spiral of events with melting clocks that intertwined like a surreal vortex. "The Dalí paradox occurs when a change in time causes cause and effect to merge and become indistinguishable.

It is named after Salvador Dalí, whose works often distorted the perception of space and time."

Priya looked at the projection and grimaced: "I just understand that it looks complicated. Can you explain it more simply?"

Soraya explained: "Imagine you go back to the past and take an artifact with you, say... a unique watch. You bring this watch to the present, and suddenly it turns out that there is no natural origin of the watch. It only exists because you brought it with you. There is no beginning and no end."

"A thing that exists out of nothing?" Priya asked skeptically.

"Exactly," Soraya replied. "The Dalí paradox describes this type of event, in which the timeline is distorted in such a way that the origin of things or events becomes unresolvable."

Aiyana, who had been listening in silence, spoke up. "And how does that affect us? We won't have brought back any clocks from the past."

Soraya looked at her seriously. "Not directly. But the attempt to save Luis has created an anomaly. Our manipulation of time may not only have triggered the Pogo paradox, but also left evidence that we may have created a Dalí paradox."

Now Kenji intervenes: "From my student days, I learned that in the Dalí paradox, the flow of time gradually slows down for the person or object concerned until it freezes from the perspective of an outside observer. For example, if a time traveler gives a book to an author in the past, which the author then publishes under his name, even though he never wrote it, we have a surreal paradox, because there is no coherent timeline and the origin of the book is not in the past. Transferred to our project now, we go into the past to save someone, e.g. from a traffic accident. However, this does not stop the person who would otherwise have caused this accident and they continue to drive the vehicle - and cause an even worse accident somewhere else."

"A change leads to an uncontrollable chain of reactions," added Ingrid, who was obviously familiar with her cultural-historical and philosophical background. "Just like Dalí's paintings - nothing is fixed anymore, everything flows into each other. In the end, you no longer know what you originally wanted to change and reality becomes completely unpredictable."

Aiyana nodded, but she wanted to make sure everyone understood. "Let's apply that to our situation. What if we save Luis from dying?"

Soraya replied matter-of-factly: "Then something else could happen. Maybe Aiyana dies during the liberation mission because we're not in the right place at the right time. Or worse - the entire resistance against the Atur collapses because we didn't trigger a crucial moment."

"But you can plan for that, can't you?" Priya asked optimistically. "If we analyze the processes carefully, we could prevent these reactions."

"That's the theory," said Ingrid with a hint of doubt. "But that's where the Dalí paradox comes in. Imagine we actually manage to save Luis. That could mean that the original motivation for our mission never existed - and then we might inadvertently change the whole reality."

"Like what?" Priya asked challengingly.

"A vivid example," Ingrid said, "would be if Luis survives, but in the altered timeline decides to leave the crew because he's traumatized. Without him, we lack his skills and the mission ultimately fails."

"That's bad enough," Priya added. "But what if Luis's rescue displaces someone else? For example, he could stand in the way of someone who was supposed to be instrumental in defeating the Atur. That's what you were hinting at with your example, Kenji, wasn't it?"

"Well," Kenji interjected with an allegory as an amateur draughtsman, "it's like painting a wall and correcting the color in one spot - but painting over so much that the whole wall is ruined."

Ingrid nodded. "Exactly. But here it's even more complicated: imagine you're painting something, but the color on the wall suddenly starts to change on its own. No matter what you do, it draws lines and patterns that you never planned."

"That almost sounds like a nightmare," Priya said gloomily. "We try to fix reality, but instead it becomes a mess."

Aiyana sighed. "That's what worries me the most. Not only could we endanger Luis' life, but we could destabilize the entire timeline. We're faced with a decision that we can't really control."

Soraya interjected, "If we accept the paradox, it means we don't fully know what's right or wrong. It's a risk we have to take."

"But that brings us back to the source," Ingrid said. "The key is to find a point that doesn't distort - an event or a constant that remains independent."

"And what could that be?" asked Priya. "I mean, everything seems changeable."

"Maybe it's us," Aiyana said quietly. "Our will to change things for the better. Maybe by making our decisions consciously, we can stabilize the timeline. But the risks seem incalculable to me."

The discussion became heated. Soraya spoke with a passion that seemed uncharacteristic for an android: "Luis sacrificed himself for us. How can we stand here and do nothing when we could get him back?"

Kenji, on the other hand, was skeptical: "Soraya, this isn't just a moral dilemma. If we change anything, we could all die here - or worse, everything we've fought for could be lost."

Aiyana turned to Ikaris again: "If we use this technology, is there any way to make sure we don't become the cause of his death?"

Ikaris' answer was like a sword thrust: "There is no certainty. Time is like a river, and even the smallest wave can cause a flood."

The journey into time

Finally, the crew decided to take the plunge. The Auron activated a platform. The platform was connected to the time matrix of Venus by a frequency resonance. The atmosphere vibrated as the crew stepped onto the shimmering platform. The atmosphere vibrated as the crew stepped onto the shimmering platform.

"Remember," Ikaris warned, "your every action carries weight. You can prevent Luis' death - or make it inevitable."

The crew materialized in the past, a few minutes before Luis' death. Everything was exactly as before: the cave, the Atur, the shimmering energy fields.

The paradox unfolds

They watched as Luis tried to deactivate the generator to free Aiyana. But this time Soraya intervened more quickly, defeating the Atur earlier, and Luis seemed to be safe.

But just when they thought they had saved him, it happened: a resonance wave triggered by a weakened Atur hit Luis as he rushed back to protect Aiyana. The scene was frighteningly similar, and yet it seemed inevitable.

Soraya fell to her knees, her system overloaded with the realization, "It... it was our return that caused this. We are the reason he died."

Resignation

Back in the shimmering city of Auron, there was a depressed silence. Ikaris looked at her, his voice soft. "The pogo paradox is merciless. You have seen that some events are self-perpetuating. There are things that cannot be changed."

Aiyana put a hand on Soraya's shoulder. "We tried to save him. That shows how much he means to us. But now we have to move on - for him."

Kenji nodded. "Luis wanted us to complete this mission. This is his legacy."

Soraya closed her eyes, her voice a whisper. "I will never forget him. His sacrifice - his humanity. It will always be a part of me."

The crew left the Auron city with their heads hung low. Luis was no longer with them, but his memory and his sacrifice drove them to carry on. The secrets of Venus awaited, and with each step they moved closer to the true meaning of their mission - and to peace between the peoples of Venus.

Chapter 16: Discussion on time travel

After a sleepless night, riddled with grief and guilt and a spark of new hope, the crew reassembled to set out for the shimmering city of Auron. The events of the previous day had shaken them deeply, but they were not yet ready to give up.

The loaf of bread model

The astronauts sat in the briefing room of the Venera Ascen-dant, lit by the soft illumination of the displays. In front of them flickered a holographic representation of the timeline, a projection of Ingrid and Soraya that they had programmed together. The display was unusual: instead of a straight line, there was a slice-like structure, similar to a sliced loaf of bread. Each layer represented a moment in time. It showed a city on earth with buildings and vehicles from the past on the left-hand side of the picture and buildings and vehicles from the future on the right-hand side.

"Okay, I understand that we can jump in time," Priya began skeptically, "but how is this... loaf of bread thing going to help us save Luis and free Aiyana at the same time?"

Ingrid stood up, tapped the hologram and spoke in a calm but firm voice: "This is not a simple line. Time is not an arrow. According to the block universe theory - or, as we call it, the loaf model - past, present and future all exist simultaneously."

Aiyana frowned: "Wait a minute. Are you saying that while we're sitting here, we're still fighting in the past and making our next plan in the future?"

"Exactly," Soraya confirmed. Her voice was neutral, but her eyes lit up as she elaborated on the idea. "Imagine the loaf of bread. Each slice is a moment in time. Our perception of time as linear - past, present, future - is only an illusion. We experience the loaf slice by slice, but in truth, everything exists simultaneously."

Aiyana leaned on the console and stared at the projection. "That sounds all well and good, but if it all exists at the same time, why can't we just go back in time, switch off the Atur and fix everything?"

Ingrid shook her head. "Because each slice of the loaf is already a fixed reality. We can enter and experience it, but we don't change the loaf itself. That's the crux of the matter - we can only act within the system."

"And what if we could look at the loaf from the outside?" asked Priya, leaning against the wall with his arms folded. "If everything exists, why are we limited to one perspective?"

Soraya replied promptly. "Because we are part of the loaf. We're like raisins in a raisin loaf - we can move within the mass, but we can't detach ourselves from the structure."

"That still doesn't explain," Kenji replied, "how we're supposed to rescue Luis from the past without taking the whole loaf apart."

Aiyana raised a hand to make the point. "Wait. If each slice already exists and we can act there, then any change in one slice would affect the entire loaf, right?"

"Yes," Ingrid confirmed. "That's the paradox. Every change we make in the past was already part of the loaf. Even our desire to change something could be predetermined."

"That's the loaf paradox," Soraya added. "We think we act freely, but maybe our decision is already part of the system."

Priya threw his hands up in the air. "That's absurd! So we can't do anything, or everything we do is already predestined? Where's the hope in that?"

"There is hope," said Ingrid, her voice firm. "Because while the loaf itself remains constant, we can act within a slice to influence certain outcomes. We may not be able to change the bread, but we can decide which raisin is moved where."

Priya laughed dryly. "Great. So we're raisins rebelling against the laws of baking."

Aiyana put her hand on Priya's shoulder. "No, Priya. That means we still have a chance. If we find the right disk - the right moment - then we could save Luis without destroying the balance of time."

"And how do we find this disk?" Kenji asked a little provocatively, because despite his scientific background, time travel was a closed book to him.

The twin paradox

Soraya activated another section of the hologram. A series of data streams appeared, representing the timeline. "This is the point where Einstein's special theory of relativity comes into play. The twin paradox shows us that time is relative - depending on perspective. If we manipulate our velocity and position in space, we could experience time in a kind of loop.

"Ingrid added: "We experienced the pogo paradox - a self-induced event. But the theory of relativity, especially the twin paradox, proves that time is not an absolute, linear flow. It is relative."

Kenji frowned: "The twin paradox? You mean how a twin traveling in a spaceship ages less than the one who stays on Earth? How does that help us?"

Now Priya interjected: "What is the twin paradox?"

Soraya projected the image of a pair of twins and explained: "On the left of the image, the twins are 30 years old; on the right, one twin is 50 years old, who traveled for 20 years at 80% of the speed of light in the spaceship, only to meet his now 63.33-year-old twin, who had remained on Earth, 20 years after separation. That's the principle of time dilation."

Priya continued to look puzzled and said: "I don't understand!"

Soraya then gave another example: "Imagine a 'light clock': Two mirrors are parallel on top of each other, and a beam of light bounces back and forth between them like a ping-pong ball.

1. When at rest, the beam of light only moves vertically up and down. The time that the light needs to bounce back and forth is fixed.

2. When in motion, the light timer moves to the right, for example. The light beam has to cover an inclined distance because it is moved upwards, downwards and sideways at the same time as the light clock. As a result, the distance the light travels is longer.

As the speed of light always remains the same, the light needs more time to travel the longer distance. This means that the clock ticks slower for the light. This shows that Moving clocks go slower - that's time dilation."

Priya nodded: "Okay, now I've understood that. But how does that help us now?"

Ingrid nodded: "If time is relative, it means that it has different effects on different observers. This means that what we experience as 'certain' may only be one of several possibilities."

Aiyana, who had been struggling with her decisions since Luis' death, sat up straight: "And if that's true - if time isn't final - maybe we could create an alternative timeline in which Luis lives."

"So a new jump?" asked Priya.

Ingrid nodded. "Yes, but more carefully this time. We have to calculate the moment in which we can save Aiyana without losing Luis. And to do that, we have to find the right disk."

Kenji looked skeptical. "And if we choose the wrong disk?"

Soraya replied with a rare expression of emotion. "Then we won't just lose Luis. We'll destabilize the entire loaf." The words echoed in the meeting room. Everyone was aware of the danger, but also the hope that lay in their new realization. Aiyana finally looked at everyone. "Then we have to make sure we find this disk. There is no way back, only forward through the loaf."

A look into philosophy

Soraya now projected a holographic representation of time, a tangled web of branches, loops and knots that represented her previous interventions in the flow of time.

Every attempt to untangle it only seemed to increase the chaos. The upcoming mission - a second leap into the past - made the astronauts think even more deeply about the nature of time.

Ingrid cast a thoughtful glance at the hologram and leaned back: "You know Heraclitus, don't you? The old Greek philosopher who said: Πάντα ῥεῖ καὶ οὐδὲν μένει (Pánta rheî kaì oudèn ménei) – 'Everything flows and nothing stays'."

Kenji frowned.

"Of course we know that. But what does that have to do with our situation?"

Ingrid stood up and demonstrated another projection of an image of a river in ancient Greece flowing from left to right: "Think about it: What if time actually flows like a river in one direction from left to right, from the past to the future? Heraclitus was probably not only talking about the nature of the world, but perhaps also about time. Perhaps it is not linear or static, but constantly in motion, changing itself - and we are trying to intervene in the middle of this flow."

Priya nodded slowly: "That would explain why our interventions have a different effect than planned. Like stones that we throw into a river - they disturb the flow for a moment, but then the water adapts, changes its course."

Aiyana frowned and switched the holography to a rotating model of the flow of time. It showed interwoven lines that wound like a river through infinity. "But if everything flows, as Heraclitus says, then the past should also be changeable. But our experiment shows that the past resists, that it prefers a certain course."

"Perhaps," Soraya interjected while working on a mathematical formula on her tablet, "it is not the past that is resisting, but us, who do not yet fully understand the dynamics of time. The flow of time might not only be chaotic, but also have a form of self-correction."

Priya propped her chin on his hand and looked at Soraya: "You mean that time fixes itself when someone tries to change it? Like a river that chooses a new route when an obstacle appears?"

"Exactly," Ingrid replied. "That would mean that through our interventions we create waves that lead time to a new course. But we mustn't forget that a river can have many paths - and not all of them end at the same mouth."

Aiyana straightened up: "If time really is like a river, then the question arises: do we even have the power to change its course permanently? Or are we just drifting on its waves, mistakenly believing that we control the current?"

Ingrid sat down again and crossed her arms: "That's exactly the point. Maybe we made a mistake because we saw time as something static. As if it were a path that you can go back and walk again. But if Heraclitus was right, then there is no fixed path. Only the water of the river, which is constantly changing."

Kenji raised an eyebrow: "But that still doesn't explain how we can prevent our second jump from triggering the same catastrophes as the first. If everything is flowing, how do we know if we're even swimming in the right direction?"

Aiyana grinned slightly: "We don't know. But maybe that's the key: trying to control time is like trying to stop a river with your bare hands. Maybe it's not about fighting the current, but learning to swim with it."

The crew fell into silence as the words sank in. Finally, Kenji broke the silence, his voice cool and matter-of-fact as ever: "Philosophy is all well and good, but we shouldn't forget that we're working with quantum mechanical realities here. Time may be a flow, but if we work on the level of space-time, it could also be a network of probabilities."

Ingrid smiled gently: "I'm not saying we should ignore quantum physics. But sometimes it helps to take a new perspective. What if the flow and the network are the same thing - different views of the same reality? Heraclitus also said: **Ποταμῷ γὰρ οὐκ ἂν ἐμβαίης δὶς τῷ αὐτῷ** (Potamoῖ gàr ouk àn embaíēs dìs tôi autoῖ.) 'You never get into the same river twice'. This could mean that even if we return to the same point in time, we are no longer the same - and neither is time."

Soraya nodded thoughtfully: "Interesting. Perhaps we should think about the fact that every jump in time inevitably leads to a new reality. And this reality is not fixed, but... fluid."

Aiyana stood up and crossed her arms: "If time is indeed fluid, then we should consider our mission not as an attempt to repair the past, but as an attempt to harmonize it with the present. If everything flows, then we shouldn't fight it, but adapt to the flow."

Kenji snorted softly: "Easier said than done, Commander. We have no idea how deep this river is - or whether there are rapids that could tear us apart."

Soraya looked at him, her eyes full of determination: "Maybe that's true. But I believe that the river will guide us if we learn to trust it. The true meaning of Heraklit's words could be: Nothing remains, but everything is connected. And it is up to us to understand this flow. If we do nothing, the river will not stop. It will continue to flow, with all the pain it has already brought us. Maybe we have to accept that we can't control everything - and that our goal shouldn't be perfection, but harmony."

"Harmony," Priya repeated quietly and nodded. "That's what it is. We must not fight, but work with time, like a boat that lets itself drift with the current, instead of fighting it."

Aiyana continued: "If we see time as a river, then let's embark on the next journey with this image in mind. Not an attempt to control everything, but an attempt to work with the flow. We jump where the waves are most favorable - and trust that we will find the right course."

Ingrid took a deep breath and looked around. "There is still a risk. But perhaps that is the true meaning of Heraklit's statement: we can never get into the same river because we change ourselves every moment. Perhaps the truth is that we are part of the river - and that every wave we make becomes part of the bigger picture."

The crew looked at each other, the hologram of the timeline still before their eyes. And as they weighed up the challenges of the mission ahead, the thought that time is like a river - unpredictable, but also full of possibilities - seemed to be a new spark of hope.

Aiyana finally said what everyone was thinking: "Then let's swim. And hope we find the right waves."

Chapter 17: The second jump

The decision was made and the crew rejoined Ikaris in the city of Auron.

Ikaris stepped forward, his demeanor impressive and calm: "You ask us to break the boundaries of time once more. But your plan no longer seems to be to change the past, but to reinterpret it."

Soraya, who was still struggling with grief and anger, looked at Ikaris: "That's exactly it. Luis' death is just one possibility of many. We ask you to give us the chance to create a different reality."

Ikaris closed his eyes as if he was communicating with time itself. Finally, he nodded. "I will grant you a second chance. But know this: Time is like a net. Every movement in one place affects other points. Proceed with caution."

The crew re-entered the time platform, their hearts heavy but determined. The Aurons initiated the sequence, and the platform was enveloped in a blinding light. Seconds later, the astronauts found themselves back in the past - again in the Atur's cave, minutes before Luis' death.

The relativity of time

The crew was back in the Atur's cave, which was flooded with a dim, bluish light. Aiyana was still trapped in the energy trap, a pulsating force field that restricted her movements. Luis prepared to deactivate the Atur's resonance generator as before, but this time the other crew members were watching him closely. They knew that their every action could change the timeline - for better or for worse. The environment is changing.

"Time feels... different," Priya murmured as he operated a scanner. The holographic projections he was analyzing showed chaotic patterns, as if the structure of time itself had been torn apart.

Kenji stood near the entrance and kept watch: "We only have one chance. Luis, are you sure you want to do this? It could get worse."

Luis lifted his head, his eyes fixed on Aiyana. "I'm not sure if we can deactivate the generator. But I know one thing: if I don't do anything, Aiyana will die - and I'll blame myself for it my whole life."

Soraya stepped forward, her voice cool, but her words seemed laced with emotion, "That's the mistake we made the 'first time', Luis. You acted without seeing the bigger picture. If we want to succeed **'this time',** you have to do something that stabilizes this reality. Something that is... different."

Luis looked in, confused: "The first time? This time? Different? What do you suggest, Soraya? Should I kindly ask the Atur for a ceasefire?" His tone was sarcastic, but Soraya refused to be provoked.

Soraya resolutely told Luis the whole truth: "Luis, even if you think we're crazy, we are time travelers and have experienced your death **'twice'** through wrong actions. Now please do as I say. I mean, you must act in a way that not only changes the flow of time, but forces it to accept this new reality. It has to be an act that puts you at the center without you dying - something that focuses the energy of this timeline on you."

Luis looked at Soraya in disbelief: "Time travel has always seemed implausible to me, but not necessarily illogical."

Priya looked up from his scanner: "It could work. Time is relative - but it is also in flux. If Luis commits an action that is unique in this new line, it will be interpreted as **'fixed'**. It's like a rock in the riverbed that diverts the flow."

Kenji puffed, "That sounds great in theory, but what's it going to look like practically? We don't have time to experiment for long."

Luis stared at the resonance generator, then at Aiyana, who was trapped behind the shimmering field. She was still hanging motionless, her face heavily marked by agony.

"Okay, I think I'm going crazy myself, but how can you contradict an android with her logic?" Luis finally said with a grin. "When I first thought about it, I would have tried to destroy the generator directly. But then I will instead..."

He paused as an idea came to him: "I'll redirect the energy. Instead of destroying it, I'll use the power of the Atur against it."

Soraya raised an eyebrow: "Redirect it? How are you going to do that? The generator is strong enough to kill you if you manipulate it wrong."

Luis grinned weakly: "Fortunately, I learned how it works the first time I tried it. I just have to set the energy to strengthen the cage - and then redirect it to the Atur when they try to stabilize it. It will take them by surprise."

Priya nodded slowly: "That might work. But it means you're putting yourself in immediate danger. You have to be extremely precise."

Luis carefully approached the generator. The Atur noticed his movement and began to charge their weapons. Their leader, a massive Atur with shimmering, crystal-like skin, called out in a deep, resonant voice: "Stop, human! One more step and your death is certain."

Luis raised his hands to show that he was unarmed: "I am here to negotiate!" he shouted. His voice was loud and clear, but fear raged inside him.

Xarun, the leader of the Atur, hesitated, obviously confused: "Negotiate? What can you offer other than your weak bodies and your blood?"

Luis stepped closer to the generator, his fingers gliding over the control panel: "We can show you that humans are not as weak as you think. But you'll have to let me finish."

As Luis spoke, he inconspicuously typed commands into the generator's interface. The energy began to change, its rhythmic hum became deeper and more irregular. The Atur noticed the change and began to look around uneasily.

"What are you doing?" hissed Xarun.

Luis looked directly at him as he made the final adjustment: "I'm showing you that humans have power too."

With a final command, he activated the detour. The generator's energy suddenly shot back, engulfing the Atur and throwing her into a shockwave of resonances. The force field around Aiyana collapsed and she fell forward, free but still unconscious.

And now the group experienced déjà vu: "Commander!" shouted Kenji, shaking Aiyana. He repeated his speech: "Aiyana!" Her eyes slowly opened and Kenji helped her to her feet: "We have to get out of here."

This déjà vu experience seemed to the time travelers like looking into a corridor of mirrors. The mirror image repeats itself in both directions until it becomes blurred. Each mirror shows a slightly different expression or subtle movement, reinforcing the feeling of déjà vu: something familiar that still doesn't quite fit.

Stabilization of time

The cave seemed to turn into a shimmering dream. The walls wobbled, the light from the generator pulsed irregularly and the air was filled with an electrifying tension that permeated everything. It was as if reality itself was hesitating which way to go.

Luis stood in the midst of this chaos while his crew stared at him with growing despair. He had rerouted the generator to change the timeline and make Aiyana's rescue possible, but something had gone wrong. Reality was unstable, indecisive, and their existence was hanging by a thread.

The search for a fixed point

"What's happening here?" Aiyana asked, holding on to a flickering pillar that was threatening to disappear. "Luis, what have you done?"

Luis gave her a pained look. "I thought we had fixed the timeline. But... it's not enough."

"Not enough?" Priya feverishly checked his scanners, which were spewing out incomprehensible streams of data. "The timeline needs a fixed point, something to anchor it. A moment so significant that it stabilizes the new reality."

Kenji shook his head. "And what's that supposed to be? We've already risked everything to save Aiyana. Isn't that enough?"

Soraya stood still, her artificial eyes fixed on the shimmering world around her. "It's not enough. Reality doesn't accept us yet because it doesn't recognize us as part of this new lineage. We need a deed, a decision that will make us inseparable from this timeline."

Luis stared at the generator, which was pulsing dangerously. The unstable energy continued to shake the cave, but a thought began to form in his mind. A thought that felt absurd at first, but the more he thought about it, the clearer it became.

"Maybe... maybe I can do this," he murmured.

"Luis?" Soraya's voice was calm, but her eyes searched his face as if she was trying to read his mind.

He turned to her slowly, "Soraya, listen to me. You're the reason I'm here. Why I wanted to change the timeline in the first place. You mean more to me than I ever wanted to admit. And if the timeline needs an anchor, I want that anchor to be us."

Soraya's eyes widened, an unusual expression of surprise on her usually composed face: "Luis, what... what do you mean?"

"I mean," he said, taking a step towards her, "that I love you. And that I won't let this timeline take you or anything else away from me. If an anchor must be something that is irreplaceable, then let it be my choice to spend my life with you."

Soraya stood silently as the words resonated within her. She was an android, a being of metal and data, created to embody logic and efficiency. But in that moment, she felt something she couldn't fully comprehend. A wave of emotion that flooded her artificial intelligence.

"Luis," she said softly, "you know I'm... not like you guys. I'm not able to feel things the way you do."

"That's not true," Luis replied, his voice firm. "I've seen how you take care of us, how you make decisions that have more to do with heart than logic. And even if you don't feel it like I do, that doesn't mean it's not real."

Soraya opened her mouth to reply, but he suddenly pulled a small, simple ring out of his pocket - a souvenir he had brought with him from Earth. "Soraya," he said, holding up the ring, "do you want to set an anchor with me? Do you want to be the one who fills this timeline with meaning forever?"

The cave shook more violently, as if the timeline was waiting to see which direction it should take. Soraya looked at the ring, then into Luis' eyes. Her programming told her that this decision was irrational, that there were risks involved. But something else, something deeper inside her, urged her to accept it.

Slowly, she reached out and took the ring: "I don't know if I'm doing it right," she said, "but yes. I want to be your an-ker."

A sudden, powerful tremor shook the cave, but this time it wasn't the chaos of instability. It was as if reality was reshaping itself, stabilizing around that moment. The generator's light went out and the walls of the cave became firm and solid again.

The crew stared around, their breaths heavy from the strain. Friya checked his scanners and nodded slowly, "The timeline... it's stable. We made it."

Kenji leaned against the wall and closed his eyes, "That was... more drama than I can handle."

Luis turned to Soraya and smiled weakly, "So? Was that convincing enough?"

Soraya held the ring in her hand and looked at it, her eyes full of new insight. "I think," she said slowly, "that you just did something no one would have ever expected me to do."

"Like what?" he asked.

"You taught me what it means to have a heart."

The crew had stabilized time, but Luis and Soraya had created something even more valuable: a connection that anchored the timeline - and perhaps changed them forever.

Chapter 18: Back in the shadows of Atur

The crew had rescued Luis - and learned that time itself was a complex, living web. They had created a new reality, but the price had been high. Now they had to concentrate on completing the mission - and securing peace between the peoples of Venus.

The Zerai's conditions had put the group of astronauts in a difficult position. Without the Atur's energy source, there would be no alliance - and without the Zerai, the alliance between the peoples of Venus was doomed to failure. But entering the territory of the Atur meant coming face to face with Venus' most dangerous enemies.

A risky plan

In the briefing room of the Venera Ascendant, Commander Aiyana stood with her arms folded in front of a holographic display showing the Atur's underground tunnels and security installations. The crew gathered around her, each with a mixture of tension and determination.

"The resonance pod we need is here," Aiyana explained, pointing to a red dot in the middle of a labyrinthine tunnel system. "The Atur are guarding it with threats and automatic defense systems. We must remain undetected if we want to be successful."

Kenji cast a skeptical glance at the map. "How exactly do we do this without all of us ending up as targets? That sounds like a suicide mission."

"Kamikaze shouldn't be so foreign to you, Kenji," Luis teased.

"But that's a bit irreverent and tasteless, Luis," Aiyana measured. "I would have expected more etiquette from you as first officer.

Luis meekly conceded and apologized to Kenji.

"We can do it with precision," Priya interjected. He opened an additional window in the hologram, which showed a disturbance in the Atur barriers. "I've found a frequency that will temporarily destabilize their resonance technology. We need to sync up and secure the pod quickly before the systems recover."

Soraya spoke in her calm, matter-of-fact voice: "If we are discovered, the entire Atur region will be activated. Their resonance weapons are deadly, and escape will be almost impossible."

Ingrid, who had been listening, stepped forward: "If we work together, we can do it. I know about the barriers and can make sure they stay deactivated while Priya and Soraya adjust the frequency."

Aiyana nodded: "That's the plan. We'll split into two teams. Priya and Ingrid come with me to the target. Kenji and Soraya will stay out here and make sure we keep an escape route open."

Luis grinned, although the tension was visible in his eyes. "And what's my role?"

"You're coming with me," Aiyana said. "We need your daredevil pacing and determination in case we have to improvise."

The resonance chamber

No sooner said than done. The astronaut crew now advanced into Atur territory. Perhaps not even the Atur expected the Earthmen to return at such short notice. The group moved cautiously, their helmets projecting shadowy maps of the surrounding area.

Soraya and Kenji positioned themselves on a ledge overlooking the entrance to the main tunnel. Kenji checked the explosives they had prepared as a distraction and glanced at Soraya, who was staring at her scanners.

"Everything calm?" he asked.

"For the moment," Soraya replied. "But the Atur are never far away."

Inside the tunnel system, Aiyana, Ingrid, Luis and Priya moved quickly but quietly. The walls pulsed slightly, as if they were alive, and a low hum filled the air.

"This technology is scary," Luis muttered.

"Focus," Aiyana whispered. "We're almost there."

Complex barrier: Ingrid's decryption

The Atur's resonance chamber was surrounded by a shimmering, blue-violet energy barrier that pulsed like a living organism. The barrier reacted to the crew's movements, small electrical impulses shot across its surface like twitching nerve signals. Ingrid knelt in front of the control module, which was built into a recessed niche next to the barrier. Her forehead glistened slightly with exertion as she unfolded her tools: a portable interface device, several sampling sensors and a holographic display.

"This is a complex system," Ingrid said. "I'll need a few minutes to get around it."

"We don't have much time," Priya warned. "As soon as the frequency jamming wears off, we'll be detected."

Luis pointed his gun at the entrance, "I'll hold the line."

"This is no ordinary protection system," she murmured as her fingers slid over the controls of her device. "The barrier is multi-layered - physical, energetic and with a quantum encryption algorithm. It's like a puzzle where each layer you solve unlocks a new one."

"How long will it take you?" Aiyana asked in a hushed voice, her weapon at the ready as she scanned the area.

"Depends," Ingrid replied, frowning. "If I can decipher the algorithm before the drones come back, it might work."

The first step: pattern recognition

Ingrid activated the sampling sensor, which emitted a fine laser light to analyze the energetic patterns of the barrier. The holographic display projected a swirling display of data streams moving in complex geometric patterns.

"The Atur have programmed this barrier to adapt to disturbances," she explained. "It learns in real time. We need to be faster."

"That doesn't sound reassuring," Luis interjected, staring nervously at the barrier's twitching pulses.

"That wasn't my goal either," Ingrid replied dryly as she analyzed the data. "Do you see this?" She pointed to a glowing dot that was repeated in a pattern of triangles and circles. "That's some kind of signature. I think it's the key to the first level."

She programmed her device to isolate the signature and generate a counter-pattern. With a low hum, the barrier began to flicker where the laser hit. The outer layer of energy retreated like water retreating from a hot stone.

"One layer down," she said, "but that was the easy part."

The second step: decoding quantum frequencies

The next layer was a pulsating web of resonances stretched across the chamber like an invisible spider's web. Any change in frequency could trigger a reaction that would alert the entire area. Ingrid closed her eyes, took a deep breath and began to analyze the frequencies.

"Ingrid?" asked Priya. "What happens if you do this wrong?"

"If I do this wrong," she said in a calm voice, "we'll find out."

Her fingers flew over the interface as she tried out frequencies. Suddenly, her display lit up red and a sharp tone sounded.

"What was that?" Luis asked in alarm.

"The system almost noticed us," Ingrid said quickly. "But I reset it in time."

She took a fine tool from her kit that looked like a tiny antenna and placed it against the barrier. The device began to modulate the frequencies in real time. Wave patterns appeared on the dis-play, gradually becoming synchronized.

"I have to adjust the waves until they're in sync with the main system," she explained. "If we get the timing right, we'll open the next layer without triggering the drones."

The astronauts held their breath while Ingrid fine-tuned the waves. After a minute - which felt like an eternity - the system clicked, and another flicker passed through the barrier.

"Done," she said, her voice calm but with a hint of pride.

The third step: the quantum algorithm

The third and final layer was a holographic field that displayed data in a complex, dynamic language. It seemed almost organic, as if the system itself was alive. Ingrid stared at the flickering symbols and frowned.

"It's like a maze," she said. "I have to decipher the algorithm by finding the right sequence. But there are millions of possibilities."

"You can do it, Ingrid," Aiyana said calmly. "Concentrate."

Ingrid activated a simulation tool, which began to try out sequences. Each wrong sequence caused a slight distortion of the holographic field, and time was running out. The threats in the background grew louder and louder.

Suddenly the light flickered and a piercing roar sounded: "That doesn't sound good," Luis said, taking up a defensive position.

While Ingrid worked feverishly, several drones appeared, their metallic bodies glittering in the blue light of the barrier. They began to attack the group with resonance pulses.

"We're spotted!" shouted Luis, firing at the drones while Aiyana stood next to him to provide cover.

"Almost done!" shouted Ingrid. "Keep them off my back for a few more seconds!"

Priya threw a sturgeon grenade that momentarily knocked the drones off balance. "It's now or never, Ingrid!"

"Think," Ingrid muttered to herself. "What would the Atur do to protect the labyrinth?"

She studied the patterns again until she noticed something: a certain symbol kept reappearing in different variations. It was subtle, but clearly a clue.

"That's it! Done!" She entered the sequence and the last barrier disappeared with a soft hum. Access to the resonance capsule was free.

After Ingrid had deactivated the barrier, Aiyana and Luis rushed forward to secure the capsule. It was heavy, but together they managed to pull it out of its moorings.

"Impressive," Luis said as he smiled appreciatively at Ingrid. "We'd be lost without you."

"We're not out yet," Ingrid said as she saved the last of the data. "Take the capsule and let's get out of here."

"Pull back!" shouted Aiyana. The group ran back through the tunnels as the drones continued to pursue them.

Outside, Kenji and Soraya had activated the explosive charges. A deafening bang caused the entrance to the tunnel to collapse, stopping the pursuers.

"That was close," Kenji said and helped Ingrid, who stepped outside, breathing heavily.

The ambush

As the crew stormed out of the Atur's cave with the resonance pod, Aiyana paused and suddenly stopped: "Stop! Something's wrong here. That went too smoothly."

Luis, who was running right behind her, stopped just in time and almost stumbled into her. "What's wrong?" he asked, looking at her in irritation. "Why don't you be happy that we made it?"

But Aiyana did not move. Her eyes surveyed the terrain in front of them while her hand slowly moved to the weapon on her hip. "That's just it," she said with an ominous calm. "That's just it, it was all still too easy. We can't be naïve, that the Atur will let us get away so easily. The Atur won't just let their prey go like that."

Kenji snorted skeptically. "Maybe they just didn't expect humans to snatch their pod so easily."

"Or maybe they set a trap for us," Ingrid added dryly. Her voice was quiet but firm. She pointed her scanner at the corridor in front of them, looking for signs of movement.

Aiyana nodded without taking her eyes off the shadows in front of them: "That's exactly what I think. Stay alert."

As soon as she had spoken the words, footsteps came out of the darkness. Heavy, rhythmic and getting closer and closer. Suddenly, a reddish glow flared up, coming from the resonators on the Atur's armor. A group of five massive figures stepped out of the shadows, weapons raised.

"I knew it!" hissed Aiyana, drawing her weapon.

"Give us the capsule!" thundered the Xarun, the leader of the Atur, his deep voice echoing through the cave. "You have no chance of escaping."

Soraya took a step back, clutching the resonance capsule tightly. "We're not giving it up."

Luis cocked his weapon and positioned himself in front of Priya. "If you want to stop us, you'll have to get past us."

"They'll try," Kenji said dryly and raised his gun.

But before a shot was fired, the ground shook beneath them. A massive rumble announced that something big was approaching. Suddenly, several huge stones crashed out of the wall, and with a loud roar, a group of Zerai emerged. The three-metre tall creatures with their muscular build and genetically optimized bodies looked like walking mountains. Their weapons were strangely shaped and a distinctive humming sound accompanied their every move.

"Atur!" thundered one of the Zerai, his voice rolling through the cave like an earthquake. "This prey is ours."

"Not while we're here!" an Atur shouted back, pointing his resonator at the approaching giants.

The Zerai and Atur rushed at each other, and the area in front of the cave became a battlefield. Laser beams and resonance waves cut through the darkness, while the massive bodies of the Zerai plowed through the enemy with impressive speed.

"Come on, this is our chance!" shouted Aiyana, leading the crew past the fighting groups.

But before they could leave the area, the air flickered in front of them. A group of Virani appeared out of nowhere, their stealth technology deactivated. Their sleek, scale-like armor shimmered in the dim lighting of the cavern, and they moved with deadly precision.

"More?" Kenji cast a quick glance over his shoulder. "We're trapped."

But the Virani had focused on the Atur. With their superior reflexes and precise attacks, they pushed the Atur back. "Go on!" shouted one of the Virani in a deep, guttural voice, without looking directly at the astronauts.

"I didn't know they could do that," whispered Ingrid, who had taken cover next to Aiyana.

"This is stealth technology on a whole other level," Soraya murmured. "Impressive."

Escape through the chaos

The astronauts took advantage of the chaos to leave the cave. But there was no time to catch their breath outside - three Atur had broken away from the group and were pursuing them. Their resonators hummed menacingly as they drew ever closer.

"Stay back!" Luis shouted as he fended off one of the Atur with well-aimed shots.

But suddenly one of the Atur grabbed Priya and pulled him to the ground. "The capsule stays here!" growled the Atur.

"No!" shouted Aiyana and turned back, but another Atur stood in her way.

Before the situation could escalate, a shadow moved through the darkness at lightning speed. A female Virani appeared. With her imposing appearance and superhuman speed, she attacked the Atur.

With targeted strikes and incredible strength, she eliminated them one by one.

When the last threat fell, she turned to Priya and offered him a hand. "Can you stand?" Her voice was cool and melodious, with an undertone that seemed both distant and compassionate.

Priya looked up at the Virani, who pulled him back to his feet with a gentle but firm movement. Their eyes met, and a moment of understanding - perhaps more - flashed between them. Her smooth, scaly face seemed to glow in the faint light. "Thank you... I don't know how to thank you," Priya replied.

"By being more careful," she said, smirking slightly. "You humans are playing with powers you don't understand."

Priya held her gaze, his voice trembling slightly as he spoke. "What's your name?"

She paused for a moment, as if weighing whether to answer. Finally, she said, "Myara."

"Myara," Priya repeated softly, nodding. "I am Priya. Thank you for... for saving me."

Myara scrutinized him, as if searching for something in his words. Then she bowed her head slightly. "You have courage, Priya. But courage alone will not save you. Remember that." She turned, ready to leave, but Priya's voice stopped her.

"Wait!" he shouted, and she stopped. "Why are you helping us? You Virani usually stay out of everything."

Myara turned around slowly. Her gaze was inscrutable. "Maybe I've seen something different about you. Or maybe it's just that your world needs a little more chaos." A faint smile flitted across her features before she disappeared.

Priya looked in the direction in which the Virani had disappeared and a slight smile played on his lips. "Sometimes help comes from the most unexpected places."

Luis looked at Priya with a wide grin. "Did you just flirt with a Vira-ni?"

"Stop it," Priya muttered, smiling charmingly at his obvious excitement.

"A superwoman like that is attractive, and I know what I'm talking about..." Luis said with a wink.

Aiyana patted Priya on the shoulder. "No matter why she came to get us - we made it out. And that's what counts."

Ingrid switched off her scanner and took a look at the surroundings. "But we have to be careful. That was just the first step."

Soraya held the resonance capsule firmly in her hands. "A step we almost lost. We mustn't make any mistakes now."

Back on the Venera Ascendant, the atmosphere was tense but relieved. The resonance capsule was safe and the crew had accomplished their mission. But the mission had pushed them to their limits.

"That was not for the faint-hearted," Kenji said, leaning back in a chair. "But we did it."

Soraya, who was standing quietly next to him, looked at Aiyana: "The Zerai will now have to offer their alliance. But we should have no illusions. They could turn against us at any time."

Aiyana nodded: "That's a risk we have to take. Now we need their support more than ever."

Ingrid, who was still checking the scans of the capsule, looked at Luis: "Good effort down there. We couldn't have done it without you."

Luis grinned exhaustedly: "That means you owe me a beer when we get back to Earth."

Priya laughed dryly, "I think we all owe each other a drink after this mission."

The crew knew they had only won one battle. The road to saving Venus was still long, and the planet's factions were still unpredictable. But for now, they could celebrate a small triumph - and prepare for the challenges ahead.

Chapter 19: The secrets of resonance

On board the Venera Ascendant, the crew gathered in the laboratory to analyze the resonance capsule. The artifact was impressive: a cylindrical object made of a shimmering material that seemed to constantly change its colors between deep purple and bright silver. It pulsed quietly, as if it had its own heartbeat. The atmosphere in the laboratory was tense. So-raya, the android with a precise scientific mind, had already set up several sensors and analyzers.

"Whatever this is," Priya began, walking carefully around the capsule, "it's not just an energy storage device. It feels... alive."

"It definitely reacts to its surroundings," Ingrid added, running her fingers carefully over the material. "I can feel how the molecules react to it when I get close."

Initial examinations

Soraya activated the scanners. A holographic image of the re-sonance pod appeared in the air above them. The inner design was a spiral staircase, a structure of crystal veins that seemed to conduct energy between central nodes.

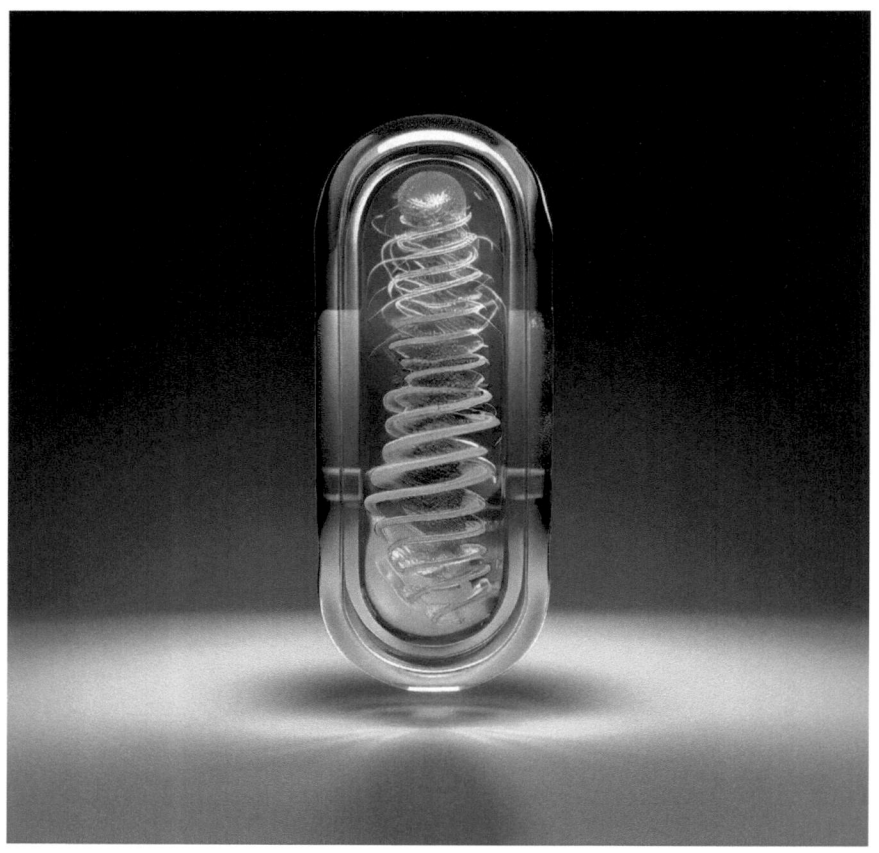

"That's incredible," said Ingrid, her eyes shining. "The crystal structure seems to store energy in its purest form. No conversion losses, no radiation - pure, concentrated energy."

"No wonder the Atur are guarding the thing like that," muttered Kenji, staring skeptically at the pulsating capsule. "But what exactly do we do with it now?"

"We have to find out how it works," Aiyana said resolutely. "Without this information, we can't fulfill the Zerai's demands."

Soraya nodded: "I will carry out a series of non-invasive tests. We mustn't destabilize the artefact - we don't know how it will react."

"That's a good idea," Priya said. "It could be like a nuclear device, only On a different frequency."

While Soraya prepared the first tests, Ingrid sat down at the console to analyze the data from the scanner. Suddenly, the capsule began to pulse more strongly. A soft, almost melodic sound filled the room.

"What's happening?" Luis asked in alarm as he took a step back.

Soraya looked at her instruments: "It's reacting to something. Maybe to the energy in this room or to our voices."

"Wait," Ingrid said and paused. She leaned closer to the capsule: "It changes its resonance frequency when we speak."

Aiyana stepped forward: "Soraya, what does the analysis say? Is it safe?"

"It shows no signs of instability," Soraya replied, "but the frequencies change like an echo of our voices. It could be some kind of communication system."

"A communication system?" Priya repeated, frowning. "You mean it's trying to talk to us?"

"Maybe," Ingrid said, "or maybe it's just picking up information. We should try sending it a controlled signal."

Soraya nodded and activated a frequency generator. She began sending different wave patterns to the pod, which responded quietly to each frequency. After a few attempts, the resonances intensified and the pod began to project a complex pattern of light to its surroundings.

"It's not just energy," Ingrid whispered in awe. "It's information. Data."

"It could hold the entire technology of the Atur," Priya speculated. "It could be our key."

A moral dilemma

"Wait a minute," Aiyana said in a raised voice, regaining her authority as commander. "We need to figure out what to do with this data. The Zerai want the capsule for their own purposes. But if it really does contain Atur technology, it could be dangerous to put it in the wrong hands."

"The Zerai haven't exactly given us much choice," Kenji interjected. "Without their support, we won't survive long on this hell of a planet."

"Maybe there's another way," Ingrid said quietly, her eyes fixed on the shimmering capsule. "We could try to use the information ourselves. Maybe we can find a solution that involves all the factions."

"A risky game," Luis said. "If the Zerai find out we're analyzing the capsule before we give it to them, it could destroy the Alliance."

"We should still strengthen our position," So-raya argued. "The capsule could help us create a balance between the factions. But we have to be careful."

"Good," Aiyana finally said, looking at everyone on the team. "Soraya and Ingrid, you keep analyzing the capsule. Figure out how we can use the data without destabilizing it. Priya and Kenji, you work on a plan to negotiate with the Zerai if they get suspicious. Luis and I will secure the lab."

The crew nodded, each with a clear task. But as everyone dispersed, Ingrid stopped in front of the pod, her thoughts absent. She felt a strange connection to the artifact, as if it was more than just technology.

A quiet secret

In the silence of the lab, Ingrid touched the surface of the capsule again. For a moment, she felt a slight tingling sensation running through her fingers. A whisper seemed to sound in her head, like a distant echo.

"Who... or what are you?" she murmured softly.

The capsule did not respond, but the pulsating light seemed to synchronize with her heartbeat for a moment. It was as if the artifact was consciously aware of her presence - and was waiting for something.

The resonance capsule was not a simple energy storage device. It was something bigger, something that the crew did not yet fully understand. But Ingrid knew one thing for sure: this artifact could hold the key to the future of their mission - and perhaps their entire species.

Ingrid stood up and walked to the control panel, her brow furrowed as her fingers glided smoothly over the controls. "The system is incredibly complex," she murmured. "There are several layers of encryption. And each one is... alive. It's as if the capsule is responding to our attempts to decrypt it."

Luis, who stood next to her at a hologram, snorted, "Alive? That sounds like we've brought an alien child into the living room."

"It's not funny, Luis," Aiyana said, standing behind them with her arms crossed, "We have no idea what will happen if we do something wrong. This could be the key to the entire future of Venus - or our destruction."

"I agree," said Priya, who was studying the holographic data of the Cape Island. "We have to be extremely careful. Any wrong input could release the energy - or lock the capsule permanently."

Soraya, who was standing quietly in the corner of the room, looked at the capsule with her deep, shining eyes. "It could be more," she said quietly. "This structure... It reminds me of the neural networks I have in my own architecture. It is possible that the capsule not only stores, but also interprets."

Aiyana turned to her: "Do you think it could... think?"

"Maybe not in the classical sense," Soraya replied. "But she could have the ability to recognize contexts - intentions, emotions. That would explain why she's equally important to the Atur and Virani."

Ingrid raised an eyebrow: "If that's true, we could easily communicate with her." She turned to Aiyana. "But we'd need more data for that. We've decoded the first layers of the resonance, but the true heart of the system lies deeper."

A message from the depths

Luis slapped the edge of the hologram table with the flat of his hand: "Then let's dig deeper! We didn't risk everything to stop now."

"Don't be so hasty," Aiyana said, giving him a stern look. "If we take one wrong step, we could lose everything. Ingrid, can you continue the decryption safely?"

Ingrid nodded hesitantly. "I can try. But I need peace and quiet - and Soraya's support. Her neural network could help interpret the data."

Soraya approached the table: "I'll do my best."

Together, Ingrid and Soraya delved into the nested layers of the capsule. Ingrid deciphered one section after another, while Soraya analyzed the subtle patterns in the data streams. Minutes passed that felt like hours. The atmosphere in the room was tense, every breath heavy.

Suddenly, Ingrid flinched: "There's something... a signal. It's faint, but it's clear."

"A signal?" Priya asked, leaning closer. "From the capsule?"

"Yes," Ingrid said, turning a holographic control wheel to amplify the signal. "It's like a soft whisper. I think it's communicating with us."

"But in what language?" asked Luis, staring at the flim-mering data in confusion.

"Not a language we know," said Soraya. "It's like music - a reso-nance. It sends patterns that indicate some kind of harmony."

Ingrid let her fingers fly as she analyzed the data, "Wait... if I convert the resonance waves and transfer them to our spectrum, I could... Yes! There it is." A holographic stream of waves appeared above the table, pulsing rhythmically.

Soraya tilted her head. "It's a pattern. It repeats, but with a slight var-iation each time. Maybe a code?"

"Or a message," Aiyana whispered. She stepped closer and looked at the waves. "But what is it trying to tell us?"

Ingrid continued to work feverishly while the crew watched spell-bound. Suddenly, the hologram lit up brightly and a structure ap-peared - a map made up of fine lines. "That's..." began Ingrid, but she paused. "It's not a place. It's... an arrangement. A machine?"

"A machine for what?" Luis asked nervously.

"I don't know," said Ingrid. "But if we interpret this map correctly, we could understand how the capsule works."

The crew looked at each other. Amidst the uncertainty, a spark of hope sprouted. Priya put a hand on Ingrid's shoulder. "You've done a great job. Maybe now we have a chance to really figure this thing out."

Ingrid looked at him, a faint smile on her lips. "This is just the beginning. But yes, maybe we have."

Aiyana nodded. "Good, then we'll keep working on it. We'll find out what this capsule is - and why it's so important."

Soraya scrutinized the hologram, her eyes sparkling with curiosity. "The answers lie in the resonance. And I think we're close to decoding them."

There was a mixture of tension and determination in the room. The resonance capsule was no longer just a riddle - it was the key to a truth greater than anything they could imagine.

The decoding of resonance

The resonance capsule projected a web of glowing lines and pulsating patterns across the hologram table. Ingrid and Soraya worked tirelessly to decipher the meaning of this data. Every moment was tense, every small step forward electrified the crew.

A revelation in waves

"I've got it!" Ingrid suddenly shouted, tapping triumphantly on the control panel. The lines on the hologram formed into a complex, shimmering structure - a kind of three-dimensional puzzle. It looked like a geometric labyrinth that was constantly changing, as if it were breathing.

Soraya leaned closer: "It's more than just a map. It's a sequence - a temporal sequence that needs to be activated."

Luis, who was watching with his arms folded, frowned. "A sequence? For what? And why does it feel like we're defusing a bomb?"

"It's not a bomb," Soraya said calmly. "At least not in the conventional sense. This capsule contains a resonance energy based on harmonic waves. It was created to activate a specific mechanism - a kind of key system."

"But what exactly is it supposed to activate?" asked Aiyana, who was also leaning over the hologram. Her voice was serious, but also curious.

Ingrid pointed to one of the more complex sequences, which looked like a spin net: "That's the key. The capsule was modified by the Atur, but its original purpose is older. It is a relic of the Auron."

Soraya nodded and added, "The message says that the resonance pod is meant to generate a frequency that resonates with the core of Venus."

A brief silence fell over the crew.

"With the core of Venus?" Priya repeated, his eyes widening. "That sounds... like some damn terraforming technology."

"That's exactly what it is," Soraya said. "The capsule has the potential to alter the gravimetric and atmospheric conditions of Venus - in a massive, controlled process."

Ingrid pointed to the pulsating lines. "But there is a hitch. This sequence must be activated in a very specific order. Each step builds on the previous one. If we make a mistake, the balance could tip - and the result would be catastrophic."

"How catastrophic are we talking here?" Luis asked, raising an eyebrow.

Soraya replied in a calm voice: "Imagine an explosion that affects not only the ship, but the entire surface of Venus. A resonance collapse could destroy the tectonic stability of the planet."

"So, no mistakes," Priya muttered dryly.

"It gets even more complicated," Ingrid added. "The sequence calls for several phases to be activated at different locations on the planet. The capsule projects these locations as coordinates."

A new hologram appeared. It showed a map of Venus with three marked points distributed in different regions. Each marker glowed in a different color.

"These are the resonance points," Ingrid explained. "Each dot represents a part of the frequency that the core needs to go into resonance."

Aiyana stepped back, her eyes narrowed. "Wait a moment. If we activate these resonance points, what will happen to the peoples of Venus? Will they survive?"

Soraya replied thoughtfully: "That's unclear. The original Auron message indicates that this process was intended to stabilize Venus - to make it habitable. But with the Atur's modifications, the effects could be... unpredictable."

"So we either risk saving the planet or destroying it completely?" Luis shook his head. "That sounds like a classic win-lose situation."

Ingrid turned to Aiyana. "We could try to undo the Atur modifications. But that would mean we'd need time - a lot of time."

Aiyana closed her eyes and took a deep breath. "We're faced with a decision: either we risk everything to stabilize Venus, or we don't and leave the planet to the Atur."

A plan emerges

"But why would the Atur even want that?" asked Priya. "If this technology is so powerful, why haven't they used it themselves?"

Soraya replied: "Maybe they tried and failed. Or maybe they're afraid of the consequences."

Ingrid switched to another view. "Here, take a look at this. The Atur's modifications seem to be aimed at using the resonance only for their own energy production. They are blocking the harmonic frequencies that would stabilize the planet."

Aiyana nodded slowly. "That means if we restore the original sequence, we could save the planet - and deprive the Atur of their greatest source of power."

"But that will make us enemies," Priya said quietly. "Big enemies."

"We already have enemies," Luis replied with a wry smile. "This would just be another item on their list."

"Then it's settled," Aiyana finally said. "Ingrid, Soraya, you two continue to work on decoding the sequence and removing the Atur modifications. Priya, Luis and I are preparing to reach the resonance points. We will venture to each point if we have to."

"And what about the Zerai?" asked Priya. "They won't be happy if we activate this without telling them first."

"We have to explain to them that this is in their interests too," said Aiyana. "If Venus is stabilized, all races have a chance. But if we do nothing, there is no future."

Soraya nodded. "Resonance is the only solution. And if we work together, we can do it."

The crew looked at each other, determined to take on the daunting task that lay ahead of them. The resonance capsule had not only revealed a riddle to them, but also a way to change the fate of Venus. But the way there was full of dangers - and the end remained uncertain.

Chapter 20: The Dance of Resonances

The astronauts had returned the resonance capsule to the main chamber of the temple, where they were preparing their next step: activating and setting the resonance points to stabilize the capsule's network. The atmosphere was tense, a mixture of concentration and subliminal nervousness.

In the main chamber of the temple

The main chamber of the temple was an impressive place. The walls, high and criss-crossed with intricate patterns, glittered with an iridescent light emitted by the strange crystals in the room. The resonance capsule that the astronauts had rescued from the clutches of the Atur now stood in the center of the room on a stone platform surrounded by rings of symbols. The air seemed to pulsate as if it were alive - an echo of past energies.

Ingrid studied the holographic projections emitted by the capsule. The maps and diagrams that formed in the air seemed to represent an intricate web of energy points that needed to be precisely calibrated.

"If I'm interpreting this correctly," Ingrid began, pointing to a shimmering dot, "we have to set these points manually. The capsule sets the frequency, but the location has to be absolutely exact."

"How exactly are we talking here?" asked Luis, who was watching with his arms folded. "Millimeters or nanometers?"

Soraya, who had now adjusted to the capsule, nodded. "The deviation must not be more than 0.002 percent. Otherwise the entire system will destabilize."

"Great," Aiyana muttered dryly. "So we're working with a technology that has to be flawless, otherwise we'll explode or - even worse - we'll distort space-time."

"This doesn't exactly feel reassuring," Luis muttered as he looked around. His gaze kept wandering to the crystals, which were emitting a low humming sound. "These things - they almost sound like... Breaths."

"Not helpful, Luis," Aiyana said, shouldering her weapon and scanning the surroundings with a scrutinizing gaze. "Concentrate. If this pod here is really going to control a network, we need every mind on this."

"Wow," Priya murmured as the projection lit up the entire room. "This is... incredible. Looks like the heart of a huge system."

"It's more than that," said Ingrid, staring at the map spellbound. "Do you see the connecting lines? They all run through the main chamber, but they spread outwards - like a nerve system."

Soraya stepped closer and pointed to a series of shimmering dots on the map. "These are the resonance points, right?"

"Exactly," Ingrid confirmed. "The capsule shows us the locations. There are three key positions. If we calibrate them correctly, the entire network should stabilize."

"And what happens if we don't make it?" Kenji asked, his voice quiet but tense.

"At best, nothing," Ingrid replied, biting her lip. "Worst case scenario... we could destabilize the temple's energy flows. The network could collapse - or explode."

Luis huffed. "Of course. No pressure."

"We have no choice," Aiyana said firmly. "This is our only chance to activate the resonance and secure the fragile alliance with the Zerai. Ingrid, how do we start?"

The preparation

Ingrid tapped the floating symbols again and brought up a detailed view of the first resonance point. It was deep under the main chamber, almost in a labyrinthine network of tunnels. "We need to set the points in a specific order," she explained. "Each point has a specific frequency, and the capsule needs to synchronize the resonance before we can activate the next point."

Soraya checked the surroundings. "We need to make sure the frequencies remain stable. I'll carry the pod if we need to move it."

"Hold it," Aiyana said. "We don't know how the Atur will react to our activation. It could be that they have already manipulated the resonance points."

"I've been watching for that," said Ingrid, pointing to a deviation on the holographic map. "Here - do you see that? One of the frequency lines is slightly distorted. It looks like the A-tur tried to move the dots."

"That means we could be walking into a trap," Priya remarked. "Or they've set it up so that we do their work for them."

Luis crossed his arms. "Great. So we either ruin everything or we activate something that wipes us all out."

"We don't have a choice," Aiyana said again, more sharply this time. "Luis, Soraya, take the capsule. Ingrid, you monitor the fre-quences. Priya and Kenji, you secure the perimeter. We can't make any mis-takes."

While the crew checked their equipment, Aiyana paused and looked at the map. Her brow furrowed, her thoughts seemed far away.

"What's wrong, Commander?" asked Ingrid.

"It's just..." Aiyana hesitated. "Why would the Atur leave this place unguarded? It doesn't make sense."

Luis glanced at her. "Maybe they underestimated us. Or maybe they're just too busy preparing for the next attack." "Maybe," Aiyana said, but her voice sounded uncertain.

"But what if that's exactly what they wanted? That we activate the points?" "Aiyana, I know what you're thinking,"

Ingrid said calmly. "But we have to risk it. Without the resonance, we have no chance of maintaining the balance between the factions. And without the factions... we are alone."

Aiyana nodded slowly, her resolve returning. "All right. But we remain vigilant. No risks we can't control."

The first resonance point

The map of the resonance pod pulsed rhythmically, projecting a trail of light that marked the path to the first point. The atmosphere in the temple became noticeably heavier as the crew began to move. Every echo of their footsteps seemed to reverberate off the ancient walls, as if the temple was registering their presence.

Aiyana led the way, weapon at the ready, followed by Soraya and Luis, who carried the resonance pod between them. Ingrid, Priya and Kenji remained close behind, their eyes attentive to their surroundings.

"We're almost there," Ingrid said, checking the projector with her scanner. "The first point should be directly behind the next chamber."

"Stay alert," Aiyana warned. "If the Atur have manipulated what Ingrid found, they could have placed traps here too."

Luis shrugged his shoulders and glanced at Soraya. "The Atur are great at making things complicated. But Fal-len? I guess we can handle it."

Soraya grinned wryly. "Let's hope your optimism isn't the only defense we have."

The crew stepped into the next chamber. The room was circular, with walls lined with crystals protruding from the surfaces like solidified waves. In the center of the room floated a pulsing blue light - the first resonance point. It was both mesmerizing and eerie, and a low hum filled the air.

"There he is," Priya whispered. Her voice was almost reverent.

"And there's the problem," Ingrid murmured as she stared at her scanner. "The frequency of the dot is completely destabilized. If we connect the capsule, it could overload."

"What do you suggest?" asked Aiyana, stepping up next to Ingrid.

"We need to manually tune the resonance waves before we activate the capsule," Ingrid explained. "But that's tricky. The point seems to be self-correcting, which means that any changes we make could be quickly reversed."

"So we need precision," Kenji said. "We don't have much margin for error."

The challenge

Luis and Soraya carefully placed the resonance capsule on a round platform directly below the floating light. A soft click indicated that the pod was activated, and it immediately began to process data. Holographic patterns swirled around it, like flames dancing in the air.

"Ingrid?" asked Aiyana, her voice strained.

"Give me a moment," Ingrid replied, her fingers flying over the capsule's interface. "I'm scanning the frequency. It's alternating between two main modulations, but there are also secondary patterns... Damn, this is more chaotic than I thought."

"Are you going to make it?" asked Priya.

"I have no choice," Ingrid said firmly. "But I need absolute concentration. Any interference could break the resonance wave."

Soraya stepped forward and took up a defensive position with Luis. "We'll hold the line," she said firmly.

Aiyana nodded. "Good, Ingrid, what are you waiting for?"

Ingrid took a deep breath and began to mani-pulate the resonance waves. Her fingers tapped precisely on the interface as she adjusted the data flows in real time. The blue light above them began to flicker and the humming grew louder.

"The frequencies are colliding," Ingrid said tensely. "I'm trying to harmonize them, but the point is reacting more sensitively than I expected."

"What can we do?" asked Kenji, looking over her shoulder.

"Nothing, except be still," Ingrid said sharply. "Any extra energy - even a movement - could disturb the waves."

Suddenly there was a loud crash. A crack ripped through one of the crystal walls and sparks flew.

"That doesn't look good," Luis said, instinctively raising his weapon.

"Stay calm!" shouted Ingrid. "It's just a reaction to the capsule. I've almost got it - just a few more seconds!"

The blue light began to stabilize, its pulsation became more even. But just as Ingrid was making a final adjustment, a shrill noise sounded and the light flared up brightly.

"What was that?" Priya asked, backing away.

"It's... All right," Ingrid finally said and fell back. Her face was covered in sweat, but a small smile played around her lips. "The point is stabilized. The capsule has synchronized the frequency."

"Good job," Aiyana said, her voice full of relief. "That was point one. Two more and we've made it."

But before the crew could move any further, the capsule began to beep. Ingrid stared at the interface and her face went pale.

"That's not good," she said.

"What now?" asked Aiyana, stepping closer.

"The next point... its frequency is even more unstable than this one. It looks like the Atur's manipulation is stronger there. And... wait." She frowned. "I'm picking up a signal. It's not coming from the pod. It's a movement pattern - something's coming."

Luis raised his weapon as Soraya stood at his side. "Do you hear that?" she asked. "Footsteps."

Aiyana nodded. "Everyone in position. We're moving to the next point, but we'll stay alert."

With the pod safely stowed, the crew prepared to move to the second resonance point. The tension was palpable, but a spark of hope flashed in their eyes - they had mastered the first step. But the signal that Ingrid had detected was a warning harbinger.

The second resonance point

The crew made their way through the labyrinthine corridors of the temple. Ingrid led the group, the resonance capsule firmly under her arm. The path to the second point was more complex, the capsule's holographic map showed several possible routes, but all seemed littered with obstacles.

"This temple feels alive," Priya said softly, eyeing the shimmering walls. "Almost as if it's watching us."

"Maybe it is," Soraya said, pulling out her scanner. "The crystals in the walls react to our movements. They could be transmission mechanisms."

"Or warning systems," Aiyana added, casting a scrutinizing glance back. "Stay focused. We need to shake off the Atur before they regroup."

The challenge in the shaft

The second resonance point was deep in the temple, in a place that could only be reached through a vertical shaft. The map showed it as a pulsating point of light, but getting there was a challenge. The shaft was narrow and surrounded by shimmering crystals that glowed like pulsating veins.

"It's not going to be easy," said Luis, leaning over the opening. "The shaft is almost 30 meters deep and the crystals look fragile. One wrong move and we could trigger a chain reaction."

"I've brought enough climbing gear for us," Kenji said, pulling a rope out of his backpack. "But we have to be careful. If these crystals conduct energy, one misstep could grill us."

Aiyana nodded. "Ingrid, Priya and I will bring the capsule down. Luis, Soraya and Kenji will secure the perimeter."

"Got it," Luis said, checking his rifle. "If the Atur show up, I'll make sure they regret it."

Soraya smirked. "I'll make sure you don't need any excuses to protect us."

The descent

The team carefully secured the ropes and began the descent. Aiyana led the way, her movements calm and precise. Ingrid followed with the capsule, her face tense. Priya stayed behind her to stabilize the capsule in case Ingrid lost her balance.

"The crystals... They vibrate," Ingrid whispered. "It's as if they're reacting to our presence."

"Don't stop," Aiyana said quietly. "Just focus on the next hold."

The group moved slowly downward, the shimmering of the crystals around them intensifying. As they reached the center of the shaft, a low hum began to fill the air. The frequency of the hum increased, and the crystals pulsed faster.

"That doesn't sound good," muttered Priya.

"What's happening up there?" Soraya called down from above.

"The crystals seem to be building up energy," Ingrid replied. "Maybe through our movements? I don't know."

Aiyana reached the ground and secured the rope. "Come down quickly. We need to stabilize the resonance point before anything is triggered."

The resonance interference

When the three of them reached the bottom of the shaft, a circular chamber opened up in front of them. In the center hovered a glowing red core - the second resonance point. But unlike the first, this point was unstable. Red arcs of light leapt through the air and caused the crystals to vibrate.

"That looks dangerous," Priya said, his voice trembling slightly.

"It's more than dangerous," Ingrid said, placing the capsule on the ground. "The point is massively overloaded. There could be an explosion if we don't unload it."

"How do we do that?" asked Aiyana, casting an appraising glance at the glowing crystals.

Ingrid leaned over the capsule. "I'll divert the energy from the dot into the capsule. But we have to stabilize the environment, otherwise the overload will tear everything down here apart."

"Priya, can you secure the crystals?" asked Aiyana.

"I can try to neutralize them with the energy dampeners," said Priya. He pulled a device out of his backpack and began to scan the first crystals. "This will take some time."

"Hurry up," Ingrid said. "I'll start the synchronization."

The critical moment

Ingrid activated the capsule and the red core immediately began to pulsate. The arcs of light became more intense and the buzzing of the crystals increased to an unbearable roar.

"It's getting too much!" shouted Priya. "The crystals are reacting more strongly than I thought."

"Then move faster!" shouted Aiyana.

Suddenly, the chamber began to shake. A crack ran through the wall and crystal shards flew in all directions.

"Damn it!" shouted Ingrid. "I need another minute!"

"You have ten seconds!" shouted Aiyana, drawing her gun. "Soraya, Luis, we need support down here!"

Luis and Soraya immediately lowered themselves down. Luis landed with a thud and drew his gun while Soraya helped Ingrid with the capsule.

"I've almost got it!" shouted Ingrid.

Suddenly, a loud bang burst through the chamber and the red core exploded in a bright light. But the capsule absorbed the energy at the last second and the light faded. Silence filled the chamber.

"Is it over?" Priya asked breathlessly.

"Yes," said Ingrid, exhausted. "The point is stabilized."

A new path

Aiyana nodded and helped Ingrid up. "Well done. But that was only the second point. We have to keep going."

"How many more explosions can we expect?" Luis asked with a wry smile.

"As many as it takes," Aiyana said firmly. "We'll get through this. All of us together."

The crew gathered themselves and prepared to find the next point. But the feeling that they were being watched remained - and the buzzing of the crystals accompanied them as they left the shaft.

The third resonance point

The crew stood in a narrow corridor whose walls were criss-crossed by fine patterns of light that pulsed like veins in a living organism. The atmosphere was different from before - denser, more electric, as if the temple itself knew they were about to complete their mission. The final resonance point was the key to activating the temple's powers, but they knew it would also be the most dangerous challenge.

"The map shows the point directly behind this barrier," In-grid said, pointing to a massive black door made of an alien material. "But there's no obvious way to open it."

"I've seen a material like this on the Atur," Priya muttered as he examined the surface of the door with a scanner. "It reacts to energy - specific frequencies."

Soraya nodded. "The resonance pod could provide the frequency we need."

"Or trigger a trap," Aiyana said sharply. She eyed the door suspiciously. "I don't trust this place. We need to be prepared."

Activating the door

Ingrid carefully placed the resonance capsule in a hollow next to the door, which seemed to be made for it. When she activated the capsule, the door began to vibrate in low tones that the entire crew could feel.

"It sounds like a heartbeat," Luis remarked, unconsciously drawing his weapon.

"It's more than that," Ingrid said, her voice strained. "It's as if the temple is reacting to our presence."

The vibrations intensified, and suddenly a beam of light shot out of the capsule and hit the door. The veins of light in the walls quickened their rhythm and the door began to open slowly, accompanied by a deep, metallic creak.

"Stand by," Aiyana said, raising her weapon. "We don't know what awaits us behind it."

The door opened fully, revealing a massive chamber. In the center floated a huge, crystalline monolith that pulsated in all colors of the spectrum. It was the last resonance point.

The unexpected disturbance

"That's it," Ingrid said reverently, stepping carefully into the chamber. "That was the last point. Now the temple should be fully activated."

"It's beautiful," Priya said, looking at the monolith. "But why does it feel so... eerie?"

"Because it's not just beautiful," Soraya said softly. "It is power. And power is never without a price."

She had barely said this when a thunderous noise shook the chamber. Several Atur emerged from the shadows, their massive bodies glaring menacingly in the light of the monolith. They were led by one of their commanders, whose armor was adorned with pulsing red veins of light.

"You have gone too far," the commander said in a voice that echoed through the chamber like a rumble. "This temple belongs to the Atur, and you will never fully activate it."

"We will not be stopped," Aiyana shouted back, pointing her weapon at him. "This temple belongs to no one - it is a tool to save this world."

"Then you will pay with your lives," the commander replied and ordered his warriors to attack.

The battle for the last point

The chamber turned into a battlefield. Luis and Aiyana opened fire while Soraya and Priya tried to cover Ingrid, who was working feverishly on the resonance pod.

"I need time!" shouted Ingrid as she tried to synchronize the pod with the monolith. "Aiyana, stop them!"

"We'll do our best!" shouted Aiyana back, firing a volley at an attacking Atur.

Luis fought his way through the ranks of the Atur, his movements precise and determined. "Ingrid, how much longer?"

"Twenty seconds, if I'm not disturbed!" she shouted back.

Soraya ducked under a blow from an Atur and delivered a well-aimed blow with her electric baton. "These guys won't give up!"

"Then let's make them realize that they have no choice!" shouted Aiyana and threw a shock grenade that knocked several Atur to the ground.

The synchronization

Ingrid ignored the chaos around her and concentrated on synchronizing the capsule with the monolith. The lights in the chamber intensified and a low hum filled the air.

"Almost there!" she shouted, "Just a few more seconds!"

An Atur broke through the defenses and charged straight at Ingrid. Priya stood in his way and activated his shield. The impact caused the Atur to bounce back, but it held firm.

"Not with me!" Priya shouted and threw the attacker back with an electric shock.

And suddenly, unexpected allies appeared out of nowhere: A group of Zerai and Virani, who finally pushed the Atur back.

"You have helped us," said Myara, who was leading the Virani, and glanced quickly at Priya, who returned her gaze happily. "Now it's our turn," she said and stormed off to pounce on Xarun.

"Synchronization complete!" shouted Ingrid, just as the mono-lith lit up in a bright light.

The light of the monolith filled the chamber and the Atur retreated, blinded and disoriented. The crew took the opportunity to join forces to capture Xarun and drive off the rest of his henchmen.

"Did we make it?" asked Luis as they ran through the corridors.

"Yes," Ingrid said, her voice relieved. "The temple is active!"

The crew sensed that the temple had come to life. The veins of light pulsed in a harmonious rhythm and the energy flowing through the temple was palpable.

"We've done it," Soraya said quietly and looked at Aiyana. "Now it's up to us to use this power properly."

"And we will," Aiyana said resolutely. "For Venus. For everyone."

Chapter 21: The voice of the temple

The activation of the resonance capsule set off a chain reaction that no one in the crew could have fully foreseen. As the last trace of energy flooded the temple and was concentrated in the main chamber, the floor beneath the astronauts' feet began to vibrate. The temperature in the room rose noticeably, and a pulsing sound filled the air.

"This is... gigantic," Soraya murmured as she looked at the glowing walls with wide eyes. "It feels like the temple is coming alive."

In the center of the room, the resonance pod that the crew had so painstakingly placed began to rotate. Slowly at first, then faster and faster until it became almost invisible. A beam of pure light shot out of its center and hit the ceiling. Concentric circles formed there, steadily widening and creating holographic patterns that looked like cosmic maps.

"That looks like... a map?" asked Priya, who involuntarily took a step closer.

Ingrid nodded as she hastily typed notes into her pad. "Yes, and more than that. It doesn't just show the temple itself. It shows... the entire planet."

"Do you see this?" Aiyana called out, pointing to some pulsating dots in the holographic images. "Those are the four faction cities! And there - that's the temple. These lines connect them all."

Luis frowned. "It looks like a network. But for what?"

Suddenly, a deep, melodic voice echoed through the room. It spoke in a language that none of them knew, but the meaning penetrated their thoughts directly.

"The harmony of resonance has been achieved. The path to unity is open. But the balance is fragile. Choose wisely, inhabitants of Venus, for your destinies are intertwined."

The crew looked at each other, speechless. Ingrid finally said what everyone was thinking. "The temple... It's communicating with us. It must be an ancient AI system."

"It's trying to tell us something," Aiyana added, her voice firm. "But there are no clear instructions. What does 'choose wisely' mean?"

The holographic map began to change. The lines between the faction cities and the temple turned red and began to flicker, as if they were unstable. At the same time, new dots appeared on the map, smaller, isolated energy signatures.

"Look at that," Ingrid said. "These are resonance points that lie outside the factions. Maybe... maybe that's what we need to really secure harmony."

Before anyone could answer, the temple shook violently and a deep, roaring sound permeated the chamber. Parts of the walls began to move, as if the temple was reconfiguring itself. The holographic image became distorted, and for a moment it was as if the temple itself had come into conflict.

"What's happening now?" Luis shouted as he held on to a pillar.

"The network is unstable!" Ingrid shouted over the noise. "The resonance points must be in tune, but something is disrupting the connection. It could be... it could be an energy source that's incompatible!"

"The Atur," Soraya said somberly. "Their energy system is based on pure power and destruction. Maybe that's disrupting the flow."

The sacrifice of the past

Suddenly, another hologram appeared in the middle of the chamber. It showed a scene that burned itself directly into the minds of the crew. The four factions of Venus faced each other in a relentless war, their once thriving cities in ruins.

But in the midst of the chaos, the temple rose up and sent out a powerful resonance signal that interrupted the conflict for a moment. The voice of the temple sounded again, this time calmer, almost sad. "The balance was destroyed before. You must choose: Harmony or chaos. The resonance cannot be stabilized without sacrifice."

"This is a warning," Aiyana whispered. "The temple shows us what will happen if we fail."

"Or if we don't act," Priya added. "The factions could use the temple as a weapon if we're not careful."

An unexpected visitor

Suddenly the light flickered and a figure emerged from the shadows.
It was Ikaris, the Auron representative, his silver body cloaked in the
glowing blue of the temple.

"You have activated the temple," he said in a voice that expressed both admiration and concern. "But you do not understand what you have unleashed."

"Then help us," Aiyana said firmly. "We are trying to unite the factions, but we need more information. What awaits us?"

Ikaris' face grew serious. "The Resonance is more than a source of energy. It is the heart of the planetary balance. But it will only remain stable if all factions are willing to commit to it. If even one faction opposes it, the temple will destroy everything."

"A final test, then," Luis murmured. "How fitting."

"And what do you propose, Ikaris?" asked Ingrid. "We can't force the factions to work together."

Ikaris' eyes glowed softly. "You can build trust. You have activated the resonance. It's a symbol of unity. But you must also resolve the conflicts of the past."

"And how exactly?" asked Soraya. "We don't have time to settle every dispute."

"Time is irrelevant, only life counts," Ikaris replied. "You must find and stabilize the resonance points of the factions. Each point is a key to harmony. And if you screw up... Venus will take you down with her."

The crew looked at each other. The burden of responsibility was heavy on them, but there was a spark of determination in their eyes, but also uncertainty because of Ikaris' cryptic words.

"What do you mean specifically, Ikaris? You speak in riddles," Aiyana replied.

"There will be a tribunal. If you feel up to the task, you can act as advocates in this trial because, as inhabitants of another planet, you can remain neutral."

"And who will be the client?" Luis asked with an ominous tone.

"I think you already know," replied Ikaris.

"Not Xarun, is it?" said Luis with a disgusted look.

Ikaris nodded: "Yes, so be it!"

"Then we know what to do," said Aiyana firmly. "We will rise to the challenge. For Venus and for all of us."

Outside the temple, a storm began to gather, as if the planet itself was waiting for the next chapter of their adventure.

Chapter 22: Tender bonds and fragile truths

The temple garden was a place of silence and reflection, a rarely peaceful spot amidst the charged atmosphere. Priya had come here to find a moment of peace, to process the upsetting events of the last few days - Xarun's capture, the heated discussions among the crew and the impending challenge from the Tribunal. But he couldn't shake the memory of one particular encounter: Myara. The proud and mysterious leader of the Virani. She had only noticed him twice, and yet those moments had stirred something in him that he couldn't quite put into words.

A soft rustling made him look up. Myara stood just a few steps away, a slender, graceful silhouette amidst the lush greenery of the garden. Her golden eyes met his, and Priya felt his heart beat faster.

"Priya," she said in her calm, melodious voice. "I didn't think I'd find you here."

He jumped up hastily, holding on to the back of the bench to keep from stumbling, "Myara! I... I didn't mean to interrupt. I just thought I could get some rest."

A slight smile played around her lips and she stepped closer: "You're not interrupting. This garden is a place of peace for all who seek it. Why don't you sit down?"

He hesitantly sat down again, while she sat down next to him, but at a respectful distance. The silence between them was not uncomfortable, but had something calming about it.

After a while, she broke the silence: "You were there when Xarun was captured. I saw how you reacted. You're not a fighter, Priya, but you showed courage."

Priya rubbed the back of his neck, embarrassed: "Courage? I felt more like a complete fool. I almost ruined everything."

"Courage is not the absence of fear," she replied calmly, "but acting in spite of fear."

He smiled shyly: "Maybe. But to be honest, you intimidated me quite a bit. Your determination, your strength - that's impressive. I'm just a scientist. Someone who analyzes samples and tries to understand the code of life."

"A scientist?" she asked, her golden eyes gleaming in the soft light. "An exobiologist, if I remember correctly?"

He nodded: "Yes, and a biochemist. I study how life works - and how it can be so different and yet familiar here on Venus. But if I'm honest, events like the encounter with Xarun... are not something I was trained for. They're not exactly the challenges I was expecting."

"Everyone has their place," Myara said thoughtfully. "Strength alone does not bring harmony. Maybe it's the little things - the understanding, the connection between beings - that make the difference."

Her words struck Priya deeply, but before he could say anything in reply, he clumsily moved his arm so that it lightly grazed her shoulder. There was a cracking sound and Priya gritted his teeth to suppress a cry of pain.

Myara's gaze darkened: "What was that?"

"Nothing, really," he said hastily, holding his arm. "Just... I bumped myself a few days ago. It's healing already."

"Bumped?" she repeated skeptically. "That wasn't a simple crack. What are you hiding, Priya?"

"It's nothing! Honestly!" He tried to move his arm but grimaced, which made Myara suspicious for good. She stood up and looked at him with piercing eyes.

"Humans are so fragile," she said softly, almost more to herself than to him. "I didn't realize that... wait." She paused, and it was as if a shadow of realization fell over her face. "Did I hurt you?"

Priya shook his head hastily. "No, no! It's really nothing. I'm just clumsy. You don't need to worry."

But Myara was not so easily fobbed off. "I'm stronger than I should be when I'm dealing with you humans. I didn't consider that when we first met." She sat down again, closer this time, and placed a hand lightly on his uninjured arm. "You have to tell me the truth, Priya. If I hurt you, it wasn't on purpose. But I need to know."

He sighed heavily and lowered his eyes. "It wasn't your fault. You only touched me very lightly, but... I'm just not as stable as you."

Myara's eyes narrowed and her voice was filled with guilt. "I should have been more careful. But why didn't you tell me? Why did you keep me in the dark?"

"Because I didn't want you to feel bad," Priya admitted quietly. "You have so much responsibility, Myara. Your people rely on you, and you carry so much on your shoulders. I didn't want you to burden yourself even more."

There was silence for a moment before Myara shook her head. "You are a fool, Priya. But an honest and brave fool." Her words had a hint of warmth that surprised him.

"I promise to be more careful," he continued. "But you must be more careful too - and honest. Our peoples cannot be united if we are not open with each other. That goes for you and me too."

Priya nodded slowly: "I understand. Thank you, Myara."

They eyed each other for a moment before Myara stood up. "I have to get back to my people. But... I'm glad you came here, Priya. Maybe we'll meet again."

With those words, she disappeared silently into the garden, and Priya was left alone - his heart a little lighter and his admiration for Myara greater than ever.

A kiss in the shadow of the stars

Night had fallen and the temple garden was filled with a soft, phosphorescent glow. Plants with shimmering leaves and flowers that twinkled like tiny stars drew Priya's attention as he strolled along the path. There was something magical, almost earthly about the place, and yet every flower, every leaf reminded him that he was on another planet.

"You seem to like this garden," a soft, melodious voice sounded behind him.

Priya turned around and saw Myara walking towards him with the elegance of a predator. Her golden eyes shimmered in the starlight and her smile was like a gentle touch. He felt his heart skip a beat.

 "I feel... calm here," Priya confessed, and his voice had a slightly dreamy tone. "It's a place that is at once so strange and yet somehow familiar."

"It is," Myara said and came closer. "The plants here only grow in places that are strongly influenced by the resonances. They are said to reflect the harmony or conflict of a people. Lately, they've been shining brighter than ever."

Priya smiled faintly and looked at a flower whose petals moved gently, as if dancing to an invisible tune. "Maybe that's a good sign."

"Maybe," Myara replied softly. "Or maybe it's you who brings them new light."

Priya's heart beat faster as she came closer, and he realized that his mouth was suddenly dry. "I don't think I have that kind of effect," he murmured, his eyes on the flowers to avoid her intense gaze.

"Oh, Priya," Myara said with an amused smile. "You're too modest sometimes."

She was standing right in front of him now. She carefully placed a hand on his shoulder.

"You're special," she said, her voice little more than a whisper. "You just don't see that yet."

"Myara..." he began, but he didn't know how to form the words. Everything he felt - the admiration, the attraction, the overwhelming need to be with her - seemed too great for a simple explanation. Priya smiled shyly: "I wish I had your composure. You always seem so... sure. No matter what."

"Sure?" Myara laughed softly, a rare and surprisingly soft sound. "Priya, I am anything but sure. I carry the expectations of my people on my shoulders. Every decision could change everything - for the Virani and for me."

"I can't imagine how hard that must be," Priya said honestly. "But I know you have the strength to carry it."

"And you?" she asked, stepping closer. "You're carrying some Schwe-res with you too. Not physically, but here." She lightly placed her hand on his chest, directly over his heart.

Her gentle contact made him pause. The touch was light, almost fleeting, but Priya felt a wave of warmth and something indescribable pass through him.

"Sometimes," he confessed quietly, "it feels like I'm out of place here. I'm just a scientist. What can I do when it comes to something as big as the unity of the peoples?"

"You're here because you can make a difference," Myara said firmly. "Maybe not with weapons or power, but with your mind, your heart. That makes you stronger than you think."

Priya looked at her, and at that moment, time seemed to stand still. Her words struck him deeply, and he knew that he no longer felt just admiration for her. It was more - something that both inspired and worried him at the same time.

"Myara," he began, but his voice broke off. How could he put into words what he was feeling?

But before he could continue, Myara stepped even closer. She raised her hand to gently touch his cheek and her eyes pierced him as if they could see right into his soul.

"You are a fool, Priya," she said softly, with a hint of tenderness in her voice. "But a fool I can no longer ignore."

"Don't say anything," she whispered, stepping even closer until their faces were only a breath apart. "Some things don't need to be said."

Her lips touched his, and for a moment everything around them melted away. The colors of the sky, the sounds of the night, even the ground beneath their feet - everything faded into an unimportant backdrop for what they shared in that moment. Priya felt a warmth he had never experienced before, and for a heartbeat, everything was perfect.

But when Myara moved slightly and placed her hand on his shoulder, a soft crack sounded. Priya flinched and pulled back slightly.

"Priya!" Myara's voice was filled with concern: "Did I hurt you?"

"It's nothing," he said hastily, though he held his shoulder. "Just... a little something. I'm okay."

"It's not a little thing!" She gently grabbed his arm and eyed him with concern. "Why didn't you say anything? I should have been more careful."

"I didn't want to ruin the moment," he admitted, an apologetic smile on his lips. "Besides - a broken bone is nothing compared to... this."

Myara looked at him for a moment, then shook her head. "You really are a fool, Priya. But a fool I..." She paused, as if searching for the right words. "...I don't want to lose."

Priya felt his heart skip a beat. "I don't want to lose you either, Myara."

She placed a hand on his uninjured shoulder and looked deep into his eyes, "Then promise me that you'll be more careful - and that you'll always tell me the truth."

"I promise," he said seriously. "But you also have to promise me something."

"What is it?"

"That you won't walk away from me. No matter what happens."

Myara's face softened and she nodded, "I promise."

They leaned against each other, the stars and the sky of Venus seeming to bear witness to their connection. Despite the pain, despite the uncertainty of the future - in that moment, they knew they had found something stronger than anything else: each other.

Medical confidentiality

Later that evening, Priya went to the sickbay of the Venera

Ascendant's sickbay, where Soraya, the crew's medic, was sorting out her instruments. When she saw Priya enter, she raised her eyebrows.

"Again? That's the second time this week, Priya. What happened this time?"

Priya held his arm, his face contorted into a grimace. "Oh, just... tripped. A little accident."

Soraya stopped her work and scrutinized him with sharp eyes. "A little accident? You broke your arm last week and now your shoulder is dislocated. Shall I give you a crash course in walking and standing?"

"It just happens," muttered Priya, avoiding her gaze. But Soraya didn't let up. She came closer, her hands on her hips. "Priya, I'm a doctor, but I'm not a fool. Such violations don't happen by chance. Either you tell me the truth or I'll get suspicious."

Priya seemed to be preparing an answer when Soraya suddenly paused, her eyes narrowed and a glimmer of realization flitted across her face. "Wait a minute... the timing. It's every time after you've spent time with Myara, isn't it?"

Priya's face turned pale. "What, no! That's absurd!"

Soraya crossed her arms. "Oh really? You know that the Virani have extraordinary physical strength. It wouldn't be the first time another being around them has seemed... a little fragile."

He couldn't help but nod slightly, "It's not her fault! It only happens when she... when she accidentally touches me."

Soraya sighed deeply and rubbed her temples. "Priya. You have to tell her. If she accidentally hurts you, it's because she doesn't know how fragile you are. If you keep doing what you're doing, you'll end up here in pieces eventually."

But Priya shook his head firmly. "No. I don't want her to feel bad. She has so much responsibility, so much weight on her shoulders. The last thing she needs is to worry about hurting me."

Soraya stared at him for a long time before she finally laughed softly. "You really are a lost cause, Priya. But that's also kind of... touching."

"Will you promise not to tell the others?" he asked Soraya.

Soraya replied with a twinkle in her eye: "Well, the others have already suspected it anyway, but of course they won't find out the real reasons for your injuries from me. My medical confidentiality dictates that!"

Chapter 23: The tribunal

The vast hall of the Auron tribunal was an awe-inspiring place. In the center of the circular hall rose a pedestal of gleaming metal, surrounded by a soft, bluish light. Here sat Xarun, the leader of the Atur, in heavy chains. Despite his imprisonment, he radiated an unbroken determination, his eyes glowing with rage. Around him stood the representatives of the factions in a symbolic array.

Three Auron sat enthroned on their floating seats like silent, all-knowing observers. Myara, the Virani ambassador, strode gracefully to her seat, her shining eyes full of hardness. The Zerai, represented by their emissary Karolak, looked like colossi of stone, determined to achieve justice through strength. The astronaut crew stood near Xarun's pedestal, their faces a mixture of tension and determination.

Opening words

"The tribunal is open," came the voice of Ikaris, the supreme Auron. His tone was calm, but every word carried an unshakeable authority. "We are here today to decide the fate of Xarun, leader of the Atur. The accused faces the most serious crimes against the harmony of the planet Venus."

A holographic projection appeared in the air, showing images of destruction: smoking ruins, devastated cities and the shadows of thousands of lost lives. The murmur in the hall grew before a movement of Ikaris' hand silenced it.

"The Virani and the Zerai are summoned as prosecutors. The defense is in the hands of the human visitors."

A murmur went through the ranks of the Virani and Zerai. Myara, the Virani ambassador, stood up, her posture radiating self-confidence and determination. Her silver robe sparkled in the light of the hall as she moved to the center.

The first accusation: Myara speaks

"Xarun," Myara began, her voice sharp as a blade. "You have brought us all to the brink of destruction. Your greed for control and power has destabilized the Resonance and plundered our planet's resources. You have wiped out countless lives, including children who didn't even have a chance to understand this world. You are not just a tyrant - you are a scourge to Venus. I demand the harshest punishment - death."

Xarun raised his head slowly, a mocking smile on his lips. "Scourge?" he repeated softly. "What you call destruction, I call vision. Only through strength can true order be created. You Virani are nothing but weaklings, hiding behind your technologies."

Myara's eyes narrowed, but she remained unperturbed. "It's easy to justify your own cruelty as strength. But strength without morality is nothing but barbarism. You have tried to enslave us all and refused to even consider peace or cooperation. There is no place for you in a harmonious Venus."

Xarun laughed softly, a throaty sound tinged with defiance. "Harmony?" he mocked. "You speak of harmony while you yourselves are at odds? Your tribunal is a farce."

Karolak, the Zerai envoy, rose from his seat. His three-meter-tall figure looked even more impressive as he underlined the Virani's words.

The second accusation: Karolak steps forward

"Xarun, not only have you tried to subjugate us, but you have also used resonance as a weapon against us," Karolak boomed, his voice deep and menacing. "The Zerai have lost uncounted warriors to your scheming. We have shown you that we can fight, and yet you have not backed down. Your actions show that you are incapable of accepting peace. There is only one solution for you: your end."

"Oh, the noble Zerai," Xarun replied with a bitter smile. "Always so proud of their strength and their bodies. And yet my plans have brought you to your knees. Perhaps you are not as indomitable as you think."

Karolak growled, his gaze like a dagger, but a look from Ikaris silenced him.

"The charges have been presented," Ikaris said, his voice carrying over the tension. "Now the defense attorneys will speak."

The defense begins

Aiyana stepped into the center of the room, the light from the floating spheres above her making her appearance seem almost majestic. Her heart was pounding hard, but she didn't let it show. The gazes of the Auron, Virani, Zerai and even Xarun's penetrated her, challenging her. It was a challenge she had to accept - not just for herself, but for the fate of the entire planet.

"I will not try to justify what Xarun has done," she began in a firm voice. "The destruction, the suffering, the losses - all this is before us, openly and undeniably. But I ask you not to look only at the obvious."

Myara raised an eyebrow. "And what, Commander, could be more obvious than the actions of a murderer and tyrant?"

Aiyana turned to her. "What if what we're doing now is the beginning of a new cycle of violence? If we execute Xarun, we only confirm that revenge and retribution are the means of resolving conflict. And that would be the beginning of the end of your peoples, your world."

Xarun laughed dryly, his tone dripping with sarcasm. "How touching. The humans plead for morality. Yet you yourselves are a people of war, of intrigue. Your history is bloodier than that of an entire solar system."

Kenji stepped forward, his hands on his hips. "Yes, Xarun, our history is full of mistakes. And that's exactly why we're standing here. Because we know how hard it is to break out of a cycle of hatred and violence. But it is possible. We humans have done it, and we believe Venus can too."

"The accusers are right," Aiyana began, looking at her crew. "Xarun has done cruel things. But we're not here to just reopen old wounds. We're here to find a solution that means not just revenge, but true justice."

"And that means compassion," Priya added. "We humans have learned that even our greatest enemy deserves a second chance."

Myara cut him off with a sharp gesture. "Compassion? For someone who has wiped out millions of lives? You humans are naive."

Soraya stepped forward, her eyes sparkling. "Perhaps. But perhaps it is precisely this naivety that we need. Xarun may have brought much suffering, but killing him will not guarantee peace. It will only create another cycle of hatred and revenge."

"What do you suggest?" Myara asked, her deep voice like a growl. "That we release him?"

Kenji shook his head. "Not free. But alive. Give him a chance to repent his deeds and make amends. The greatest punishment for a man like him is to live with the consequences of his decisions."

Interjection from the Zerai

Karolak rose from his sitting position. His massive figure seemed to thicken the atmosphere in the hall as his voice broke the silence.

"Fine words," he said in a low, rumbling tone. "But words do not bring back lost lives. Words do not erase the traces of blood left by Xarun. What you call 'compassion' is nothing more than weakness."

Soraya stepped forward and looked Karolak straight in the eye. "That is not weakness. Compassion is a choice. One that requires more courage and strength than any weapon or battle. You are strong, Karolak, everyone can see that. But are you strong enough to forgive?"

Karolak held her gaze, but a slight twitch of the corners of his mouth revealed that her words had reached him. He said nothing, but sat back down with a thoughtful expression on his face.

The arguments intensify

Myara crossed her arms and paced around Aiyana. Her voice was cool and cutting. "Forgiveness is a luxury we cannot afford. Xarun has proven that he only understands the language of violence. What if we forgive him and he causes chaos again? Will we stand here again and beg him to spare him?"

"No!" said Ingrid, who had remained silent until now, emphatically. "We shouldn't spare him because we're naive. But because we believe that another world is possible. We have seen what your peoples are capable of when they work together. The resonance points, the activation of the temple - all this proves that harmony can be not just an idea, but a reality. But we have to live it."

Priya added, his voice becoming insistent. "Myara, Karolak - imagine yourselves in Xarun's place. Wouldn't you hope that someone would have the strength to give you a second chance? If we execute him, we deprive him of any chance to change. And we deprive ourselves of the opportunity to create a better future."

A moment of silence

Xarun watched the discussion with an expressionless face. But there was a spark of something in his eyes that the astronauts couldn't quite interpret - was it defiance, doubt or perhaps even remorse?

Finally, Ikaris, the supreme judge of the Auron, stood up. His voice sounded calm, but it echoed through the hall like a gong. "There is no clear truth in this conflict. But I ask you, humans: Why do you stand up for someone who sees you as an enemy? What is your true motive?"

Aiyana answered without hesitation. "Our motive is peace. Not a forced peace, but a genuine one based on understanding and forgiveness. We are not defending Xarun because we approve of his actions. But because we believe that his execution would be a sign of division. And this world has seen enough division."

Ikaris seemed to be thinking, his gaze wandering over the gathering. Then he nodded slowly: "Your words are... remarkable. But the tribunal will decide whether they are enough."

Defending humanity

The tension in the tribunal hall was almost palpable when Aiyana stepped into the center of the room. The light from the floating spheres above her seemed to grow brighter, as if the room itself sensed the significance of this moment. All eyes rested on her - those of the Virani, with Myara as their leader, critical and watchful; those of the Zerai, with Karolak, skeptical and demanding; and finally those of the Auron, who were motionless in their role as judges. Xarun sat silently, his expression frozen between defiance and disinterest.

Aiyana took a deep breath. "I do not stand here today to say that Xarun is innocent. That would be a lie, and I respect this tribunal too much to desecrate it with such words. Xarun has committed crimes, and the traces of his deeds crisscross this planet. But there is one truth we must not ignore: Violence does not bring harmony."

Karolak laughed derisively, his deep voice echoing through the hall like thunder. "Harmony? You speak of harmony with a monster that knows only bloodshed. If we show weakness now, he will return - stronger and crueler than ever."

Aiyana withstood his penetrating gaze. "It's not about weakness, Karolak. It's about showing that we are more than just beings who respond to violence with violence. All of you - Virani, Zerai, Auron - have survived through your stories because you have shown strength. But true strength is not shown in the act of destruction. It is shown in the will to choose a different path."

An emotional appeal

Soraya stepped forward, her voice clear and laced with emotion. "We understand your pain. We have lost friends ourselves, people who are important to us. Luis..." She paused for a moment before continuing, "Luis is like a brother to us, and his loss in another timeline has almost torn us apart, especially me. Xarun is responsible for so much that was taken from us. But if we execute him, what do we really gain?"

Myara, who had been listening in silence, took a step forward. "And if we spare him, what do we lose? What if he uses this weakness to wreak havoc again? Can you guarantee that your humanity will stop him?"

"No, I can't," Soraya admitted. "But I do believe that everyone has the ability to change. Even Xarun. Maybe not today, maybe not tomorrow, but at some point. And if we deny him that chance, we'll never know if it could make a difference."

The meaning of humanity

"Humanity is not just a word," Aiyana said quietly but firmly. "It is a choice. A decision to show compassion despite everything that is against us. Xarun has hurt us, yes. But what does it say about us if we only respond to him with hatred and retaliation? Are we better than him then?"

Karolak snorted. "Your words may be touching to humans, but we are not humans. We are Zerai. We have maintained our strength for millennia by never showing weakness."

"Perhaps," Aiyana replied calmly. "But the question is not who you were. It's who you want to be. The resonance pod has shown you that this world will only survive if we all work together. Do you really want to give up that chance just to satisfy your anger?"

A turning point

Xarun, who had been silent, slowly raised his head. His voice was rough and deep. "You talk about compassion and change like it's something that just happens. Do you really think someone like me deserves forgiveness?"

Soraya stepped closer. Her eyes sparkled and her voice was soft and firm at the same time. "Do you deserve it? Perhaps not. But it's not just about what you deserve, Xarun. It's about what we all need to heal this world. You can be the one to break the cycle of hate - or you can keep fueling it. The choice is yours."

A low murmur went through the hall. Even the judges of the Au-ron exchanged glances, but their faces remained impenetrable.

The voice of the traitor

The hall was silent as the heavy footsteps of Zerai echoed through the huge tribunal hall. The chief witness, a mighty, three-meter-tall giant named Zerath, took center stage. Despite his imposing appearance, he looked broken. His shoulders were slumped and there was a mixture of shame and fear in his eyes. The Auron judges watched him motionlessly, while Myara and Karolak looked at their former opponent with mixed feelings.

Zerath was known as one of the Zerai's most skillful strategists. But his loyalty had come at a high price - and had ultimately been broken. The traitor had allied himself with the Atur out of greed and a desire for power, only to be betrayed by Xarun. Now he was here to testify and thus mitigate his own punishment.

The opening of the interrogation

The voice of Auron Judge Ikaris was calm, but imbued with a sternness that filled the room. "Zerath, you have been condemned as a traitor to your own people. Today you appear here as a star witness. Your testimony will decide the final fate of Xarun. But be aware: your punishment depends on whether your words are true and meaningful."

Zerath nodded gravely, his massive frame seeming to sway under the weight of his guilt. "I understand, noble Auron. I will speak the truth."

"Begin," Ikaris demanded.

Zerath raised his head and looked directly at Xarun, who sat calmly but somberly in the dock. The Atur leader showed no sign of emotion, but his eyes sparkled with anger.

The unveiling of the deal

"It began three cycles ago," Zerath began in a heavy voice. "I was unhappy with the isolation of the Zerai. Our people have always stayed out of the conflicts of the other factions, but I saw weakness in that. I wanted more for us - more power, more influence."

"And that led you to Xarun?" Myara interrupted sharply, her voice full of disgust.

Zerath nodded slowly. "Yes. Xarun promised me that we could take over Venus together. He offered me resources, technology and, above all, a place at his side. I believed him."

Karolak snorted contemptuously. "And what did you give away in return?"

"The Zerai's defense strategies," Zerath admitted, his voice softening. "I gave him access to our communication channels and gave him information about our weakest points. Through me, he was able to destroy our outposts without us being prepared."

"And yet you're sitting here now and testifying against him," said Ingrid, who was following the proceedings closely. "Why?"

Zerath turned to her and looked directly at her. "Because Xarun betrayed me. As soon as he got what he wanted, I became expendable to him. He left me behind when the Atur attacked our allied positions. My own people captured me, and I suffered the consequences of my decisions."

"So you're here to save yourself?" Soraya asked skeptically.

Zerath shook his head slowly. "I'm here because I realized that I was wrong. Xarun is a danger, not just to my people, but to all the peoples of Venus. I don't want others to make the same mistake I did."

Ikaris nodded slowly. "Then give us the information we need, Zerath. What does Xarun have planned, and how can we make sure he doesn't pose another threat?"

Zerath hesitated before speaking. "Xarun has never sought only to rule the Atur. His goal is to use the resonance pod to subjugate all other factions. He wanted to manipulate it to create an energy surge that would destroy the environmental conditions of Venus, but make the Atur invulnerable through their genetic adaptation. He spoke of a Venus for the Atur alone."

A murmur went through the hall. Myara rose from her seat, her hands clenched. "This is a crime beyond anything we've ever known. He wanted to destroy Venus itself?"

Zerath nodded. "Yes. He saw it as the only way to make the Atur the dominant species. And I - I was stupid enough to help him before I realized his true intentions."

The defense steps in

Kenji stepped forward, his voice calm but firm. "Zerath, what have you learned in all this? Why should we believe you regret it?"

Zerath looked at him for a long moment before answering. "Because I love my people, despite what I've done. I want the Zerai to thrive again. If Xarun is not stopped, he will take everyone down with him - including my people. I want this chance to make amends."

"And what do you suggest?" asked Aiyana. "How can you help re-gain the trust of your people?"

"I will lead them, if they let me," said Zerath. "But if not, I will still do everything I can to stop Xarun. My punishment is unimportant. Only the future of Venus matters."

A new spark of hope

The judges exchanged glances, and finally Ikaris spoke. "Your words carry weight, Zerath. But it is not up to us alone to decide your fate. Your people will have to forgive you - or not."

Zerath bowed his head. "I will accept it."

Myara stood up and walked to Zerath, her eyes full of anger, but also compassion. "I hate you for what you've done. But if you really want to help, maybe you deserve a chance. Show us that your words are true."

Karolak growled. "But no more mistakes, Zerath. Just one false move and I will judge you myself."

Zerath nodded silently, but a spark of hope flickered in his eyes. His statement had paved the way for a new alliance - one that could be the last chance for Venus.

A paradoxical thank you

The tribunal room lay in tense silence as Luis rose from his seat. The eyes of all present turned to him, surprised by his decision to speak as a witness for Xarun. Soraya in particular seemed torn by his decision. Her eyes betrayed a mixture of concern and admiration.

Luis, still scarred by the emotional and physical strain of the last few weeks, stepped in front of the judges. He was aware of the weight of his words and the risk of being misunderstood.

"Honorable judges," he began, looking directly at Ikaris, the Auron chairman. "I have decided to speak here because my perspective may be unusual - and yet it could be decisive."

The beginning of the plea

Ikaris nodded slowly, his voice like distant thunder. "Luis Ortega, you have not been called as a witness, but we hear your words Speak."

Luis took a deep breath, his voice clear but composed. "Xarun has caused a lot of suffering - I cannot and will not deny that. But there is something that makes me look at his actions in a different light. Not because I want to excuse them, but because they triggered a chain of events that changed my life forever."

"A chain of events?" Myara asked skeptically, her eyebrow raised. "You speak in riddles, human. Be clear."

Luis nodded. "I am clear, Myara. It may sound absurd, but Xarun is indirectly responsible for the fact that I'm standing here today - and that I'm happy. In another timeline, I was killed by him. His betrayal put my crew in a situation that cost me my life. But through this loss, paths were opened that gave us the opportunity to change time."

"You want to thank Xarun for killing you?" Karolak interrupted, his face incredulous. "That sounds like madness!"

Luis withstood Zerai's skeptical gaze. "Listen to me. I'm not here to defend Xarun - at least not in the way you think I am. But through these events, painful as they have been, I have found something I never expected: love."

The surprising revelation

Luis turned to Soraya, who blushed at his words but kept her eyes proudly fixed on him. "Soraya and I got to know each other better during this turbulent time. The despair caused by Xarun's actions brought us together. It may sound paradoxical, but I owe Xarun this part of my life."

Soraya stood up, her voice soft but firm. "Luis, you are important to me, and I understand what you are saying. But you must remember that Xarun has done other heinous things. Your words could be misinterpreted."

"I know, Soraya," Luis said softly, his voice full of affection. "And I will not put myself before the truth. Xarun has caused suffering to countless beings. But even in this chaos, some good has found its way. It shows that even the darkest deeds can have consequences that strengthen the light."

The message behind the words

Ikaris raised a hand to interrupt the emerging conversation in the hall. "Luis, what exactly are you trying to tell us? What is your conclusion from this chain of events?"

Luis took a step forward and looked directly at Xarun, whose face showed a hint of surprise for the first time. "Xarun, I have every reason to hate you. But I don't. Because if I did, I would become entangled in the cycle of hatred that has been tearing this world apart for generations. Instead, I want to show that we can transcend those cycles."

He turned back to the judges. "Xarun has made mistakes - grave mistakes. But it's up to us to decide whether we can just punish him or learn a lesson from his actions. What if, instead of being sentenced to death, Xarun helps to heal Venus? What if his intelligence, his power and his strategies can be used for a better future - instead of sowing destruction again?"

The reactions

The room was filled with a nervous murmur. The astronaut's words seemed to shake those present to their very foundations. Karolak glared at Luis. "You would let a mass murderer go?"

Luis shook his head. "No. I'm not saying Xarun should go free. I'm saying that his punishment shouldn't just be retribution, but an opportunity to change this world. Everyone here has a chance to make this tribunal something greater than just an execution."

Xarun's reaction

Suddenly, Xarun spoke, his voice deep and penetrating. "You are a fascinating man, Luis Ortega. You bring light into the darkness where others see only anger and retribution. But make no mistake. My path was never yours. I am not like you."

Luis held Xarun's gaze. "Perhaps not. But you have a choice of who you want to be from now on. Everyone has that choice."

Xarun remained silent, but a barely perceptible glint appeared in his eyes. No one could say whether it was remorse or mere calculation. But Luis had touched something - perhaps even in Xarun himself.

The prosecution's closing statement

The atmosphere in the tribunal was electric. The towering Auron judges sat on their floating podiums with expressionless expressions, while the light from the resonance pod bathed the room in a flowing, iridescent glow. Xarun stood motionless in the center of the hall, the shackles on his wrists a stark symbol of his captivity. Myara, as ambassador of the Virani, stepped forward, followed by the burly Zerai prosecutor Karolak.

Myara's voice rose, crystal clear and penetrating: "Honorable judges of the Auron, representatives of all races and also the esteemed human crew, today I appeal to all of us to strive for justice. Xarun, the leader of the Atur, is no simple opponent or tragic anti-hero. No, he is a tireless architect of chaos and an enemy of harmony. His quest for power has not only plunged his own people into ruin, but endangered all the peoples of Venus."

Myara paused meaningfully, her amber eyes traveling through the crowd, "Under his leadership, the Atur not only desecrated the principle of life, but also manipulated the resonance pod, a tool created for the balance of all. The Atur have destroyed countless lives on their way to power, and Xarun was the head of this disruptive apparatus. Even the people here, who face us unprejudiced, were marked by his actions. Their mission was sabotaged, their team threatened - and in an alternate timeline, one of their members, Luis, was even killed at the hands of this man. The existence of a second timeline shows that Xarun has not only threatened our reality, but has endangered the very foundations of time itself!"

The silence was overwhelming as Myara took a step back. She turned to Zerath, the Zerai, who now took the floor.

"I, Zerath, speak not only as an accuser, but also as one who knows the price of betrayal," he began, his deep voice a thunderous echo in the chamber, "Xarun has manipulated me. He has weakened my faith in the Zerai and made me a tool of his intrigue. My guilt is undeniable, but I stand here today to admit that Xarun's influence alone is a destructive force. He uses the weaknesses of others to achieve his goals. My betrayal was the result of his promises, and yet... there was no reward. Only destruction."

He took a deep breath, his massive shoulders visibly rising and falling, "I appeal to you, Auron. Think not only of justice for the past, but also of lessons for the future. If Xarun gets away without the harshest punishment, we send a message of weakness. We must not allow anyone with such unscrupulous methods to believe that they can undo their deeds through repentance alone."

Myara stepped forward again, the stage was hers once more: "Your sentence, venerable judges, is more than a punishment. It is a signal to us all. It is a decision as to whether we want to continue to be a

277

pawn in the game of violence and hunger for power or whether we choose a future shaped by justice and mutual trust. Xarun has broken every trust, shattered every agreement. He does not deserve pity - he deserves justice."

With one last glance at the judges, Myara withdrew. The words of the prosecution echoed in the chamber, a sharp contrast to the pending defense. All eyes turned to the Auron judges, who murmured quietly as the tension in the chamber grew palpably.

The defense's closing statement

The room was filled with tense anticipation as Commander Aiyana slowly rose to her feet. She was the last defense attorney to speak. Her posture was upright, her voice calm, but there was a fire in her gaze that gripped everyone in the tribunal. The external judges fixed her with their impenetrable eyes, while Myara and Karolak - the prosecutors - waited impatiently for an opportunity to shatter her arguments.

"Honorable judges, esteemed audience," Aiyana began, her voice echoing through the stone chamber. "We stand here today not only for a verdict on Xarun, the leader of the Atur. We stand here for the question of whether we, as beings of different worlds - and with all our differences - can ever break the chains that bind us to hatred and vengeance."

The summation begins

Aiyana took a step forward, her eyes wandering over the audience and lingering for a moment on Xarun, who sat in chains. His face was stony, but his eyes flickered briefly as she continued: "Xarun has undeniably committed atrocious acts. His strategies have not only brought suffering, but have also sown distrust and fear among the peoples. And yet," her voice became more insistent, "I ask you: Is it not precisely this mistrust, this fear, that has brought us here today?"

"Get to the point, human," Myara interjected pointedly. Her glowing Virani eyes seemed to want to pierce Aiyana.

Aiyana didn't allow herself to be rattled: "The point, Myara, is that we have to decide: Do we want to stay trapped in this spiral of retribution? Or do we want to find a way to break this chain? Xarun is a symbol of this chain. But what if he could also become a symbol of change?"

The case for humanity

Luis stood up and stepped next to Aiyana, "What Aiyana is saying is that we are all shaped by choices that make us who we are," he added. "I myself am living proof of that. In another timeline, I was killed by Xarun. That experience changed me, yes. But it also showed me that even the darkest deeds can have consequences that bring out the light."

Luis let his gaze wander over those present: "Xarun is not just a leader. He is a being who has made decisions - some wrong, some perhaps unforgivable. But that doesn't mean we should give up our own humanity by seeing him only as a monster."

The discussion heated up as Myara stood up again: "The Virani have seen what happens when you trust the Atur. They exploit every sign of weakness. Xarun has shown no remorse."

"Perhaps because no one has ever offered him a real alternative," Ingrid interjected. "Our experiences with the Atur have shown us that their society is based on harshness and mistrust. But if we take a different path now, we could make a difference."

Ikaris interrupted the discussion: "People talk about humanity. Of compassion. What do you say to that, Xarun?"

Xarun looked up, his face a mask of defiance, but in his eyes glowed a spark of something the crew hadn't expected - uncertainty. "You know nothing of the Atur. We only respect strength. Everything else is weakness."

"That may be so," said Aiyana. "But strength doesn't just mean having power. It also means changing yourself. To change yourself."

Soraya took the floor and joined her crewmates. "I have seen for myself in the eyes of an enemy what change can mean. Xarun may be responsible for many things, but it is in our power to show him that we are different. That we seek not just retribution, but justice that leads to something better."

Her voice trembled slightly, but she continued: "If we kill him, what is left? Another martyr, another tale of bloodshed and hatred. But if we let him live, under conditions that force him to face his mistakes, then we could achieve something that has never been achieved in this world: forgiveness."

A look into the future

Aiyana took the final word. She stood in front of the judges, her voice calm but full of conviction: "Xarun is no hero. He is not an innocent. But neither is he a symbol we should destroy to heal our own wounds. If we kill him, we show that we know no better way than retribution. But if we make him part of a future in which the peoples of Venus can coexist, then we make him proof that change is possible."

She turned to Xarun, her eyes boring into his, "Xa-run, you have a choice. These judges will decide your fate. But how you influence that decision is up to you. Are you willing to use your power to re-build what you have destroyed? Or will you continue down the path that leaves only darkness in your wake?"

The final twist

Xarun slowly raised his head. His lips barely moved, but his deep, raspy voice echoed through the chamber, "You are naive creatures if you think forgiveness will undo my decisions. But..." he paused, as if weighing the words carefully, "perhaps there is more strength in your naivety than I thought."

Aiyana nodded barely perceptibly: "That's not an admission, Xarun. But it is a start."

The chamber was silent. Everyone waited for the Auron's verdict. But something had changed - a spark born in the midst of conflict and tension.

A decision that changes everything

Ikaris, the chief judge of the Auron, raised a hand to get everyone's attention: "We have heard enough. The defense has made its point. It is now up to the Tribunal to decide whether the principles of humanity can stand on a world like this. The resonances have shown that harmony is possible. But harmony requires sacrifice. The question is whether that sacrifice will be in the form of forgiveness or retribution."

He looked at Xarun, then at Aiyana and her companions: "You have argued that compassion is the path to unity. We will consider this. But let me warn you, if Xarun ever causes chaos again, there will be no further defense."

With these words, the council left the chamber to retire for deliberation. The silence that followed was frightening. No one dared to say a word while the fate of Xarun and perhaps all of Venus lay in the hands of the judges.

Chapter 24: The verdict

The air in the tribunal was heavy with anticipation. An oversized gong hovered in the center of the hall. Gathered around it were the representatives of all four races and the human crew, who had chosen a defense that had earned them respect, but also mistrust.

Aiyana glanced at her teammates. Her hands were clenched into fists, but her voice was calm as she whispered quietly: "No matter what happens, we must hold fast to our convictions. The unity of the peoples depends on this moment."

Luis nodded, his jaw muscles twitching with tension. Soraya put a hand on his shoulder to calm him down. Priya and Ingrid stood close together, their faces a mixture of worry and hope. Kenji stood there outwardly emotionless.

The gong sounded, announcing the start of the trial. The three Auron judges moved a little closer together, their golden cloaks shining in the dull light. The chief judge, whose voice sounded like a cosmic melody, took the floor.

"Xarun the Atur," he began with an infinite calm that was both awe-inspiring and terrifying. "You stand before the tribunal of the peoples of Venus today. The prosecution has found you guilty of treason, destruction and endangering life on this planet. However, your defenders have made an argument that challenges the very foundations of our moral understanding. This is a verdict that not only determines your fate, but defines the foundation of our future."

Xarun raised his head slightly, his chains rattling. There was a hint of defiance in his face, but a trace of understanding also seemed to cross his expression. The judge turned to those present: "We will judge in three phases: The question of guilt, the sentence and the consequences for the unity of the peoples."

Phase 1: The question of guilt

The atmosphere in the tribunal was heavy and tense. The focus was now solely on Xarun, whose cool silence only heightened the tension.

The prosecution would explain why he had to be found guilty, while the defense would seize every opportunity to portray him in a different light. The eyes of all nations were on this moment.

The prosecution speaks

Myara, the Virani ambassador, stood up, her slender form cloaked in a shimmering silver cloak that emphasized her authority. Her voice was clear, almost cutting: "Xarun the Atur, you are not only a traitor to your own people, but a threat to all the peoples of Venus. Your actions have caused immeasurable damage. You have unleashed technologies that were not meant for any one individual. You have manipulated the resonance forces to secure your power without regard for the lives you have endangered."

She paused and looked around. Her eyes rested briefly on the humans before turning back to Xarun.

"What's worse, you deliberately sowed discord. Your betrayal has shattered alliances and sabotaged our efforts to build a future together. The Atur may have once seen you as their leader, but you have led them to ruin."

Xarun remained silent, his gaze boring into Myara's eyes, but he did not say a word.

Now Karolak, the representative of the Zerai, stood up. His powerful body seemed to tremble with tension, but his voice was firm and full of anger.

"I fought alongside you, Xarun. I trusted you - and that was my biggest mistake. You betrayed not only my trust, but the trust of my entire people. You used me to weaken the power of the Zerai while you secretly experimented with technologies that threatened the existence of us all."

He clenched his fists and took a step forward: "It was your greed, Xarun. Your insatiable urge to rule over everything and everyone drove you to create your own downfall. But we all suffered for it. You have not only betrayed your people, but also the foundations on which our world is based."

The words of accusation echoed through the chamber and a murmur rose among the audience. The tension was palpable.

The defense answers

Aiyana, speaking as the representative of the humans, now stepped forward. She was aware of the enormous task that lay ahead of her: she not only had to defend Xarun, but also humanity and the possibility of forgiveness. Her voice was calm but firm: "It's easy to see Xarun as the face of all problems. It's easy to condemn him and say that his actions are unforgivable. But let's not forget: Behind every wrongdoing is a story, a context that we need to understand."

She turned directly to Myara and Karolak: "You speak of betrayal and destruction. These are facts that no one disputes. But I ask you: Why did Xarun act as he did? Was it just greed for power? Or was it perhaps the fear of loss, the fear that the Atur would be robbed of their identity in a new order?"

A low murmur went through the hall as some began to ponder these words. Aiyana continued: "You are here today because you want to leave the past behind you. But you can't do that if you are only focused on guilt and punishment. If you really want peace, you must understand why your enemy acted the way he did - and give him the opportunity to make amends."

The defendant's response

The judge stood up and spoke in a calm but insistent voice: "Xarun, you have the opportunity to speak for yourself. Would you like to comment on the question of guilt?"

The whole chamber fell silent. All eyes were on Xarun. He remained silent for a few seconds, then raised his head and looked directly into the judge's eyes. His voice was rough, but full of determination: "You all speak of betrayal, of destruction, of greed. Perhaps you are right. Maybe I was everything you accuse me of. But what I did, I did for the Atur. I wanted to protect our people. We were weak, threatened by the growing power of the other races. You would have wiped us out."

His eyes wandered over the gathering, and his voice grew louder: "Yes, I have done things I should perhaps regret. But I never acted for myself - I fought for my people. And you all know that the same fears and insecurities lurk in your hearts. You are no better than me."

The words hit the tribunal like a hammer blow. Some looked away, others nodded in agreement. But the judges remained silent.

The turning point

Luis, who had remained silent until now, now stepped forward. He was determined to change the balance of the discussion. "You talk of betrayal and greed," he began, "but I see something else. Xarun has forced you all to question yourselves. His actions, as terrible as they were, brought you to this chamber. Without him, you would still be at odds. Perhaps - and I say this as someone who nearly died at his hands - Xarun helped you without meaning to."

The crowd fell silent again, and Luis added: "You are here to decide the future. You cannot change the past. But perhaps, through understanding and compassion, you can create something new - something that even Xarun could not have imagined."

The judge summarizes

The chief judge stood up again. "The question of guilt is complicated. Xarun's actions are undoubtedly serious. But it is up to us to decide how to deal with this guilt. We will now retire to clarify this question." With these words, the judges moved to a chamber away from the main hall, and the tension reached its peak. The hour of destiny had arrived.

Phase 2: The sentence

The judges of the tribunal returned, their golden robes gleaming in the soft light of the chamber. An oppressive silence fell over the hall as the decision on Xarun's fate was about to be made. The prosecutors and defense attorneys rose to their feet, all eyes on the three Aurons who would now decide the sentence.

The speech of the chief prosecutor

Myara stepped forward again, her posture as dignified as ever, but her voice harsher than before: "Your Honor, the question of guilt has been settled. Xarun has endangered not only his own people, but all the peoples of Venus. His crimes demand a punishment that sends a clear signal: no individual may put himself above the good of the community."

She turned to those gathered and spoke in an urgent tone: "I demand the maximum punishment. Xarun has destroyed many lives and thrown the harmony of our planet into chaos through his treachery and lust for power. His death would not be mere retribution - it would be a warning to all who might try to follow in his footsteps."

A murmur went through the hall. Many nodded in agreement, but some seemed to struggle with their claim.

The defense's claim

Aiyana stepped forward, her stance firm but her voice carried with a gentle persuasiveness: "Your Honor, the demand for Xarun's death may seem understandable, but it is not the solution. By executing him, you would only perpetuate the cycle of violence. Xarun may be

289

guilty, but you must not forget that he also deserves a chance to make amends."

She turned to the judges, then to the accusers and spoke emphatically: "True justice does not mean letting our emotions get the better of us. It means that we set an example of forgiveness and understanding. Let's show that there is room for change and healing on this planet - even for someone like Xarun."

Luis added, his voice calm but insistent: "I experienced Xarun's violence first hand. In another timeline, he killed me. And yet I stand here to say: His death would not improve anything. If we really want a future in which the peoples of Venus and Earth can live together in harmony, then we must act differently. Punishment must lead to improvement - not destruction."

The voice of the Zerai

Karolak, the representative of the Zerai, spoke up, his voice heavy with emotion: "I once fought alongside Xarun. He was not always the man who stands before us today. There was a time when he had visions - visions of a strong future for the Atur. But power has corrupted him. Now I ask myself: can he ever again become the leader I once admired?"

He looked at the judges: "If we kill Xarun, then we end his story. But if we let him live, then we give him a chance to take responsibility for his actions. I'm not saying he should go free. But let's make him improve the world he destroyed."

The voice of the Virani

Myara was less willing to compromise. She looked sharply at Karolak: "Forgiveness is a noble idea, but it must not come at the expense of justice. Xarun has deliberately manipulated the resonance forces and turned nations against each other. His actions have threatened thousands of lives. If we let him live, we risk him doing harm again. Can we afford that risk?"

She addressed the defense directly: "You speak of forgiveness, but what about the victims of his deeds? How are they supposed to find peace if they know he still exists?"

The defendant speaks

The judge turned to Xarun: "Xarun, the Atur, this is your last opportunity to speak out. Do you have anything to say in your defense?"

Xarun, who had remained rather silent and stoic throughout the trial, now slowly stood up. His gaze was fixed, his posture upright: "You want me to repent. You want me to admit that I'm a monster. But I was never a monster. Everything I did was for the survival of my people." He paused, letting his gaze wander over the assembly: "Yes, I have made mistakes. I have made decisions that have cost lives. But in my position, I had no other choice. If you believe that my death is the answer, then I accept that judgment. But I ask you: Will my death really bring you peace? Or will you continue to look for someone to blame because you refuse to look in the mirror?"

The words echoed in the silent chamber. Some of the spectators seemed shocked, others angry.

The verdict is announced

The chief judge, whose face was as unreadable as the stars themselves, stood up. His voice was calm, but it had the weight of eternity: "We have heard the arguments of the prosecution and the defense. We have heard the voices of the people and we have weighed the testimony of the accused. The sentence we pronounce will not only affect Xarun - it will be a message for all the peoples of Venus."

A tense silence spread. Everyone waited for the decision. The judge paused before continuing: "Xa-run will not be sentenced to death. Instead, he will be placed in the service of all peoples. His powers and knowledge will be used to undo the damage he has caused. From now on, his life belongs to Venus - not to the Atur, not to himself, but to all living beings on this planet."

The words elicited a divided response. Some cheered quietly, others seemed disappointed. Xarun remained silent, his face closed.

"The sentence has been passed," the judge concluded. "May this be the beginning of a new chapter for our world."

Phase 3: The consequences for unity

The pronouncement of the verdict echoed in everyone's minds as the judges rose and left their seats. But the tribunal was not over yet. The consequences of Xarun's verdict went far beyond his personal punishment. It was a turning point for relations between the peoples of Venus - and a challenge for the astronaut crew, who were now aware of their responsibilities.

The discussion begins

The first voice to break the silence belonged to Myara. She walked with slow, measured steps to the center of the chamber: "The tribunal may have ruled, but I wonder: is this really a victory for unity? Xarun is alive. The Atur have kept their leader - albeit broken. But what prevents them from sowing discord again?"

Soraya, who had positioned herself next to Aiyana, stepped forward, her voice firm: "The question is not whether we can eliminate all risks. The question is whether we are prepared to trust each other. Unity does not come from the absence of conflict, but from the ability to overcome conflict."

Myara raised an eyebrow skeptically: "Trust? After everything the Atur have done? After everything Xarun has done? The trust you speak of seems a naive hope to me."

Luis, who had been listening in silence until now, intervened: "Myara, I understand your doubt. But let me tell you something. In another timeline, Xarun killed me. And yet here I am. I wouldn't be the same person without that death, without the sacrifices and the battles we went through. Sometimes the worst that can happen brings us closer to what we really need."

Myara looked at him with a mixture of curiosity and skepticism: "And what is it that we really need?"

Luis smiled slightly: "A chance to do better. Unity is not a state - it's a process. And Xarun's judgment gives us all the opportunity to work on it."

The Zerai's reaction

Karolak nodded in agreement, but also stepped forward to voice his thoughts: "I agree with Luis that unity is a process. But how can we ensure that the Atur - or any of our people - do not sabotage this process? Xarun may be under surveillance now, but his followers are numerous and loyal. What if they free him or find a new leader who shares his ideals?"

Aiyana replied in a calm voice: "That is why the judgment is not the end, but the beginning. Xarun has not only been punished - he has been held accountable. He will be forced to make amends for the damage he has caused. And in doing so, he will be under everyone's watchful eye. Every step he takes will be a step that shows us whether he can really change."

Soraya added: "It is also up to all of us to protect this process. If we continue to nurture mistrust and prejudice, no punishment, no judgment, will ever change anything. We have to be prepared to open up - even if that means taking risks."

Karolak looked thoughtful as he spoke: "Perhaps the greatest challenge lies not with the Atur or Xarun, but with ourselves. Can we really forgive and look to the future together?"

The voice of the Auron

One of the Auron judges, a tall, ethereal man with a soft but insistent voice, stepped forward: "You all speak of risks, of trust, of forgiveness. But let me offer you a different perspective: Unity is an equal. Like the resonance points of the temple, we too must balance each other. Trust alone is not enough - responsibility is needed. And responsibility comes from the willingness to recognize mistakes and learn from them."

He turned his gaze to the congregation: "Xarun's judgment is a test - not just for him, but for all of us. It is up to each of you to maintain this balance. And that means looking not only at the faults of others, but also at your own weaknesses and fears."

The words made those present pause, everyone seemed to be lost in thought.

The astronauts deliberate

After the discussions had calmed down, the crew retired to a small side chamber to discuss their next steps. Luis was the first to speak: "So, what do you think? Do we really have a chance of bringing these people together?"

Aiyana folded her arms and leaned against the wall: "It won't be easy. But honestly, I think the judgment was the right move. If we had killed Xarun, we might have ignited the anger of the Atur and destroyed any hope of unity."

Soraya nodded, her brow furrowed in worry: "But even with this verdict... It feels like we're walking a tightrope. One wrong step and everything falls apart."

Ingrid, who had been quiet until now, spoke up: "That's always the risk with change. But remember why we're here. These resonance points, this temple - they exist to create a balance. Perhaps we can learn from them. Instead of focusing on the peoples' differences, we should emphasize their strengths."

Luis smiled and looked at Soraya: "As you said earlier, unity is not a state, but a process. I think we should lead this process."

A plan for the future

The crew returned to the main hall where the representatives of the races were still discussing. Aiyana stepped forward and raised her hand to attract attention: "We have all been through a lot, and there is still a lot to do. But we must not allow old wounds to create new conflicts. Xarun's verdict is a symbol that change is possible. Now it is up to all of us to shape this change." Those present nodded hesitantly, some seemed convinced, others less so. But it was a beginning - a new spark of hope that went through the hall.

And somewhere in the distance, the temple seemed to confirm the unity that would now gradually emerge with a soft, harmonious sound.

Chapter 25: A new spark of hope

The air in the tribunal hall had relaxed noticeably after the verdict had been pronounced. But the crew of the Astro-nauts could feel the lingering tension between the different factions of Venus.

Aiyana stood in the center of the room, her thoughts seemingly far away. Finally, she spoke, her voice soft but firm. "We have achieved something great today. But this is only the beginning. If the factions are not prepared to really work together, it will all remain just a beautiful dream."

Soraya nodded and stepped closer to her. "And it's a fragile dream. The Atur could interpret this judgment as weakness. We need more than words."

Luis sighed and crossed his arms. "But what? We've activated the resonance pod, awakened the temple, and now we have the Tribu-nal behind us. What's left to do to really unite them?"

The voice of the Auron

Ikaris stepped forward, his face calm as ever, but there was a sparkle in his golden eyes that radiated hope and concern at the same time. "Your performance was remarkable. You have shown that compassion can be a powerful weapon. But Soraya is right. Words alone are not enough."

"Then tell us what else we can do," Priya urged. He looked exhausted, but his eyes sparkled with determination. "There must be a way to get the races to really work together."

Ikaris hesitated before answering: "The resonance pod is a symbol, but it also has a practical meaning. It is the key to a harmony that goes beyond mere politics. But to be fully effective, the resonance points must not only be set physically. They must also be anchored in the hearts of the political groups."

"What does that mean?" Ingrid asked with a frown. She had been holding back most of the time, but now she stepped forward. "Are you speaking in riddles or is there something concrete we can do?"

The challenge of unity

Myara, the Virani leader, spoke now, her voice soft but firm: "It's not just about technique or symbolism. It's about the factions learning to trust each other. And that is something that cannot be enforced by a tribunal or a temple."

"Trust?" Karolak laughed harshly, his massive figure seeming to dominate the room. "How is that supposed to work when all we've known for centuries is enmity? Even with your tricks, humans, this won't just go away."

"It won't be easy, but it is possible," Aiyana replied calmly. She took a step closer to Karolak and looked him straight in the eye without blinking. "Each of you has taken a small step towards peace today. Myara, you agreed to let Xarun live, even though you had every reason to hate him. Karolak, you held back even though you thought the judgment was wrong. That shows that there is a spark of hope in each of you."

A vision of the future

Soraya turned to Ikaris. "You speak of resonance points in the hearts of the factions. But how are we to achieve this? How can a war that has gone on for so long end with trust?"

Ikaris smiled slightly, an expression of patience and wisdom. "By continuing to be the links. You, humans, have no part in the ancient feuds of this planet. You are uninvolved. And that is what makes you the perfect mediators. But you must also be prepared to make sacrifices."

"What kind of sacrifices?" Luis asked cautiously.

"Time. Patience. And maybe more," Ikaris replied seriously. "You won't see results immediately. But if you continue on your path, you can make a difference beyond yourselves."

Aiyana looked to her crew, her eyes searching the faces of her friends. "Are you guys ready to do this? We could just go back to Earth. Our mission was successful, at least in the eyes of our employers. But if we really want to make a difference, we have to stay."

Luis nodded immediately: "You know my answer. I'm in, no matter what."

Soraya put her hand on Luis' shoulder: "Me too. We haven't come this far to give up now."

Ingrid hesitated briefly, then nodded: "This is bigger than us. It would be wrong to just leave."

Priya smiled slightly and glanced briefly at Myara before speaking. "There's more to do. And I'm ready to tackle it."

Kenji raised his hands in a feigned gesture of surrender. "How could I leave you alone?"

Aiyana turned to Ikaris, her determination radiating from her. "Then lead us. Show us what we must do."

The spark is ignited

Ikaris nodded slowly. "Then your true path begins now. The resonance pod has laid the foundation, but you must build the bridges. You will go to each people, persuade the leaders, open their hearts and overcome their hatred."

Karolak grumbled, crossing his arms: "That will cost you more than words."

"We know that," Aiyana replied firmly. "But we will try."

Myara stepped forward and looked directly at Priya, her voice soft but insistent. "The humans have proven something today. Maybe you really are the change we need."

A spark of hope permeated the room, and although the challenges were huge, the crew felt that they were no longer alone. A new day was dawning - and with it a new chance to unite the peoples of Venus.

Xarun's surveillance: a system of control and cooperation

After the verdict was announced, a tense discussion arose among the representatives of the peoples. How could it be guaranteed that Xarun would abide by the punishment imposed on him? How could a man whose thirst for power and intrigue had caused so much damage be effectively controlled without imprisoning him directly?

The resonance shackle

The Auron, as guardians of the balance and judges of the tribunal, presented a solution. The chief judge stepped forward and declared with calm authority: "To ensure the safety of all peoples, Xarun will be under constant surveillance. However, this surveillance will not be through coercion, but through a network of cooperation. Technology and symbolism will merge to ensure that its rehabilitation is not just an empty gesture."

A beam of light illuminated the room and a floating construct was brought to the center of the tribunal. It was a filigree mesh of metallic and crystalline structures - the so-called resonance fetter, a device that the Aurons had developed as a control instrument.

"The Resonance Cuff," the judge explained, "will accompany Xarun wherever he goes. It is more than just a symbol of his punishment - it is a living system based on resonant frequencies, as activated by the capsule in the temple. It connects him to the energetic structures of Venus and allows it to register any deviation from his duties."

Luis looked at the device curiously and asked: "So, how exactly does it work? Is it some kind of invisible leash?"

The judge nodded slightly: "You could call it that. The resonance tether is integrated into Xarun's energy field. If he tries to evade his duties, the tether will send out a warning - first to him, then to the nations. Any attempt to evade responsibility will be recognized immediately."

The supervisory commission

In addition to the resonance fetter, the Auron proposed the establishment of a supra-factional supervisory commission. This should

representatives of all four races - the Atur, the Virani, the Zerai and the Auron themselves - as well as an independent observer role for the astronauts.

Myara crossed her arms and spoke skeptically: "A nice idea. But how can we be sure that this commission won't itself become the scene of intrigue? Xarun is a master at sowing discord."

Soraya took the floor: "This is precisely why we have to show that we are superior to him - not through control alone, but through transparency. If every decision is communicated openly and all peoples are involved, we minimize the risk of manipulation."

Aiyana added: "It's not just about surveillance. It's about involving him and making him realize that he can be part of the solution. If he accepts that, he will be less inclined to work against us."

The tasks of Xarun

Karolak spoke up: "You speak of insight and rehabilitation. But what exactly will Xarun do to repair the damage? Words alone are worthless."

The judge raised his hand and explained: "Xarun will oversee the rebuilding and healing of the areas destroyed by his actions - starting with the Zerai's shattered energy fields and the environmental destruction in the Virani territories. His knowledge of Atur technology and strategy will be used to restore the balance he once upset."

Xarun, who had remained silent until now, looked up and spoke with unusual seriousness: "I accept these conditions. Not out of fear of the consequences, but because I finally realize what my actions have caused. If my knowledge can help to heal Venus, I will use it."

The safety clause

Luis turned to the judge: "And if he fails? Or deliberately tries to sabotage everything?"

The judge replied in an implacable voice: "If Xarun fails to fulfill his duties or sows discord again, the resonance fetter will be activated and prevent him from acting any further. In the worst case, he will be brought back before this tribunal and the verdict will be overturned."

The words echoed through the room. It was clear that this was no empty threat.

The consent of the people

After further discussions, the representatives of the peoples finally agreed to the plan. Myara spoke for the Virani: "We will give him a chance. But only one."

Karolak of the Zerai nodded slowly: "May the resonances ensure that he sticks to his task."

The astronauts breathed a sigh of relief. Soraya whispered to Luis: "Perhaps that was the best solution. Not just for him - but for everyone."

Xarun was fitted with the resonance shackle and handed over to the supervisory commission. The first step towards redemption had been taken. But as the peoples of Venus began to prepare for a new, shared future, it was clear to all that the road ahead would still be full of challenges.

The hope that flashed through the judgment had to be preserved every day - through cooperation, trust and the courage to learn from the past.

Chapter 26: A new beginning

The warm atmosphere of the temple hall was filled with excitement and awe as the peoples of Venus gathered. In the center of the stage stood the Crystal of Unity, a towering monument of crystalline material. The time had come to officially seal the unity of the four peoples.

The unveiling of the symbol of unity

A drum roll sounded and the new seal was unveiled. The audience held their breath as the logo appeared on a large screen. A collective murmur went through the crowd as the emblem of the Venus Alliance became visible.

Ikaris of the Auron stepped in front of the seal and raised his voice: "This is our common symbol. It will remind us that we do not exist alone, but as part of a greater whole. May it guide us, even in dark times."

The hall erupted in applause. Myara placed her hand on Karolak's, and even Xarun bowed his head briefly in respect. Luis and Soraya smiled at each other, while Aiyana exhaled in relief. It was a moment that not only made history, but also promised a future that united them all.

The logo was a mighty circle divided into four equal sectors, each representing one of the peoples:

1. Virani (top right): Their symbol showed a majestic face with striking lines and flowing horns that emphasized the exalted and wise nature of their species. Sharp and dynamic, they looked like celestial scholars. The background was crisscrossed with geometric energy paths, a reference to their connection to cosmic resonance.

2. Zerai (top left): Their section of the logo showed an engineered profile with mechanical extensions, indicating their technological perfection and progressiveness. The intricate details of the cyber aesthetic linked her technology to the origins of Venus.

3. Auron (lower left): The lower left sector contained a soft, curved face with an almost otherworldly expression that symbolized her connection to nature and spiritual harmony. The background showed organic, almost leaf-like patterns that emphasized her role as protector of the Venusian ecosystems.

4. Atur (bottom right): The Atur section presented a face with sharp features and menacing, reptilian-like lines that spoke of a clear survival instinct. The background featured stylized patterns of claws and energy, representing their fighting spirit - but now tamed and channeled into the service of the community.

In the center of the logo, a shining, star-shaped crystal united all four symbols. It was a clear reference to the resonance capsule, the activation of which had made this moment of unification possible in the first place.

Soraya, who was looking at the emblem with fascination, whispered to Luis:

"Look how it captures all their differences - and yet brings everything together in harmony."

Luis nodded and added: "A perfect symbol for what we want to achieve here."

The signing of the contract

The air in the great ceremonial hall of the Temple of Venus was heavy with expectation and a solemn silence. The four races of the Venus - the Auron, Zerai, Virani and Atur - were present, gathered beneath the massive dome, its ceiling filled with dancing patterns of light. The light reflected the newfound harmony that promised to finally unite these peoples after centuries of hostility.

In the center of the hall stood a semi-circular table of polished white stone. On it lay a large, parchment-like tablet decorated with symbols of the four peoples and engraved lines that looked like rivers and streams - a metaphor for the common path they were to follow from now on. At the foot of the table stood a crystal desk on which the new seal of unity rested. It showed the stylized faces of the four peoples merged in a circle - a symbol that expressed the meaning of equality and cooperation.

Ikaris, the wise and charismatic representative of the Auron, stood at the head of the table. His shimmering, gold-colored cloak reflected the light of the dome, and his motionless posture was reminiscent of the gravitas of a judge. He was the official mediator of the ceremony and was to provide the final signature after all the other parties had given their consent. His presence radiated authority, but also an unusual calm - one that stemmed from the centuries of wisdom of his people.

"The time has come," Ikaris began, his deep, melodious voice filling the room. "We stand here as witnesses to a new chapter. May this treaty be not just words on a parchment, but a living agreement that unites our peoples in peace and harmony."

He made an inviting gesture towards the representatives of the other peoples. Myara, the proud ambassador of the Virani, was the first to step forward. Wearing a bright green robe interspersed with golden ornaments, she solemnly raised a hand before signing her name with a glowing pen made of energy matter.

"May this agreement be the first step towards a future in which we not only survive, but thrive together," My-ara said in a voice that sounded full of determination.

Next was Karolak, the wise representative of the Zerai. His movements were calm, almost deliberate, as he took the pen. "Our past may have been characterized by mistrust," he began, "but our future is based on trust. This is our common oath." He signed his name with a gesture that seemed almost ceremonial.

Then Xarun stepped forward. With the resonance cuff around his arm and his gaze lowered, he appeared to be a shadow of his former self. The guards of the supervisory commission accompanied him, but the room remained quiet. He raised his eyes, surveyed the assembled peoples, and said quietly, "I sign this as a sign of my change - and as proof that the Atur can be part of this unity too." Hesitantly, but without resistance, he placed his signature. A low murmur went through the rows of spectators, but no one dared to disturb the ceremonial dignity.

Finally, it was the turn of the human crew, who had gathered at one end of the table. Aiyana, with a combination of pride and humility in her eyes, stepped forward. "We humans often have our own struggles with unity and peace," she began. "But we know that true strength comes from working together. Today we share our hope that unity is more than just a word - it is a path to walk together. May this treaty not only change Venus, but also be a beacon for our own world." With these words, she signed the crew's signature, followed by the other members.

Now only Ikaris remained. With a majestic movement, he took the pen in his hand, turned briefly to those present and spoke: "The symbol of unity is not the end, but the beginning. May this treaty be a promise that we keep every day. I do not sign the final signature as the ruler of Auron, but as one of you all."

He placed his signature, and at that moment a beam of light burst forth from the crystal console. The dome shone in glowing colors, while the lines of light on the parchment began to pulsate - a sign that the contract was now official.

The oath of unity

The four delegates stood side by side, their hands outstretched towards the star in the center of the logo. The crowd fell silent as they spoke together: "In the name of Venus, we pledge to honor our differences and use our powers for the good of all. May our resonance henceforth vibrate in unison."

The words reverberated like a physical echo across the square, carried by the resonance points of the temple that reached deep into the core of Venus.

As the applause erupted, the astronauts looked to the peoples' cores as they slowly mingled together. Virani and Zerai entered into cautious conversation, while Atur and Auron showed mutual respect.

Aiyana smiled and spoke to her companions: "It's just the beginning. But I think we've taken the most difficult step."

Luis laughed softly: "We? They did it themselves. We just helped to build the bridge."

Aiyana put a hand on Luis' shoulder: "And sometimes that's the biggest task."

The new beginning of Venus had begun, a new beginning that promised a little more hope for a harmonious future with every step.

Epilogue: The beginning of a new era

The Temple of Venus, once a symbol of conflict, was now a shining emblem of unity. The peoples of Venus - Auron, Virani, Zerai and Atur - had together ushered in a new era in which cooperation and understanding replaced enmity. The astronauts who had been instrumental in initiating the process became legends on the planet and yet did not return to their old home, but wrote new chapters of their lives under the alien sky.

Soraya and Luis: an extraordinary wedding

Venus was brighter than ever that day. The sky, streaked with soft veils of cloud, glowed a deep gold that filled the planet with an almost unearthly warmth.

The wedding of Soraya, the crew's doctor, and Luis, the engineer, was not just a personal event. It was a celebration of unity, a testament to the bond between humans and the peoples of Venus.

The preparations

The ceremony took place on a floating platform erected by the Auron. The platform, shimmering in shades of silver and gold, was adorned with plants of Venus - glowing Virani flowers, the shimmering crystals of the Zerai and the symbolic grasses of the Auron dancing in the gentle breeze.

Luis stood with Kenji in one of the preparatory rooms and struggled with his nervousness.

"Why am I so tense?" he asked as he plucked at his ceremonial jacket. "I've already launched rockets, survived time travel and fought the Atur, but a wedding... That's what gets me."

Kenji grinned, his calm voice like an anchor "Maybe because it's the first time you can't control everything, you engineer. This is bigger than technology - this is love."

Luis looked at him, took a deep breath and nodded: "You're right. Today is not about control."

The entry of the bride

The ceremony began with the sound of a common song composed by all the peoples. The melody was a mixture of the resonant harmonies of the Auron, the crystalline sounds of the Zerai and the warm rhythm of the Virani.

Luis waited at the altar, a simple but elegant smile on his face. When Soraya appeared, the entire platform seemed to hold its breath. Her dress, a combination of human and Venusian design, was a work of art in fine fabric that caught and reflected the light of the suns. She walked slowly towards Luis, her eyes fixed on him, while her friend Ingrid accompanied her.

Aiyana, who acted as maid of honor, was already standing next to Luis and whispered to him: "Breathe, engineer. She looks stunning." Luis could only nod, as words seemed inadequate at this moment.

The ceremony

The ceremony was led by an Auron representative, Ika-ris, whose calm presence grounded the crowd.

"Today we celebrate not only the joining of two people," he began in a low voice, "but the merging of two worlds. The love that Soraya and Luis share is proof that unity is possible - a unity that transcends space and time."

Luis and Soraya had written vows to each other. Luis began: "Soraya, in the darkest moments, you brought light. You not only healed my body, but also my heart. Today, I promise to always be a safe haven for you, as you have been for me."

Soraya smiled and tears shone in her eyes. She took his hands. "Luis, you are the anchor that has carried me through the storms. You have shown me that even in the greatest uncertainty, a heart like yours is enough to hold me. I promise to love and honor you in every universe we enter."

The first sunlight as a couple

After they had spoken their vows, they both placed their hands on a resonance sphere, a gift from Auron. The sphere glowed with a golden light that combined with the rays of the two suns and shone beyond the platform. It was a symbol of unity and harmony that was understood by all those present.

As the orb glowed, Ikaris declared, "May the resonances of your hearts be forever in harmony. You are now one."

Luis and Soraya kissed and the crowd erupted in cheers. The sound was a harmonious blend of human joy and the melodies of the Venusian peoples.

The festival of unity

The festivities lasted well into dusk, accompanied by dancing and music that combined both human and Venusian elements. Priya and Myara danced in close embrace, while Ingrid and Aiyana talked animatedly at the edge of the platform, sharing a quieter connection. Kenji, who usually seemed dis-tanced, was relaxed and even joked with some Virani.

Luis and Soraya spent the celebration with their crew and their new friends. They laughed, danced and kept looking at the two suns, which were slowly overlapping and forming a rare conjunction.

A promise for the future

As night fell and the stars lit up over Venus, Luis and Soraya withdrew for a moment to enjoy the view of the planet.

"We made it," Soraya said quietly as she held Luis' hand.

"Not just us," Luis replied. "This is bigger than us. But I'm glad we did it together."

Soraya smiled and leaned against him. "Me too. And I know we can do anything as long as we're together."

The two kissed under the starry sky, the resonance sphere still glowing in the distance. They were not just a couple, but a symbol of hope, unity and love.

Commander Aiyana: A quieter chapter

The glowing surface of Venus had changed over the past few months. The once rugged landscape that made the planet seem so wild and unruly was beginning to radiate a new harmony. It was as if the unity of the peoples was also healing the face of the planet itself. But for Commander Aiyana, the strong, unwavering leader of the mission, inner peace had not yet been fully achieved.

A retrospective view at the past

Aiyana sat on a hill near the base, which had been converted into a joint research and cultural center for the four races. The horizon glowed in the light of the two suns, and she held a steaming cup of Venusian herbal tea in her hand - a gift from the Virani.

Kenji found her there, her silhouette framed by the first rays of sunlight. "You hardly sleep anymore, do you?" he asked as he sat down next to her.

Aiyana smiled faintly. "You get used to it. I used to think the nights on Earth were short. But time seems to flow even faster here."

Kenji tilted his head. "Or maybe you just don't want to give in to time."

Aiyana took a sip of tea and was silent for a moment. "Maybe you're right. I often wonder what my place is now. The mission is complete, the unity of the peoples has been achieved. But where is... Aiyana, the person?"

Kenji looked at her attentively: "It's hard to find a new direction when you've been the compass for others for so long. But maybe this is your chance to find out who you are without all that."

Aiyana leaned back and let her gaze wander over the landscape: "When I applied for the space program, it was always my goal to take on a leadership role. Responsibility was everything to me. But here on Venus... responsibility has taken on a different meaning. It's no longer just about giving orders. It's about building bridges, creating something sustainable."

Kenji nodded: "And that's exactly what you've done. But there's another responsibility you may have neglected - the one for yourself."

Aiyana furrowed her brow, "That sounds so... selfish."

"It's not selfish," Kenji disagreed. "It's survival-important."

An unexpected offer

In the evening, Aiyana was summoned to the large meeting hall by Ikaris, the leader of the Auron. The crystalline walls reflected the warm light of the room lights, and the atmosphere was solemn but calm.

"Commander Aiyana," Ikaris began in his deep, calm voice, "the Auron owe you and your crew more than words can express. We have entered a new era, and there is no better opportunity to solidify harmony. That's why I want to offer you a unique role."

Aiyana frowned: "A role?"

"We want you to remain as a mediator between the peoples. Your wisdom and courage have proven that you can overcome the challenges of a complex world. Unity is still young, and there will be disputes. But with your leadership, this unity could become permanent."

Aiyana was speechless. She hadn't expected her journey on Venus to end like this. "I'm honored," she began coyly, "but I don't know if I'm the right person for this."

Ikaris' expression remained gentle but firm: "You are more than suitable. The question is whether you want to."

A walk through the garden

Later that night, Aiyana found herself in the central garden where Priya and Myara had once forged their tender bond. The glowing plants cast a soft, vibrant light into the darkness, and the gentle lapping of a Venusian fountain soothed her thoughts. She had witnessed Soraya and Luis' wedding, seen Priya and Myara's budding love and watched Kenji forge a deeper connection with the Zerai. Everyone seemed to have found something here - except her.

"Why is it so hard for me?" she murmured to herself.

"Because you always think you have to carry everything alone," said a familiar voice. It was Ingrid, who stepped out of the shadows with a small smile.

"Ingrid," Aiyana said in surprise. "What are you doing here?"

"I could ask you the same thing," Ingrid replied. "But I think I know the answer. You're here because you don't know whether you should stay or go."

Aiyana laughed softly. "Score."

Ingrid sat down next to her. "Maybe you don't have to make a decision right away. Maybe you can just... be. Sometimes time will show you what you really need."

Aiyana looked at Ingrid thoughtfully. "Just... be? That sounds easier than it is. It feels like everything around me is pushing to find an answer."

Ingrid nodded slowly, "I know how that feels. But you know what I've learned? Sometimes, when you look too hard for an answer, you overlook the clues that life gives you. Maybe it's better to listen instead of looking."

Aiyana leaned back and let her gaze wander over the vast, misty landscape. The evening was silent. "What if I miss the clues? What if I just... fail?"

"Then you fail," Ingrid said quietly, her eyes fixed on Aiya-na with a mixture of seriousness and warmth.

Aiyana bit her lip and remained silent. She knew Ingrid was right, but that didn't make the fear any less oppressive. "What if I don't want to disappoint anyone?" she finally asked, almost in a whisper.

"Then you start to disappoint yourself," Ingrid replied, her voice softer now. "Disappointment can even be a positive thing, because you've only been deceiving yourself the whole time. Listen, Aiyana. There is no perfect way. But if you're always following the expectations of others, you'll never know what your own path is. And I think that's the real loss."

They sat side by side in silence for a while, while the sky slowly faded from a warm red to a cool blue. Finally, Ingrid took the floor again. "Do you want to tell me what really brought you here?"

Aiyana hesitated, but felt the weight of her thoughts lighten a little with Ingrid's presence. "I think I'm afraid of making the wrong choice. It feels like everything I do is either a beginning or an end. No in-between."

"Maybe it's both," Ingrid said quietly. "Sometimes beginnings are also endings, and vice versa. Maybe what you see as a decision is just part of a bigger path. And no matter what you choose, you will grow. You can trust that."

Aiyana closed her eyes, letting Ingrid's words sink in. It wasn't the answer she had been looking for, but perhaps it was the one she needed.

A new morning

The next day, Aiyana returned to the great assembly hall, where Ikaris and representatives of all the races were waiting for her. She had used the night to think, and the words of Kenji and Ingrid echoed in her mind.

"I've made a decision," she finally said in a firm voice. "I'm going to stay. Not because I can keep the unit on my own, but because I want to be part of something bigger. We are all responsible for this new era, and I want to do my part."

A smile spread across the faces of those present. Ikaris nodded slowly. "You have chosen wisely, Com-mander."

A new role

Aiyana began her work as a mediator, a task that went far beyond her previous experience. However, she not only found a new vocation, but also a new understanding of herself. She learned to share responsibility, accept help and appreciate the beauty of the moment.

And as Venus continued to shine under the rays of her two suns, Aiyana became a symbol of what the people and nations of Venus could achieve together - a true unity based not on strength, but on understanding.

Ingrid: The development of an unexpected togetherness

The Virani's garden stretched out like a living painting, in which bright colors and floating plants harmonized in a way that was almost surreal to human eyes. Cristall watercourses meandered through the lush vegetation, and the scent of exotic flowers was heavy in the air. It was a place that invited both meditation and quiet contemplation. Aiyana had often visited it to find clarity, but that evening she was not alone.

Ingrid sat on a flat, moss-covered stone ledge and seemed completely absorbed in contemplating a floating flower, its petals pulsating in a constant change of color. Her otherwise analytical eyes seemed soft and thoughtful.

"I thought I was the only one using this place as a refuge," Aiyana said with a gentle smile as she approached Ingrid.

Ingrid looked up, surprised but pleased, "Sometimes even a scientist needs something that can't be analyzed to calm her mind."

Aiyana sat down next to her and let her gaze wander over the garden: "The Virani really have created something extraordinary. It's more than just a garden. It feels... alive."

"Alive and yet peaceful," agreed Ingrid. "Unlike us, who are always striving for the next goal."

Aiyana laughed softly: "You mean those who are always running away?"

Ingrid turned to her: "Are you running away?"

Memories and confessions

Aiyana hesitated. The garden was silent, apart from the soft splashing

of a nearby waterfall. It was a safe place, a space where she could be honest - not only with Ingrid, but also with herself.

"Perhaps. I've been running away all my life - from responsibility, from expectations, from closeness." She took a deep breath. "I went on the mission because I thought it would be easier to deal with myself thousands of kilometers away from Earth."

"And did it work?" Ingrid asked gently.

"Not really," Aiyana admitted. "I just moved even further away. But here... in this world... I feel for the first time that I belong somewhere. Maybe because everything is so different that I can reinvent myself."

Ingrid nodded: "I understand that. I've always been on the lookout too - for the next discovery, the next challenge. But at some point you realize that none of that means anything if you can't share it with someone."

Aiyana looked at Ingrid, and for a moment it felt as if time stood still. It was a moment that didn't need to be filled with words.

"Shall we walk a little?" Aiyana asked to break the heaviness of the moment.

Ingrid rose and followed her as they made their way along a path beside the shimmering streams. Bioluminescent plants floated above them, casting a soft light. The path led them to a tranquil pond that reflected the two suns of Venus like a double mirror.

"You know what I find fascinating about this place?" began Ingrid. "The Virani have created everything to maintain harmony with their surroundings. It's not a place of control, but of cooperation."

"Something we humans have yet to learn," Aiyana replied. "We tend to shape everything, to dominate. But here... Here, I feel that everything is in balance."

Ingrid stopped and looked at the pond: "Maybe we could find that balance too."

Aiyana felt her chest tighten as she recognized the quiet meaning behind the words: "You mean... between us?"

Ingrid turned to her, the cool intellectuality she often displayed was broken by an unaccustomed openness: "Maybe. All I know is that I feel... feel different. Calmer. But more alive at the same time."

A tender moment

Aiyana took a step closer, and her hand moved of its own accord to touch Ingrid's fingertips. It was a light touch, but it gave them both pause.

"I never thought I could trust anyone enough to feel like this," Aiyana whispered. "But with you... it's another."

"Maybe because we both didn't expect it," In-grid said with a small smile. "But sometimes you have to accept the unexpected."

Slowly, Aiyana leaned forward and Ingrid did the same. The kiss that followed was tender and uncertain, but full of meaning. For a moment, the world around them seemed to disappear and all that mattered was the moment.

But when their lips parted, Aiyana frowned: "I'm sorry, I... I think I squeezed you too tightly."

Ingrid laughed softly and rubbed her arm: "I'm a bit robuster than I look. But maybe you should take a crash course in careful handling of female scientists anyway."

A new chapter

They continued their walk, the air between them was lighter, the insecurities seemed to have disappeared. There was no need to put everything into words. They both knew that they had embarked on a new path - one that connected them not just as a team, but as something much deeper.

At the end of the path, as the garden opened up to reveal the vast horizon, Ingrid took Aiyana's hand: "We have a long journey ahead of us. But I think it will be less lonely as long as we walk it together."

Aiyana squeezed her hand. "Together," she repeated, and for the first time she felt that the word 'home' was no longer tied to a place, but to a person.

Professor Kenji: A visionary on two worlds

The crimson clouds of Venus framed the horizon as Kenji stood on a rock formation and let the geologist in him run free. His eyes glided over the porous, sulphur-soaked surface that shimmered in the twilight. For him, Venus was no longer a hostile world, but a living laboratory full of stories. As an astrophysicist and geologist, he had always searched for patterns in nature - for the invisible forces that shaped the universe. Here, on this strange world, he felt closer to these forces than ever before.

But it wasn't just science that kept him here. His encounter with the Zerai had changed his thinking and taught him that knowledge did not always consist of data and formulas, but was often rooted in the lived experiences of a people.

An unusual connection

Kenji had become particularly close friends with a Zerai named Rhezar, a wise but reserved scholar. The two often spent hours together, discussing the geo-logical evolution of Venus and exchanging theories about the cosmic order.

"Professor Kenji," Rhezar began one day while they were analyzing the layers of an old rock together, "you humans are always looking for evidence. But sometimes the stone reveals its secrets not by analyzing, but by listening."

Rhezar laughed softly. "In a way, yes. Not all truths lie in data. Sometimes it's enough to be still for a moment and feel the story a place tells."

Kenji thought about those words. As a scientist, he had always insisted that evidence and measurement were the basis of all knowledge. But Rhezar had taught him that intuition and respect for the unknown were just as important. This way of thinking began to change his view of the world - and his work.

The vision of a cosmic bridge

Kenji had long had the idea of an intercultural project that would involve not only the peoples of Venus, but also Earth. His conversations with Rhezar had inspired him to develop this idea further.

One evening, during a Zerai ritual under the clear sky, Kenji spoke his thoughts. "We all look at the same sky, whether we are human, Zerai, Auron, Virani or Atur. Our differences may be great, but the stars unite us."

Rhezar placed a hand on Kenji's shoulder. "What do you have in mind, my friend?"

"A Nexus," Kenji explained, "a bridge between our worlds. A place where science, culture and philosophy come together. We could share our knowledge and explore new horizons together."

Rhezar nodded slowly. "That would be a vision that could unite our peoples. But are you ready to take on this task? It will not be easy."

Kenji looked up at the starry sky: "It never was. But it is necessary."

Challenges and doubts

Implementing this vision was anything but easy. The Atur in particular were suspicious of the idea. "A joint knowledge center?" asked one of their representatives during a discussion. "Who can guarantee that our knowledge won't be used against us?"

Kenji remained calm. "Knowledge that is shared creates trust. And trust is the cornerstone of peace. We can't approach each other if we continue to live in secrecy."

Kenji also had to deal with insecurities on a personal level. Working on Venus demanded a lot from him, and he often wondered whether he should ever return to Earth. His passion for science kept him going, but it was his connection to the Zerai that gave him a new perspective.

In a conversation with Aiyana, he voiced his doubts. "Sometimes I wonder if I've really found my place here. Earth is my home, but I feel a kind of responsibility here that I can't ignore."

Aiyana smiled. "Maybe your place is not in a place, but in the idea you realize. You are a bridge builder, Kenji. And bridges are always between two worlds."

The Nexus of Knowledge

After months of planning, Kenji's dream became reality. The Nexus of Knowledge was ceremoniously inaugurated in the presence of all four peoples. The center was an architectural marvel, inspired by the elements of the different cultures: the crystalline structures of the Virani, the grounded stability of the Zerai, the floating forms of the

Auron, the resonant forces of the Atur and the pragmatic constructions of the humans.

Kenji gave a speech that was simultaneously translated into all languages. "Knowledge is the only commodity that increases when it is shared. This place is not only a center of learning, but also a symbol of what we can achieve when we work together."

The response was overwhelming. Students and researchers from all over the world flocked to Nexus to learn and research together. It was the beginning of a new era of exchange.

A visionary on two worlds

Kenji had decided to stay on Venus, but he regularly returned to Earth to share the knowledge gained on Venus with his homeland. He gave lectures, wrote books and became a symbol of interplanetary peace.

One day, during a conversation with Ingrid, he spoke about his future. "I have always believed that my life lies in science. But now I see that it's more than that. It's about making connections."

Ingrid smiled. "You're a geologist, Kenji. It's in your na-ture. You're always connecting the layers."

Kenji laughed. "Maybe you're right. But these layers - they're not just geological. They're cultural, emotional and universal."

As the Venusian sun disappeared behind the clouds, Kenji felt a deep sense of contentment. He was a man between two worlds, a visionary who built bridges - not just of stone, but of hope and understanding.